Dying Art

Malcolm Hollingdrake

Print ISBN 978-1-912175-39-0

Dedicated to
Debbie Hollingdrake
who never lost faith.

A note from the author

There have been many forgers and fakers throughout history going back to Roman times, each snaring the innocent and the greedy, each preying on the naïvety of hope and wealth. Can you believe that in the latter part of the twentieth century, some of the biggest art frauds took place against the growing forensic, scientific ability to investigate the very substance that makes a painting specific, not only to a date or time, but to a particular artist? So why do these fakes continue to plague both actual and on-line auction houses?

Over the last decade, television has been instrumental in demonstrating the power of art and antiques, the potential to find a hidden gem secreted amongst the detritus, flotsam and jetsam of the car boot sale or attic! It is this very desire, to make a fortune, that places the naïve in the clutches of those who have the ability to create something that will deceive, tempt and tantalise.

Between the years 1989 and 2006, a family from the north of England managed to develop an operation that would do just this. They would produce a large number of forgeries. They would go on to sell these fakes, not to the innocent or the aspiring private dealer, but to galleries, museums, auction houses and private wealthy collectors who were surrounded by experts and accrue well over a million pounds.

How was this possible? Not only were they capable of producing quality fakes, both two-dimensional and three-dimensional, but they also managed to develop a system of creating false, yet realistic provenance, the history of the piece. And the real key to their success was to keep it all within the family, a family who did it for the challenge. Although amassing wealth from the illegal trade, it was a wealth that stayed hidden; there were no fancy cars nor the usual trappings of ill-gotten gain.

So why did they fail? Thankfully, some specialists have a keener eye than others. Suspicions were raised when the forger was only too willing to lower the price when probing questions were being asked and doubts were being cast. Once the alarm bell had been rung, others listened. The dominoes began to fall, slowly at first, but the end result would be staggering.

It has been said, by the police in the know, that allegedly, forty per cent of art works traded through online websites may well be the work of forgers. It is always wise to go through reputable dealers and remember that when buying at auction: caveat emptor – let the buyer beware.

The foreground in a picture is always unattractive … Art demands that the interest of the canvas should be placed in the far distance, where lies take refuge …

(Louis-Ferdinand Celine)

Prologue

The sadistic murder of a female colleague leaves DCI Cyril Bennett reeling and wracked by an impossible burden of guilt. The attack had been wrought by an old adversary, seeking revenge, after Bennett had disturbed and closed down his lucrative trade in a previous case. Her kidnap and murder had been a contrived test, a challenge that Bennett had eagerly, yet naïvely accepted.

All he had needed was his ability as a good detective, his professional skills to out-think and out-manoeuvre the criminal. If he were to succeed in this, as he had always done in the past, then he would reach his colleague before she could be sacrificed on the altar of revenge. That belief had been foolish, the murderer was always one arrogant step ahead, for this crime had been long in the planning.

Seeing a colleague's damaged corpse propped against a gravestone was, to all concerned, the final, crushing blow. Even though Cyril was down and broken, he was most certainly not out of the game. Moving his final piece in the evil contest, this last, calculated strategy would cost the detective dearly. Liz was not the only person to die that day, a huge part of Cyril died too as the seeds of doubt inevitably took hold, quickly killing his self-belief. Guilt, always lurking, followed swiftly to bury it.

Cyril did not think that he would be able to function anymore, let alone work, so he withdrew to the security of his past.

What he needed was time and care.

Chapter One

July

The summer rain was relentless. Manchester was famous for two football clubs, M People, The Hacienda Club and the ability to attract wet weather. As he crossed Mosley Street, after a Metrolink tram had shaken the ground, a warning bell added to the rumble of the wheels on the track.

The Manchester Art Gallery was an impressive building but he had little inclination to stop for a moment and stare. The rain seemed to have found a greater enthusiasm and was now driving almost horizontally. He quickly mounted the steps and entered, shaking the umbrella under the shelter of the portico. Research had a lot to answer for but here he would see a fine collection of the works he wished to study at first hand and his qualifications would allow very close inspection.

The gallery entrance was busy and he deposited his coat and umbrella receiving a cloakroom ticket in return. He moved to the Reception checking his watch, he was a few minutes early.

'Good morning, I have an appointment with a Miss Tonge. My name is Green. Dr Darwin Green.' He smiled and wiped a drop of water that ran from his hair.

'Still raining a little?' The Receptionist's smile said everything as she picked up the phone. 'She'll be along in two ticks. Please take a seat.'

Dr Green sat looking at the flight of stone steps that led from the entrance to the galleries. Two green-patinated, bronze, statues filled each plinth. He stared at them.

'Dr Green?'

Green turned and looked at the attractive young lady who held out her hand, which he shook.

'As I mentioned on the phone, the Valette paintings that you wish to see are not on public display. I've brought them to one of the education rooms for you to study.' She passed him a pair of white, cotton gloves.

'It's busy today.'

'Whenever we have heavy rain we see many more visitors. The gallery is dry, warm and, more importantly, it's free.' She pulled a face and smiled as if to suggest it was ever thus.

Within five minutes, she had left him with the three Valette oil paintings. None was large and all illustrated a moment in Manchester's social history during a key time, its industrial peak. The grim, sombre-coloured oils depicted a window into the past. His expert eye checked the coloured pigments, the board and the back of each painting. This, to people like Darwin, revealed much more than the painting itself.

It would take him twenty minutes to study and photograph each work and then he would head back to the station and home. As he drew his observations to a close, he removed a small, padded envelope from the side of his laptop case. From this he extracted a small oil painting, which he laid between the others. He scrutinised the paintings again, one after the other and then came back to the outsider that he had introduced. *Bloody hell that's good*! He whispered to himself. He picked it up and slipping a jeweller's loupe into his eye he inspected the painting close up. *Bloody good indeed.*

He opened his eye fully and the loop immediately dropped onto his open palm. Happy with the result, he slipped the painting back into the envelope and into the bag.

***

August

The sun hung like a limp, yellow balloon in the early morning Yorkshire sky; it was neither high nor low but at a height that was blinding both for the few drivers and even fewer pedestrians alike. It would prove to be far from innocent. For Nathalie Gray, it was a total nuisance. Each step of this part of her morning run was becoming unacceptably difficult. The lack of suitable pavement was also a hindrance.

'Merde!' she whispered under her breath as her foot dipped into the third pothole within a hundred yards. She made a mental note to wear sunglasses on her next run.

She had pounded the same route for four consecutive mornings and this was the first day of sunshine; she was so ill-prepared. Within the hour she would be back at the hotel, she would have breakfasted and be heading for the Conference Centre and the Antiques and Fine Art Fair. It was the penultimate day of her annual working pilgrimage to Harrogate. The songs of Jack Savoretti caressed her ears, blocking out the surrounding sounds; there were few, not surprisingly, considering where she was and the time of day.

The silver-grey Lexus had passed her ten minutes previously. The driver knew Nathalie's route, she had run a convenient distance behind her each day, but today was to be different, very different. Monica parked the car at the side of the road and waited. There was no tail of grey smoke from the exhaust of the now stationary vehicle. The driver, ever alert, was sensing her pending and approaching prey. The hybrid car sat ready to pounce; it would do so electrically and silently. The driver checked the rear-view mirror and yawned. The occasional early morning and late night were tolerable, but four in a row were proving unacceptable, especially considering the exercise.

She lowered herself into the seat as the runner came into view. Pulling down the sun visor with her gloved hand, she slipped on a pair of sunglasses. Within seconds, Nathalie was closing on the car, now a dark silhouette ahead in her path. The driver saw her turn her head as if checking there were nothing approaching from behind in preparation for rounding the parked car, unlikely considering the time of the morning, but it was more instinctive.

She quickly veered to the right and ran around the parked obstacle, unaware of the driver's presence. She checked her watch and, in spite of the dazzling sun, she was still on schedule.

It was then, when she was a hundred yards past the parked car, that she suddenly pulled up abruptly as a startled rabbit sprang from the hedge. It paused briefly before darting, bob-tailed across her immediate path and vanishing magically into the far hedge. Nathalie raised her hand, shielding the sun so as to allow her eyes to focus on the white, swiftly-disappearing tail. A smile came to her lips. *It's like 'Watership Down'*, she thought, her breathing slowly steadying as she bent at the waist to take a deep inhale. It would be the last thing that would pass through her mind as the blinding sun was swiftly snuffed like a candle flame touched by wet fingers. Her breathing stopped seconds later.

***

Monica Mac stared at the crazed windscreen. Her gloved hands gripped the wheel and a huge smile moved across her lips. She whispered, 'Yes!' to herself in a triumphant gesture. It had taken days of planning. She had stood and watched from outside the hotel from the day her victim had arrived in Harrogate; she had followed her to the Conference Centre daily and she had even followed her into the ladies and struck up a conversation about the weather if her memory were correct. She had planned every detail noting Nathalie's habits and her routines.

Monica lowered herself yet again into the seat as a car approached from behind. It sped past, the driver concentrating on the blinding road ahead. She took one final look around the inside of the car, ensuring that she had left nothing, before collecting the small bag from the passenger seat and climbing out.

The sun was sparkling, diamond-like on the fractured glass screen where Nathalie's head had made contact. Within seconds, Monica looked down at the contorted, blood-covered face staring back blindly with open eyes. One white earphone had been dislodged from her left ear and lay bizarrely like a thin, albino worm next to her head. Most of the twisted torso was buried beneath the car, apart from a leg that protruded from beneath the front wheel. Two pieces of bone had punctured the green leggings but there was little blood. The training shoe that had been torn from the foot was swiftly kicked to dispatch it under the car. She leaned towards the body, lifted it away from the tarmac and removed the hotel key card that was tucked beside her phone in her sleeve armband. She then slid the key card into her own armband. It was no coincidence that their running gear was a near match.

Monica sprayed the inside of the vehicle with lighter fuel, flicked open the Zippo lighter, lit the fluid and then tossed them into the car. She started to jog down the road, her back to the sun and the growing flames that would slowly incinerate any evidence. She headed towards the town centre and Nathalie Gray's hotel. To approaching cars, she was but a silhouette! There would be no vehicles coming the other way, the fire should ensure that.

She was soon on Crescent Road and slowed as she approached Parliament Street; the traffic was busy there and she jogged on the spot waiting for a break in the stream of vehicles. It amazed her how just one hour could transform the town's traffic.

From the sixth floor an observer saw her appear. He watched her less than perfect running style and shook his head. Buildings soon masked her approach as she stopped for the crossing. He turned away and went to shower.

As she ran up King's Road towards the Grand Hotel, she focussed on Nathalie's routine and followed it to the letter. She ran up the steps before pausing, her head lowered taking in breaths as Nathalie had always done. She then entered the foyer nodding at the Receptionist. Keeping her sunglasses on, she made for the stairs. She had followed Nathalie on one occasion to determine her routine. Once on Level Four, she turned right and stopped at room 434. Within minutes she had collected a laptop and iPad and was crossing the foyer. The Receptionist looked up a little confused as to why she was going out again, dressed for her run, carrying a laptop but said nothing; she had learned over the years that some guests had the strangest of habits.

***

DS David Owen's head thumped as his hand reached out unsuccessfully for the screaming mobile phone that danced and vibrated on the bedside table. He was, however, successful in knocking over a half-drunk mug of stale tea, quickly followed by the bedside lamp. The lampshade clattered to the floor and rolled in a semi-circle before coming to rest against the wall.

'Shit!' came immediately to his lips as he welcomed the morning.

He sat upright and opened his eyes; light pierced the gap in the curtains bringing a semblance of reality to his cloudy world. His phone continued to move like a small, flat fish in a polluted pool before it collided with the marooned teabag.

'Shit!' he uttered again followed by, 'Bloody hell fire!'

He swung his legs out of bed and collected the drenched phone.

'Owen!' he barked, annoyed at drips that hit his shoulder before running down his chest like cold tea tears. He wiped them off with his free hand before wiping his hand on the sheet.

'When? Right. SOCO? Twenty minutes …' He checked his watch. '… tops. And Shakti,' he paused, 'thanks.'

***

DC Shakti Misra stood leaning on her car, the smell of burning rubber mixed with an acidic aroma still polluted the morning air. The dark shadow of smoke lingered and ensnared the upper leaf canopy of the bordering trees to the left of the scene, like a dark pall. She watched as the ethereal form changed shape and density as if moved by invisible hands. The blue flashing lights from the fire engine attracted her attention and she again focussed on the yellow-clad figures moving efficiently to clear and secure the scene. She had to admit that she felt attracted to the men in uniform and it brought a smile to her lips. She shuffled with uncomfortable guilt.

A dark grey Skoda stopped lower down the road and Shakti immediately recognised Dr Julie Pritchett, one of four Home Office Pathologists working within the North East; she was followed by her assistant, Hannah Peters. The Crime Scene Manager moved past Shakti towards the Doctor and they talked for a few moments. Julie and Hannah donned the necessary protective clothing and collected the tools of their trade before moving towards the taped area.

'Morning, Doctor, DC Shakti Misra, we've met before. DS Owen is on his way. How's—?' She wanted to ask after her boss, DCI Cyril Bennett, who was still on compassionate leave, but then stopped herself. Even though Julie and Cyril were close, she realised that it was neither the time nor the place.

Julie smiled. She paused in front of Shakti and whispered to her. 'I'll tell him you asked, he'll be pleased. He's doing very well but still a bit of a misanthrope so, in my honest opinion, he needs a bit more time.' She smiled and rested a reassuring hand on Shakti's shoulder. *When did Cyril listen to anyone?* Julie thought before recovering her composure. 'I believe we have a bad one here.'

On hearing the news Shakti felt a degree of relief, but then focussed on the job in hand. 'Strange one. A body under the car and from what I've seen badly charred from the fire that may have been deliberate. First call came in just after five forty-five but by then the whole thing was an inferno. SOCOs are waiting for clearance to move in when it's safe to do so but at this stage we know only that we have a burned-out vehicle and a fatality. The vehicle's a hybrid and the fire people have a standard operating procedure for dealing with it so it's taken a little longer than anticipated.'

Julie saw the Crime Scene Manager wave to her. She picked up her bag and smiled at Shakti before moving towards the cordoned area where she spoke with the Senior Fire Officer to ensure that the area was safe to work. She knew that it would be only a brief assessment until the body was back in the operating room and lab, particularly as only a small portion of the torso was visible.

Shakti saw Owen's car pull to the side of the Skoda. She watched as he climbed out of the car and lumbered up the slight incline towards her, noting that his tie was loose and his top button undone. He rubbed his eyes as he approached and stifled a yawn.

'Doctor is there now. You OK, Sir?'

Owen observed the scene. The sun was higher now allowing a clearer view. He spotted Hannah Peters and raised an eyebrow. 'Yes, thanks, the morning started badly and from what I'm looking at it could get worse.'

'A body, believed to be female, trapped under what's left of the vehicle. No driver, no witnesses. Could be a hit and run, could be a deliberate act, could be anything. There've been a number of accidents this morning on account of the intensity of the low sun, interestingly mostly on easterly routes.'

Owen moved towards the cordon. The fire officers had finished clearing their equipment but remained on scene until the body had been recovered once the vehicle had been lifted. He watched Julie direct Hannah, taking photographs before moving towards him.

'Jesus! What a way to start a day! What can I tell you?' Julie removed her suit and the mask that hung at her throat before bagging them. 'Female, considering the teeth. My assumption at this stage is that she's in her twenties or thirties. The intensity of the fire has destroyed all of her facial features. Considering the distance that the body travelled beneath the vehicle, I'd surmise that the car was moving fairly quickly when it collided with the victim. Initially, the body struck the front of the car and was then tossed into the air. I'd imagine that part of the torso landed somewhere on the vehicle and then would have been thrown either forwards or sideways. What is strange, Sergeant, is that normally the car would stop and the body would be positioned a short distance from the vehicle. In this instance, the body is under the car, suggesting to me that once the victim was prostrate, the car was deliberately driven over the victim. There appear to be no tyre marks to indicate an emergency stop! You might be dealing with a hit and run but I see it, at this stage, as a deliberate attack.

'What's interesting is the type of car. It's a hybrid, it can travel silently! Seeing that she has the remains of earpieces suggests that she was also listening to music and so she'd have been unaware of its approach. Why people run and cycle with them in is beyond me ... I see a number of victims, usually traffic accidents.'

Owen made notes, rarely looking at her as she spoke, but occasionally glancing at the burned-out car. As she collected her bag he turned his gaze on her hoping that she would mention Cyril but she quickly removed her overshoes and gloves and walked to her car.

'May I attend?' Owen watched her open the car door.

'My pleasure, Owen. I'll give you a call.'

Shakti moved and placed a hand on Owen's shoulder. 'The car was stolen from Ripley last night. It's just been phoned through.'

Owen took a deep breath. 'Watch this until it gets cleared and then when the SOCOs have finished I'll see you back at the station.'

***

Dr Darwin Green opened the MacBook Pro after running his hand over the cover. The screen lit revealing a screensaver depicting a painting by a northern artist. The colours were vivid, the brush strokes eager and positive.

'*You certainly knew your stuff, girl,*' he said to himself.

He closed the lid and put it with the iPad into a travel bag. Before making his way to meet the others for breakfast, he checked the time and made a call. There was still no answer.

Chapter Two

The sound of Big Ben's chimes erupted from the mobile phone next to Cyril's bed; he had maintained a rigorous, daily routine since being signed unfit for duty. It didn't wake him. He had been awake since first light. Like most nights, this one was no different; he had suffered the sweats, seen the faces, clear and seemingly alive, heard the screams and cries. Each, although only a dream, was a fine ingredient of the same, seemingly real nocturnal flashbacks or '*sleep terrors*' as his counsellor called them. He had also fully grasped the tag that had been attached to his medical problem, Post Traumatic Stress Disorder and felt stupid to hang on to it. *Christ, that only happens to people who've witnessed their colleagues mutilated or blown to pieces before their very eyes*, he thought; the same thought he had entertained since the diagnosis.

He had not witnessed Liz's death, he had seen only the aftermath. What truly tore him apart was the guilt, the belief that he had not done enough, that he was losing his edge, his professional skills and that his possible incompetence had in some way brought about her death. He had gone over and over the case repeatedly to see whether he had missed a vital clue that, if acted upon at the pertinent moment, might have changed the outcome of the case and therefore saved his colleague's life. He had found none.

He was lying back against two pillows, his electronic cigarette firmly in hand. The faint crackle from the cigarette's atomizer, brought alive by his pressing the button, seemed loud in the still air. He inhaled deeply feeling the minty vapour tickle his throat; the shallow, crackling sound was the only noise that disturbed the moment of tranquillity. He stared ahead and focussed on the minute pieces of dust that floated, like small aircraft, trapped in the thin shafts of sunlight penetrating the blinds. The vapour added miniature, cumulonimbus clouds to the scene. Its silver light, needle-thin, suddenly reminded him of pins and his mind turned darker as Liz's face yet again swam into view.

He jumped out of bed and pulled the cord, frantically opening the blinds more fully, ridding the room of the needles of light. He needed a coffee.

***

Owen stared at the china cup and saucer in the cupboard. It belonged to Cyril. He would only drink from a china cup and a saucer; it was written in stone, like a tidy desk, a good shave, pressed pants and shiny shoes, like please and thank you! The cup sat upside down on the shelf giving the appearance of a white, shiny, bowler hat. He lifted it out and ran his thick finger round the rim; his action was almost reverent. He pretended to hold it as if drinking tea and immediately his little finger jutted out as if on a spring.

'Come on Flash, get your arse back in gear … there was nothing you or I or any other copper on this earth could've done to change the outcome … it's not your fault!' he said out loud. He stared at the cup and felt a sudden sadness, not only for Liz but also for Cyril. 'We can do nothing for the dead, only for the living.' It made him reflect on his own dark moments after his mother's death when he was a young teenager. How that seemed so long ago.

Cyril had long held the nickname, Flash, but few people now dared say it to his face, only very close colleagues and even closer friends. He had not earned it because he was always immaculately dressed as many new officers incorrectly presumed. When he was a cadet, he had picked up the nickname, Gordon, after Gordon Bennett, the man behind the Gordon Bennett Trophy, but then someone mentioned Flash Gordon and so the sobriquet, *Flash*, stuck. This fact had been lost to most people in the mists of time.

Replacing the cup onto the saucer, he returned it to its usual place and took his own Harrogate Festival Anniversary mug. He popped in a teabag, two spoons of sugar and the milk before adding the water. He let it fuse naturally. The interior of the mug was ringed like an ancient oak, stained strand lines marking the many unfinished brews.

Owen trundled back to his desk, the tea bag floating in the sludge-like liquid that dribbled down the edge of the mug before leaving a Hansel and Gretel spot path along the floor. He had only just settled when his phone rang.

'DS Owen. Sir, on my way.'

He left the drink and made his way to the Chief Constable's office. The secretary smiled as he approached.

'Good or bad news? Do I need an exercise book down the bum of my trousers?' Owen's face cracked into a huge smile as he said it.

'Caned a lot at school, Owen?'

'Once or twice, never my fault, I'll have you know.' He winked and grinned, a grin that reminded her of a cheeky school kid.

Shaking her head, she picked up the phone. 'DS Owen to see you.' She put the phone down. 'You may enter the lion's den.' It was her turn to wink.

'Ah! DS Owen, David. I want to introduce you to your temporary, new boss, DI Claire. Helen, David Owen, known as Owen. The Detective Inspector has been moved across from York. Helen tells me you've met before. Is that so?'

Owen immediately recognised the lady and quickly recalled that they both had surnames that could also be Christian names. 'Yes, Sir, on a couple of occasions.' He turned towards Helen and held out his hand. 'Good to have you with us, Ma'am.'

Somehow the words seemed hollow and did not ring true and it was acknowledged. Helen knew that this moment was difficult and hoped that her smile would be interpreted as sincere.

'I know you and Bennett are a great pairing and I'm sure it won't be long before he returns. I'm also confident that you'll give DI Claire every assistance during her time in Harrogate. It's difficult for her too, she knows Cyril very well. Anyway, let's get on. I've organised a team briefing in the next ten minutes and I'd like you to make the introductions, Owen, and then give Helen the heads up on the cases.'

Owen watched the Chief Constable's gaze move to the mountain of papers that cluttered his desk, layer after layer held in position by pebbles of various sizes. He knew it was time to leave.

***

The briefing was just that, brief, and after a few smiles and handshakes, the team dispersed and Owen sat with Helen and went through the cases they were presently dealing with. He did not need to give her the details relating to Cyril's absence, they were well known. Shakti entered, breaking an embarrassing, lengthening pause.

'This morning's victim we believe is a Nathalie Gray, twenty-eight. Checked into the Grand Hotel five days ago. She was attending the Fine Art and Antiques Fair working for Freshman's Fine Art Dealers. The last sighting was today about two hours ago. Mr Freeman Freshman rang to say that she hadn't turned up for the briefing and that she'd been seen leaving the hotel for a second morning run, taking a laptop with her. No answer from her mobile, no answer from her room. DC Park is going to the hotel now.'

'Rather premature concern from Mr Freeman Freshman. Is that his real name?' Helen Claire asked immediately.

'DC Shakti Misra meet DI Helen Claire, taking over from DCI Bennett, temporarily like.'

Shakti leaned over and shook Helen's hand exchanging smiles that held more curiosity than warmth.

'As far as I know. I've not run any checks as yet. Poor woman was only found this morning so I'm as surprised as anyone that they're looking for a missing person.'

'Did Mr Freshman call in personally?' Owen asked. His face pulled as if deep in thought.

'Phone call … I have the log here.' Shakti slid the paper across the table and both Helen and Owen read it.

'She's not turned up for work … she's always punctual and reliable. Instead of pursuing innocent motorists maybe you can direct a few of your boys in blue to get off their backsides and look for my employee.' Owen read parts of the telephone transcript before pushing the paper back across the table. 'She's probably buggered off, he sounds a right knob.' Owen turned to Helen and raised a hand. 'Excuse my French, Ma'am.'

'999 call too, I see!' Helen's expression suggested that she had seen it all before.

'Least it wasn't a request for a lift to the station to report it!'

This brought a smile to everyone's faces and it seemed as if any ice there might have been had started to thaw.

'We'll go and see the obnoxious, Freeman Freshman and maybe your rank might make him think before he opens his unpleasant mouth. What on earth were his parents thinking? Freeman Freshman indeed! Shakti, find out what you can about Nathalie Gray and start getting things together in …?'

'I'll use Incident Room 2, Ma'am.'

'Enthusiastic! She's new, the novelty will soon wear off,' Owen said whilst smiling and then winking at Helen.

Shakti just shook her head and whispered something about men under her breath. Owen went to his desk and picked up the tea he had brewed an hour earlier. The teabag, still an island, was now encircled by beige, milky rings. Even he looked twice but then he tilted his head back and drank the lot leaving the teabag stranded in the bottom.

'Waste not, want not,' he mumbled as he quickly followed Helen.

***

Cyril Bennett walked towards Montpellier Hill after crossing The Stray just before Beech Grove. The pathway took him away from the now-busy road and into the shadows of the trees. Two joggers ran past in the opposite direction and he nodded politely whilst moving to the side of the path. His plan for the morning was to look at the progress of a new art gallery being readied, followed by a tea and scone in Betty's Tea Room before his weekly visit to the counsellor.

He turned down St Mary's Walk and could see the covers still on the windows, preventing the inquisitive from monitoring the progress of the refurbishment. Above the shop front was a new and extremely modern sign, *'Focus North Gallery'* written beneath in a delicate script, *'Dealers in Quality, Northern Art.'* Cyril smiled inwardly. He had received an invitation to the opening night and had been delighted to see a catalogue full of some very distinguished northern artists, mostly from the past, but with some modern new talent. The paintings he was interested in were those of Adolphe Valette and L.S. Lowry. To see them *'in the flesh'* filled him with a rare excitement. He checked his watch and then shook his wrist before looking again. He would just see if anyone was working inside. He tried to look through a small gap in the masked-up window but there was nothing to discern.

***

Helen and Owen walked into the Harrogate Conference Centre, a building that always reminded Owen of the UFO depicted on the cover of an ELO album. It was neither attractive nor ugly, it just seemed to fit the space, but it was a far cry from the magnificent Royal Hall that nestled next door, the Kursaal as it was known.

The foyer was busy and Helen went straight to the Reception desk, identifying herself with her warrant card. She was immediately escorted within the labyrinthine building to the stand occupied by Freshman. Positioning herself beside Owen, she watched as Freshman described a painting to a potential client. A large oil rested on a gilt easel. He was all flowing hands and false smiles.

'Looks like he's selling snake oil!' Helen whispered, behind a raised hand.

Owen observed him carefully, unimpressed by the mustard tweed jacket, green trousers and what appeared to be hand-made shoes.

'It's the bow tie, and the colours! Would you trust him with your hard-earned cash?'

Freshman moved away from the potential customer and noticed the couple looking in his direction. He smiled and nodded before approaching them.

'May I help? Some wonderful paintings and sculptures to tempt you, today.'

Owen raised his eyebrows and waited for Helen to show her ID. If he could not eat it or drink it he was not interested!

'Mr Freeman Freshman?'

Freshman smiled again and held out a hand. Neither Helen nor Owen acknowledged it.

'Detective Inspector Claire.' She turned briefly to her left. 'DS Owen. We've come to present you with a large bill for wasting police time.'

Freshman just laughed. 'Bugger me, the Old Bill demanding money! Shouldn't you be out looking for Nathalie Gray rather than wasting my time? I've a bloody stall to run that costs a fortune. I provided you with all the information on the phone.'

'No, you rang an emergency number which, for your information, is a punishable offence, because, Mr Freshman, your call was abusive. Now, before you speak again, my Sergeant here is going to warn you, not caution you at this stage, but warn you that if you verbally abuse me he will arrest you. Is that clear?'

Freshman's facial expression changed and his mouth fell open.

'Good, we have an understanding. Now we need fifteen minutes of your time. It can be somewhere private here or back at the station. Your choice.'

Owen liked what he was hearing and smiled inwardly before stretching to his full height.

Freshman turned to his assistant. 'I'll be ten minutes.'
'He'll be longer,' said Owen.

***

Cyril tried to look into the covered windows but could see nothing. The opening of this gallery seemed to give him hope, a light at the end of a dark, personal tunnel. For the first time since Liz's death, he experienced a positive emotion, he felt a flutter of excitement and he smiled. 'I can't wait,' he said to himself. He turned away and set off up Montpellier Hill. There was the usual queue forming outside the café, it was always a Mecca for tourists but he popped inside, smiled and was immediately shown to a seat. It paid to shop all year round!

Within forty minutes Cyril was sitting in a familiar office, an office he had occupied for an hour a week for the past six weeks. He was fortunate that St Andrew's, a large Police Welfare Centre, was situated in Harrogate. It was here that his Police Welfare Officer, whilst liaising with his GP, had designed his rehabilitation programme. In some ways he had grown accustomed to the surroundings, they offered neither threats nor promises, only truths. It was an oasis, free from guilt and fear. It had not always been the case. He remembered that the first two occasions had been traumatic, he had been ill at ease and in some way in denial that he should be there at all. It was only Caroline's skilful and patient questioning and focus that had unwrapped the protective sheath that Cyril had wound around himself and even more tightly around his emotions. But now, he felt totally at ease and although admitting that he looked forward to his weekly visit might be an exaggeration, he did not consider it to be an unnecessary burden. If the truth be known, he now saw his counsellor as his guardian angel. If anyone could get him sorted, then he had confidence that she could. He took from his pocket the work she had asked him to prepare.

***

'So how long has Nathalie worked for you?'

'Three years. You know she's part French? Mother's side. That's why you have Nathalie with the h!'

Owen just wanted to slap him.

'Master's degree in History of Fine Art and a degree in Art Conservation: skilful painter in her own right. I have another two people who work for me, also fine art trained. One's a Dr Darwin Green, he specialises in finding 'sleepers'.' He looked up and saw Owen's puzzled expression. 'They're paintings that have been inaccurately catalogued at auction, our job is to buy them cheaply and sell them for their true value. He also wheedles out the potential fakes and believe me there are more of those floating around than many people believe, especially in the world of abstract and impressionist art. Then there's, Lynn McGowen, works freelance. She's not here this week. On holiday.'

'Her role?'

'Provenance, she searches out the history of a piece. Bloody time-consuming and a pain in the arse of a job, too.'

'Can we talk about Ms Gray otherwise you'll be here all day.' Helen felt as though he were avoiding the real questions. 'Why did you ring so quickly, she'd not been missing long and weren't you staying at the same hotel?'

'Precisely, we always met for breakfast and then came here, it's only next door, takes a minute. We'd have a briefing and then we'd start work, doors open at 8:30 so we need to be organised and ready. Every day we all met for breakfast but today she didn't show. When I questioned Reception, they told me that she'd appeared to go out for a second run carrying a laptop; a laptop for God's sake! That immediately raised my concerns. There was no reply from her room nor from her mob ...'

Owen's phone rang and he noted that it was DC Stuart Park. He held up his finger and Freshman stopped speaking mid-sentence. Freshman watched as Owen's head nodded up and down as he listened to the conversation. He hung up.

'Just give us a minute, please, Mr Freshman.' Owen addressed Freshman more politely than he had done all interview and moved Helen away. 'Stuart's checked the CCTV taken from the corridors and the hotel foyer. In his opinion, the girl leaving for the first run is not the same girl who returned, similar, but in his opinion, not the same. However, the girl who returned left after visiting Nathalie's room. He's checking street CCTV to see if he can notice any difference in the way the two ran. Each runner has a different gait, allegedly.'

They returned to Freshman.

'Where was I?'

'No reply from her room,' Owen prompted.

'Yes, so I tried her mobile and that just went straight to answerphone. In all the time we've worked together I've never known her miss an appointment.'

'She ran every day?'

'Yes, obsessive and I mean ran, not jogged. She had the gait of a gazelle, real spring to her run. Made it look effortless.'

'Do you have an up–to-date picture of her?'

'Yes, from this year's Fine Art brochure, we're all in. I have one on the stand.'

Helen and Owen collected the brochure before starting to make their way to meet DC Park at the hotel next door. Owen stopped and turned back to Freshman. 'How did you all arrive in Harrogate?'

The question threw him off balance mainly because he thought it a ridiculous thing to ask. 'We have one car, Dr Green's, he arrives the night before the delivery of the goods and checks the venue. Even though we've done this before, systems change. He checks the stand, organises a drop off time for the goods and ensures that we have enough experienced porters. Nathalie arrives that evening. A driver brings all the stock in a very large van and I travel in an estate car containing the paintings and valuable sculptures. I've learned over many years not to carry all my eggs in one basket and that includes my staff.'

'Good question, Owen. Get Park to organise the collection of Nathalie's car by the end of the day.'

The hotel was positioned next to the Conference Centre. They entered the foyer and DC Park was sitting in the Reception area. He saw them immediately. He was not the only one. In the far corner, next to an exotic palm-type plant, a man lowered his broadsheet briefly and glanced at the three officers. Owen had glanced over as he saw the movement of the paper in his peripheral vision. He looked at the man briefly; his goatee beard gave him a distinguished, theatrical appearance. He then turned away as he saw the paper raised. *A thespian,* Owen thought. The man chanced a look by moving the paper sideways and watched them walk behind the Reception desk and disappear. He folded his paper, put it back in the rack and left.

Owen, Stuart Park and Helen checked the CCTC footage against the image Owen held and they all agreed that they were looking for a different woman.

Chapter Three

Owen did not mind an autopsy, it seemed to stimulate his imagination. This examination, however, was a little different. He had never seen a badly burned corpse and he was astonished by how the human body contorted when subjected to intense heat. Looking down at the figure on the post-mortem table, it reminded him of the stone figures from Pompeii he had seen in his school history books.

Julie's face was covered with a Perspex visor. She worked methodically alongside two colleagues. One appeared to be Hannah. She was photographing the charred remains as directed. It seemed strange hearing Julie's voice enhanced over the speaker above his head. A small microphone was clipped to her visor.

'We discovered her mobile phone strapped to her left sleeve. She'd fallen onto it and that offered a degree of protection from the heat even though the subcutaneous fatty tissues had ignited because it was under the body. Some damage occurred but it has been protected. It's been couriered through to Forensics to see if anything can be recovered. DNA matched the samples taken from the toothbrush found in her hotel room, so here you see, Nathalie Gray.'

'I note two things, Doctor, the position of the corpse …'

'It's what's referred to as a pugilistic attitude caused in simple terms by the contraction of the spinal muscles, resulting in marked opisthotonus, in an attitude adopted by boxers.'

'And the cuts, were they from the collision?'

'No, they're heat ruptures. I must say, Owen, your boss would be looking positively green around the gills at this stage never mind asking very relevant questions. I'm impressed.' She smiled.

'I always liked playing with dead things when I was a kid. I remember once keeping a dead rat in a shoebox under my bed until my mother discovered it. Must have been there a week. Everyone in the house thought she was being murdered the way she screamed. I was grounded for ages if I remember correctly.'

Julie laughed, as did Hannah.

'Why keep a dead rat?'

'It was my pet. When I went on holiday for a week to Scarborough a mate said he'd look after it but he forgot to feed it. Tried to eat its way out of the cage and then tried to eat itself! Heartbroken I was.'

'You poor thing,' whispered Hannah.

'We'll take a full X-ray and that should give us more of a clue as to the cause of death. You see, in my job you tend to realise that you can never fully predict how your life will change from one day to the next. It took but a second for this young lady's dreams to be snuffed out.'

Owen knew what she meant but thought she had expressed it insensitively.

'I'll send a full report as soon as ... You may as well go. You know now that she was murdered. The physical damage and the fact that the car was deliberately torched are clear evidence.'

The car had been removed and was being forensically scrutinised. He was sure that something would be discovered with the increased scientific advances that could pinpoint the smallest fragment of evidence.

Owen returned to the Incident Room. The boards to the left were now no longer bare and slowly images and notes had been strategically added. The enlarged image was that of Nathalie Gray. She stared back at him as if demanding to know why he had not solved her murder, her eyes seemingly following his path across the room. He looked back at the image and felt a shiver down his neck. Brian Smirthwaite called him over to a desk.

'We've received the footage from both the hotel foyer and street CCTV showing the girl, but more likely the girls as we now think. It's been enhanced.'

They watched the images of Nathalie leaving the hotel. It was clear, dawn was just breaking and there was little traffic. Owen noted the time that was ticking away at the bottom of the screen. Smirthwaite fast-forwarded the tape.

'Here's our girl, but is it?'

He said nothing allowing Owen to make up his own mind. Owen jotted down the time again.

'That's seventy-five minutes she's been out! Was that normal?'

'Looking at the previous days, she ran for sixty to sixty-five minutes maximum. This was the longest run of the week.' Smirthwaite knew what was coming.

'Or this second girl did the return run more slowly or the accident took longer than planned.' Owen did not disappoint.

'You can see Nathalie was wearing different clothing, only slightly but there's a reflective strip on the back of her running shoes, on the girl returning there's none. She's also wearing tight gloves.'

Both men studied the images of the mystery girl leaving the hotel with the laptop.

'Forensic analysis tells us it's a different woman, you can see when you consider the contrasting running styles. If you check the street CCTV the last sighting we have of the first girl is here.' Smirthwaite pointed to a position on a street map on the desk. 'Note again the time. She's in the dark almost as the sun wasn't up, but it's clear enough with the streetlights. Now here's a shot taken later, again note the time, which, we might assume, marks the girl's return. You can clearly note a different stride pattern.'

'Isn't that through fatigue?'

'No, slightly different height and according to our experts, different running styles.'

Owen thanked his colleague and moved to his desk. He tapped a pencil against his teeth as he considered the way in which the girl had been murdered. They had obviously tried to make others believe it to be an accident, a hit and run that was clumsily covered up. It was foolish. This was a deliberate act. His phone rang.

'Owen!' He'd picked up Cyril's way of answering, no welcome, just name and to the point.

'Owen, we found a trace of DNA under two of Nathalie Gray's finger nails on the hand that was trapped beneath her body. The melting plastic from the car's bumper had formed a protective barrier. My experience tells me that there should be enough to test.'

'Good news ...' He didn't finish.

'There's something else, the phone has also revealed some clues. Firstly, she was listening to Jack Savoretti, I don't know if that's worth anything and secondly, we've managed to extract her address book. I take it you've checked her phone records and her home address?'

He informed her that they were both in hand when he knew that the phone records had not been requested.

'Details coming over. Bye.' Julie did not linger knowing the conversation might turn to Cyril.

Owen rang Shakti. 'Nathalie Gray's phone records?'

'On file, sorted this morning. Manchester Police are searching her apartment as we speak but someone had been there before them. They'll get back to us ASAP. I can't see anything out of the ordinary with her calls, mainly to her work colleagues, her boss, Lynn McGowen and the more interesting ones to Darwin Green. Some very interesting text messages also where he's concerned but we're also checking social media sites.' Shakti's voice changed spiking Owen's interest.

'Better take a butcher's then. And Shakti, thanks for that.'

'It's my job, Sir. Expect a call from DI John Dunn from Greater Manchester.'

'Did Dr Pritchett mention Cyril when you were chatting at the crime scene?'

'Yes, said he was a bit of a misanthrope and still needed time. I didn't pursue it as I could see it was a little delicate.'

'Right ... really. Yes, delicate. Thanks. Said nothing to me and you'd think she might have knowing how close we were.'

'Lady to lady, Owen. Sometimes it's easier.'

Owen sat back and took a deep breath as he thought about his boss. He then realised that Cyril would have had the phone records nailed immediately. It did not help his mood!

***

Cyril read from the papers that he had been requested to prepare. It was as if he were reading evidence in court. He had set in his mind that it was as in British libel law, that he, the defendant, had to prove his innocence even when he believed everyone considered him guilty, guilty of professional incompetence. Caroline listened, her eyes clearly focussed on Cyril's expression and each word that was uttered. She could hear the emotion in his voice, particularly when he revealed certain information, confidential details that would normally never surface in public, triggering personal anxieties or inner anger. She waited for him to finish and then paused for thought for a few moments.

'If you were to sum up then, Cyril, what would be your conclusion now that you've gone over all of the evidence?'

Cyril lifted his electronic cigarette to his mouth but only ran it along his lips. The pause was torturous for Caroline but she was patient, never letting her eyes drift far from Cyril's gaze. It was then that she noticed the tear well in his lower lid, like a transparent blister, before bursting and rolling down his cheek. He immediately lifted a hand in defiance in the hope of shielding what he believed to be a weakness, but then lowered it knowing it was a futile gesture. His shoulders lifted and fell as his head sagged towards his chest. He began to weep.

Caroline said nothing she simply stood and left the room, closing the door quietly. It was a critical moment in his healing process and she respected the privacy that he now craved.

Ten minutes later she returned carrying a tray holding two china cups and saucers and a plate of custard creams. She placed a cup in front of Cyril who had now recovered some of his equilibrium. The silence was palpable as they drank their tea, the room like a protective cocoon, private and secure.

'Not guilty!' Cyril whispered, his words hardly audible. He looked directly at Caroline and mouthed the words, 'Thank you. I've made my mistakes like we all do but not with this. Not guilty.' He let the final two words linger on his tongue as if he were exorcising a deep-rooted, evil spirit.

'One more session, Detective Chief Inspector Bennett.' She deliberately emphasised his rank. 'I want a list of all your positive traits. In this session your modesty goes out of the window, do you understand?'

She smiled at the man sitting to her right before pushing the plate of biscuits in his direction. After a few moments, she passed him the script he had written and read out, painstakingly slowly, his collection of the evidence for Liz's case. It was a blow-by-blow account, warts and all; it was as if he had corralled the evil that had deliberately been sown, the evil that had torn him apart, rendering him lost and personally and professionally impotent.

'I want you to tear it into small fragments, they are never to be considered again as a whole script. The only thing you must remember is the bravery of your team and that team includes its leader, you, DCI Cyril Bennett, you, and that team still includes Liz. You'll always be together in memory but never together in guilt. You'll take Liz with you, a silent partner, through the rest of your career if she decides to travel with you. You'll be proud that she's there or respect her decision if she's not. Slowly, she may drift away, returning only now and again and maybe, just maybe, she may go and never return. It will be her choice, not yours.'

Cyril simply listened before finally tearing the last sheet into small pieces before depositing them in the bin, as if casting them to the four winds. He finished his tea and although he felt lighter in spirit, he felt totally exhausted.

'I'll write to your Doctor but I want you to promise me to continue with the prescribed medication. Stopping them? That's for him to decide not you.' She leaned over and shook his hand. 'Take your time, I'll leave you here until you feel you're ready to leave and I'll look forward very much to seeing you next week.'

She motioned to leave and Cyril politely stood before returning to his seat. He felt as though a huge weight had been lifted. After a few moments he pushed back his hair. 'Come on, Liz. I'm starving!' he said out loud. A thin smile came to his lips.

For the first time he had voluntarily spoken her name without feeling the grip of guilt grab and twist his stomach. For the first time he felt his inner strength returning.

***

Owen sat opposite DI Claire as they listened to the open phone line to DI John Dunn as he described the search of Nathalie Gray's apartment.

'Whoever has been through the rooms was thorough, no damage but every cupboard and drawer has been searched. We believe that some paintings have been taken, two in fact, all the others remain in situ. At the moment we know little about the contents of the property.'

'Neighbours or relatives know anything?' Helen asked optimistically.

'Tracing relatives. I think you're aware mother's French, originally lived in Sedan, northern France, father's English.'

'Yes, they now live in the village of Nun Monkton, it's just outside York. They've been informed of their daughter's death. Mother didn't seem to react to the tragic news, probably delayed shock, that's sometimes the worst of reactions. Support has been put in place. We'll interview them tomorrow. Can you send over 360 degree images of the apartment, they may be able to shed light on the missing paintings?' Owen requested.

'One of the neighbours remembers seeing a regular male visitor. The last time she saw him was one day last week but she can't be more specific. Description to follow. As I've said, there appears to be no damage to the door lock or the apartment … just thoroughly searched. Whatever they were after may still be there. Scene of Crimes Officers are in there now.'

'The male visitor could well be either her boss or her colleague, a Dr Darwin Green. Images will be with you in a mo. One thought, are there any storage facilities in the apartment, garages, lock ups?' Helen Claire enquired.

'Underground parking but nothing private.'

The conversation over, Owen looked at DI Claire. 'As a colleague once said, 'Curiouser and curiouser! Shakti's collating info on Freshman's employees, we know that none has any previous according to our records. We just need to make sure that all the names correspond to the faces and the people we're dealing with.'

'Anything on Cyril, Owen? I don't like asking too many people.'

'Shakti spoke with Julie at the crime scene. She told her that he was still a bit of a mistle thrush whatever that means. Said he needed a bit more time. Always thought a mistle thrush was a bloody bird! You live and learn, probably some medical term.'

Helen just lifted her eyebrows. 'Mistle thrush, really?'

Chapter Four

The morning briefing was longer than usual for a Friday. The Incident Room was full. People perched on the edges of desks as Owen and Helen moved paper around on the surface in front of them. The large screen on the far wall shone deep blue, emblazoned with the badge of the North Yorkshire Police. The chattering and occasional laughter seemed to fill the small space. Stuart Park leaned against the back wall as more people entered, watching the scene whilst chewing a pencil. He smiled at Owen when he looked up and nodded showing his support, he knew that Owen was a little nervous. He received a smile in appreciation.

Owen tapped the top of the desk with his pen. The chattering and laughter slowly died away.

'Morning, morning everyone. If you've read the boards and the briefing notes you'll be aware of two new interesting developments, firstly note 6c. DNA found under Nathalie Gray's nails has matched with that of Dr Darwin Green, her colleague, who's now been formally interviewed here at the station. The transcript is available and should be read. Secondly, Dr Green has shed light on the two paintings missing from Gray's apartment. They are by two northern artists ...' Owen looked down at his notes. '... One is by the artist, Alan Lowndes and the other by a French artist, Adolphe Valette, who lived in Manchester. Both paintings have a considerable value. At this stage, we don't know whether the robbery and the murder are connected or simply a coincidence so an open mind everyone, please.'

Owen's thoughts turned immediately to Cyril. 'An open mind' was one of his sayings when closing a briefing. He smiled, a smile that was not missed by many in the room for they too were thinking exactly the same.

Helen spoke. 'Forensic examination of the vehicle has so far produced little. We've nothing on the car from when it was stolen up until the time it was discovered. This was a well-organised and methodical murder if not a little clumsy. The make of car and the routes had been carefully chosen. We're putting out a call on all possible channels, including social media, seeking help from the general public, so Control is gearing up for that. I want quick responses to anything that might seem relevant but everything in time will be followed up, everything. Is that clear?'

There was a definite affirmative from the collective.

'Requests for eyewitnesses and dash cam footage of the areas involved will be emphasised. We can't establish a motive for the killing unless we can link the two incidents. House to house in the vicinity of the apartment is now complete but, so far, it's showing nothing. I can't believe, however, that this professional young woman was murdered for paintings worth in the region of thirty thousand pounds. We're looking for something much more sinister. We're interviewing Freeman Freshman today so be aware of any developments. A warrant has been issued to search both Freshman's and Green's business and private premises. Owen will allocate individual and group tasks in a minute but remember to keep things uploaded and filed, no matter how trivial you might consider that data to be. Paperwork please, paperwork uploaded to HOLMES is key to police teamwork.' Helen stood and pointed to DC Smirthwaite. 'Brian, a minute.'

(HOLMES 2 - Home Office Large Major Enquiry System – is an informational technology system that is used predominantly by UK police forces for the coordination and investigation of major incidents such as murder, terrorism and high value frauds.)

**

Cyril's morning had not begun like all the others as on this occasion the alarm woke him. In his excitement he collected the phone, stopped the alarm and rang Julie.

'Julie…' He paused waiting for some kind of acknowledgement. '… for the first time in weeks I didn't beat the alarm. Slept right through.' He waited for the response but nothing came. 'Julie?' He then heard her sob very faintly as if she were holding her hand over the phone. It was out of sheer relief.

'Well done, you! I'm thrilled Cyril, absolutely thrilled.' She laughed trying to mask the quavering in her voice. 'So, what plans have you got for today?'

'Not a lot today, but tomorrow evening, if you're free that is, I have an invitation to the opening of the new Focus North Gallery and then maybe we could have a meal, possibly Italian?'

'I'd love that, Cyril … how I would love that.'

For the first time Cyril could sense the utter relief in Julie's voice and it brought a small lump to his throat. 'Pick you up at six-thirty?'

'Wonderful! I do love you.' She blew a kiss down the phone.

'Julie,' he paused.

'Yes, Cyril?'

'I just wanted you to know that I lo…' He stopped himself. He didn't have the emotional strength. 'Six-thirty.' He hung up.

***

Freeman Freshman sat uncomfortably in Interview Room Three. Even though the door was open and the noise from the immediate surroundings was non-threatening, the austerity and formality of the room brought with it a strange sense of guilt, the guilt he had felt as a child if asked to see the Head Teacher for some unknown reason. He shuffled his feet nervously and a bead of sweat broke the surface of his forehead, but he quickly rationalised it as a normal human reaction. After all, his colleague and friend had gone missing. He removed a neatly pressed handkerchief and dabbed away the moisture.

Owen was the first to enter. His demeanour did not improve the ambience.

'You're not under caution, Mr Freshman, you're here voluntarily to help with our enquiries ...' He looked up preparing to observe the response to the next few words. '... into the death and possible murder of Nathalie Gray.'

It took a moment for the words to sink in but then Owen read the man's facial expression as one of complete shock and horror.

'Why wasn't I told sooner? Bloody hell, man. Jesus!' He put his hands to his face resting his elbows on the table. 'Who would ... why? Christ!'

'She was found the morning she went missing, died before you made the sudden 999 call. Logged at 09:45. We thought that strange. Why should you call so soon after she didn't turn up for work? Most people who have loved ones go missing tend to wait a little longer, they tend to ask around, wait a while.'

'I explained all of that when you came to the Conference Centre. We checked her room, asked at Reception, tried to contact her mobile but there was nothing. I called because it was totally out of character.' He was beginning to recover a little from the initial shock. 'Murdered?' He paused and looked Owen straight in the eye. 'Let me ask you a question, Sergeant. If you had bleeding from your arse-end this morning would you ignore it for a fortnight in the hope that it would go away or would you ring to see a doctor?'

It was Owen's turn to feel a little uncomfortable so he switched his style of questioning. Freshman might have a point.

'Was Nathalie having any problems, relationships, financial?' Owen's tone was more cordial.

Freshman shook his head. 'Not that I'm aware of, she never changed from one day to the next, never seemed to display the mysterious hormonal mood swings that most females suffer. She was always efficient and thoroughly professional. Look, I've known her for four years, maybe longer. She's never missed a day's work nor a work commitment. Her conservation work is outstanding, brilliantly logged and photographed at each stage. She's the consummate professional, she's the perfect colleague ...' He stopped himself. 'Was, sadly was!' He lowered his head again. 'Murdered? Can't believe it, sorry!'

'What about her personal relationship with Dr Darwin Green?'

'As far as I'm aware their relationship was purely professional. What makes you think there was anything going on?'

'I can assure you that Dr Green has given a full account of the relationship they shared. Finally, when did you last see Lynn McGowen?'

Freshman slipped his hand into the inside pocket of his jacket and withdrew a diary. He opened it and flicked the thin ribbon that marked the correct date. He thumbed the pages backwards. 'Here, it's nearly three weeks. She did some research on two paintings we held in stock, three days' work in total. Should see her again ...' He fingered the pages in the opposite direction. '... next week, on the sixteenth. We're attending an auction viewing in London, Dr Green will be attending that appointment too.'

'You're aware that we'll be searching your properties and we'll be getting in touch with Lynn McGowen on her return to the U.K?'

'Yes, yes and so be it. Goodness, as long as those who do it are careful. As you can imagine, considering the profession I've been in for more years than you've been on the planet, my place of work and my storage facilities contain some valuable antique artefacts. I'll be present I assume?'

At times, Freshman could be absolutely charming and at times he could be a total prat. Owen found it difficult to remain calm. 'It will be arranged.'

***

Shakti sat in the Incident Room with a few other officers, mainly working on routine paperwork. It was warm and the buzz from either a computer or a light began to irritate her. She glanced at the boards checking images of the two missing paintings; she noted beneath from the scribbled comments that they had been added to the Art Crime Register. Once on the register they would become impossible to sell commercially worldwide.

She looked back at the Forensic reports from Nathalie's apartment. DNA matches for Darwin Green, Freshman and unknown others. She had a reputation for being a party girl so things might prove to be complicated. She flicked open an address book that had been removed from a cupboard under her house phone and carefully cross-referenced the numbers that had been extracted from her phone and SIM card. Accessing iCloud information would be impossible owing to the strict enforcement of client confidentiality by Apple. She decided to list all the female names that featured. It was then that she realised that they had missed an opportunity. She picked up the phone.

'Ma'am? It's Shakti. I just had a thought whilst looking through the lists and numbers in Nathalie's address book and phone records. We've missed one element. We should check the hotels within Harrogate for the day prior to her death for couples or single females; it would be relatively easy to do just mind-blowing and boring.'

'Please organise that.'

***

Monica Mac sat in the Leeds hotel room. On the bed lay the laptop and iPad. She checked her watch. The meeting had been set up before the murder. There were two venues planned, it was always worth staying one step ahead of the police. Both hotels had been booked in different names. She felt nervous. This was always the difficult time when the job had been done and the final payment had to be made. Some tried to adjust the fee, others were grateful and simply paid and left. Today she felt uneasy. Unusually, everything had been carried out by courier, the request, the initial payment, even the details of the venues; she knew nothing of the person making the request and more importantly, she believed, nobody knew her.

She checked her watch again and moved to the door. The corridor was empty. She closed the door and made her way to the lifts. She checked for the floor and pressed the button for the nearer lift. It would prove to be a mistake.

***

Cyril stood outside Focus North Gallery and looked in the windows. A large, metal, open-mesh security grill sat behind the glass. There were no paintings, only two empty easels. The same flutter of excitement filled his stomach, the one that signalled that he was eventually feeling human again. He turned and headed for The Stray. The clear sky and the warm breeze invited a good walk.

***

DC Park stood and watched the police search of Dr Darwin Green's home; fortunately he lived within the North Yorkshire Police boundary. It was, as he had imagined, elegant and classy. Rows of grey painted bookcases lined the hallway, occasionally broken by a painting or a sculpture. There was an order about the place. This was his only residence and he had freely and openly supported the search. Searches for firearms and firearms' residue had found nothing and neither had that for illegal drugs.

'If you know what you're looking for, then ask. If it's here, then I'll show you.'

His words fell on deaf ears. DC Park wandered around, simply looking at the paintings beautifully displayed on nearly every wall. *Cyril would be in his element here,* he thought to himself.

'By Braaq, born Liverpool, lived in Harrogate. Bit out of favour at the moment but his star will rise again, believe me.'

Park did not really see any value in paintings. 'How do you justify selling something that small for so much money? It's madness in my opinion.'

'Demand. The artist is dead so there's a limited supply on the market which pushes the price up. Who would have thought we'd be paying millons of pounds for the simple efforts of a rent collector? People do, they fight for them in the auction houses.'

'As a group, you, Freshman and your colleagues live miles apart. Does that not cause difficulties?'

'Always travelling, either to auctions, sales, fairs. Makes no difference where you live. Most of my research I can do online. We meet up regularly.'

'If I may say so, for someone who has suffered a dreadful shock of having your partner murdered you're very calm.'

'Would sitting and weeping change the situation? I'm a suspect and believe me, that really makes you remain sharp. Maybe when you lot are out of my life it might hit me.'

Within an hour the search was concluded. There was nothing. Dr Darwin Green finally closed the door, poured himself a drink and relaxed. Within half an hour he had slid one of the bookcases away from the wall, opened a short door and was descending into an area of the cellar that had originally been created in the sixties as a form of nuclear bunker. Now it served a very different purpose.

***

Monica sat on the dressing table stool, her arms bound at the elbows with a thick electrician's tie. The two men stared at her, their eyes cold.

'So this is what Mr Salvatore paid you to collect? He sent this video to Gray. He didn't expect to find it back here.'

'No, he paid me to kill, Nathalie Gray. You suggested that I might bring her laptop and tablet for an extra ten grand. There they are.'

'An accident you were told, a simple accident, not a fucking clumsy, fiery hit and fucking run!'

The back of the guy's gloved hand struck Monica at the side of the head propelling her off the chair. He then rested his foot on her neck making it impossible for her to stand.

'Fuck!'

'Once you get beyond the screen saver there's nothing apart from this.'

He lifted down the laptop to allow her access to the screen. Encased within a glass box she could see a model of a fat, moustachioed policeman, his cheeks marked in red circles and his eyebrows bushy. The shadowy figure appeared and put an old penny in a slot. The glass case illuminated as the model sprang into action, its mouth opened and the body swayed backwards and forwards. The sound of laughter erupted from within the mechanical device. Nobody laughed within the room. They let it play until the laughter had stopped and the fat policeman was returned to his opening position. The light went out.

'Only one person is laughing, someone is laughing at us, laughing, Monica, and that someone is not you and it's definitely not me. It will certainly not be the person who hired you, you can bet your last penny on that. Either that bitch knew that she was being watched or we have a very, very serious problem. Now we need to know everyone you've spoken to, we need to get to know your nearest and most certainly your dearest. Believe me, my dear, you'll tell us everything, I can assure you of that.'

The foot was lifted from her neck and she was dragged to her feet.

'We're going to take a little ride. Now you'll promise to be a good girl won't you?' As he spoke, the second person slid the hypodermic into her neck and injected a mild sedative. 'You'll be able to function physically, walk, with help but talking will prove difficult. The effects should only last an hour. Come on, you have an important meeting to attend.'

One man stood to either side and they walked her along the corridor to the emergency hotel stairs. There was security coverage of all the corridors and the emergency stairs only on the ground floor. The emergency doors on this level were alarmed. Keeping faces away from the cameras was key. One man left the stairs on Level Two and pressed for a lift. If it arrived occupied then he would wait. The other held on to

Monica in the stairway. The elevator was empty and he jammed his foot against the door. Monica was helped into the corridor and was assisted towards the elevator, their heads lowered. A helping hand ensured that Monica's eyes never looked anywhere but at the carpet. The same procedure was followed as they entered the elevator. They were soon at the underground garage area. A car had been positioned as close to the elevator doors as possible, to alleviate the need to expose themselves to the number of security cameras that were strategically located to maximise safety. Within five minutes they were on the Leeds inner ring road.

***

The requests to the hotels and guest-houses were landing in their computer inboxes marked, *Police and Priority Assistance Request*. The information included a description of the woman and a number of images taken from CCTV. It was also posted on the North Yorkshire Police Facebook and Twitter pages, giving details of where she might have been seen and requesting information concerning her identity and whereabouts. Usually some saw the request immediately but for others it would take time.

Helen had also added the same images and request to the north-east evening news in the hope of wider coverage.

***

Within hours, Monica was sitting uncomfortably in the total dark, her arms still trussed behind her at the elbows. Her finger ends were numb and her tongue found the tooth that had caught the blow in the hotel room. It wobbled. It would be foolish to suggest that she was not afraid; she had been in this game too long not to know what those who needed her services were capable of. She could smell the rich and not unpleasant aroma of turpentine; it was strong and heady yet in some ways offered comfort. She moved her head searching for the slightest chink of light in her dark world but found none.

Ever since she had left the army she had decided to use the skills she had been taught, both the legitimate and those that were encouraged but were never acknowledged. She had been afraid then too on many occasions but it was a different fear, it was a fear mixed with excitement and it was quite difficult to discern which was the stronger. The one palpable sense of fear she had felt was on the penultimate patrol of her last tour, in a small village comprising broken, mudbrick homes. Many of the tall, exterior walls to the yards, predominantly the women's area, had been shattered and the occupants had left days or weeks before. She could visualise the small pieces of detritus that hinted that this was once a home, a haven. It was now a place in which to demonstrate extreme caution. Everywhere looked pretty much the same, all you were concerned about was getting back in one piece. You never knew what was on the other side of the wall.

She remembered that many of the lads had just wanted to get the hell out and home but somehow she had been in her element. It was here that they first heard the cry, muffled and almost ethereal. The message was passed down via hand signals and each soldier dropped and waited. Like now, she could feel that her senses were alive and vivid, but then she had had her sight. As medic, she was called forward and proceeded, cautiously, careful not to tread where others had been; the IED was real and this very scenario was tailor-made to let your heart rule your head. They had found two young men, left by the Taliban. One was dead. Both men were naked and from the grotesque, physical damage, severely beaten. One was propped against the blood-spattered, mudbrick wall, both legs appearing to be broken, the other, prostrate, his decapitated head on his chest. She glanced at the head, flies swarmed where the orifices should have been. She looked at the mouth, quickly turning away as she realised what had been placed there; a glance between the youth's legs confirming her thought.

The other youth could not be approached. He had been kept alive, he was bait, to draw the soldiers in the hope that the medic would immediately help. It was only experience that told them that behind him would be an IED, bomb wired to detonate once the body was moved. Her group backed away, he would remain and face a slow and agonising death whilst being quickly infested with flies. His death was, in her opinion, probably the more cruel; the other youth had simply been tortured and slaughtered.

The light came on stabbing her eyes. She closed them and listened to the footsteps approaching, but what came next she could never have predicted.

Chapter Five

The day had seemed to go on forever. Cyril had bubbled with excitement since beating the alarm. He would have liked to convince himself that it was the thought of an evening with Julie that was the catalyst for this newfound euphoria, this renewed energy that now flowed into his very being, an energy that had suddenly been rekindled. Inside, if he were truly honest, it was the paintings and the thought of collecting another one more that brought a flutter to his stomach. As a compromise, he settled to the conclusion that it might be a cocktail of both. He glanced around the room assessing potential places a new painting might hang.

'Bloody hell, Cyril, you're going to have to be a little more discerning. Wall space is becoming a premium.'

He made a coffee and settled down with the well-thumbed catalogue and price list.

***

Monica lay on her right side. Her left humerus was shattered and bone shards had penetrated the flesh and the clothing, yet she felt no pain. She glanced at her arm and it brought to mind the shattered leg protruding from beneath the car wheel. Grimacing, she remembered a saying she would often quote to her army buddies, *What's round, comes around.* She could not fail but to notice the irony and the thought of the ultimate conclusion brought the strong taste of fear to her throat. She vomited.

The light suddenly seemed blinding. All she could recall was the immediate pain as the iron bar had crashed against her left arm; the sound, like a muffled gunshot, had been the bar making contact with her bone. She immediately fell to the right side, her head making contact with the stone floor. She remembered that the pain had come a little later, intense and fiery. It seemed to fill her whole being. Now, all she could see were shoes as she tried to shuffle away. She turned her head but the light blocked the people and faces from her view.

'Where's the laptop, Monica? Monica, please, you know we don't want to fall out.'

She caught the lilt of an accent as he spoke gently and quietly.

'I got them from her room, there were no others, that's all I know. They're no good to me. What I collected, I delivered.'

The iron bar tapped the exposed ends of the shattered bone and she remembered little else. She neither saw nor felt the local anaesthetic delivered to her arm, all she felt was relief and a false belief that they accepted what she had told them. She was not usually so foolish. She was returned to the darkness.

***

The taxi pulled up outside Julie's apartment and Cyril walked up the short pathway. He rang the bell. A moment later a hand moved the vertical blinds hanging in the bay window to reveal Julie's smiling face. He was waiting to count the number of fingers she normally raised, indicating the number of minutes she needed to be ready, but on this occasion none appeared. He simply smiled. The front door opened and she appeared in a beautiful black dress with one shoulder cut away revealing her elegant shoulder. She held a grey shawl. The sun was still high and the increasing shadows spread from the trees on The Stray across the road and were just creeping into the front garden.

'Beautiful evening, Cyril. Just look at the clarity of the sky.' She thought carefully before she spoke. She wanted to say it was good to be alive but … They both looked up. The blue was rich, the leaves from the many trees dark in contrast. 'The Stray is just so pretty, my very own front garden.'

'Makes you glad to be alive,' Cyril uttered, totally undermining her understanding of his newfound strength.

It had to be said, The Stray, the two-hundred acres of grassland in the heart of the town filled with pathways and trees, was one of Harrogate's true treasures. No matter how long you had lived there, it still amazed.

She slid her hand into his before turning and kissing his cheek. 'Thank you for inviting me.'

Cyril simply smiled. 'Beautiful dress, going somewhere special?'

She squeezed him a little closer. He opened the taxi door and she slid in.

The journey took seven minutes. Already a number of people were approaching the gallery.

'It's going to be a busy evening,' he said as he collected the catalogue from the seat and handed it to Julie before paying the taxi fare.

'I'm going to buy a painting tonight, a new start,' he whispered as they stood facing the gallery window. Julie linked his arm as if to demonstrate her approval.

'I might just buy it for you.'

Cyril turned and looked at her. He did not smile, he just looked at her and she felt him pull her just a little closer.

In the window, in place of the empty easels, two paintings, both large, now filled the space. They admired them for a few moments before entering the gallery. To the left was a table containing glasses and bottles of Champagne. Cyril took two flutes and started to walk around, his eyes darting between the paintings. It was busy.

'DCI Cyril Bennett! How good of you to come and this must be Dr Julie. He never talks about anybody else any more.' He proffered a hand.

Julie blushed slightly, thrilled by what she had heard.

Simon Posthumus was a larger than life character. This was his third gallery; the first had been opened in Manchester in the eighties followed by a second in Skipton. The Harrogate Gallery was to be the jewel in the crown and that was clearly reflected in the quality, rarity and value of the exhibits for an opening show. He had known Cyril for a number of years and in the early days had offered very positive advice, almost fatherly guidance, when he had started buying at auction.

'I didn't expect to see four Lowry oils, goodness and the prices!' Cyril said, obviously impressed by the price tags of two of the larger pieces, at over eight hundred thousand pounds.

'Some signed prints too in the upstairs rooms for those who would like a bit of the man at a more reasonable cost. Five years ago you'd have got the prints for a few hundred and now they're a few thousand … a good investment if you buy right. Now, you two, I want you to meet a really special artist friend of mine who has two works in the show. His name's Ben Kelly. He's had sell out shows all over the place. Believe me he's bound to become one of the best new northern artists. Come with me!' He put his arm gently around Julie's shoulders and guided her, leaving Cyril to follow in their wake.

They moved through the crowd. Simon, like Moses, parted the people as if they were the Red Sea. 'Ben! Ben! Please meet Cyril and Julie and be careful what you say, he's a copper and she's a pathologist. She'll steal your heart, she's stolen his!' He nodded towards Cyril and laughed heartily before moving away to mingle with the other guests.

'This one of yours, Ben?' Cyril asked, looking at a woodland scene. Shafts of light penetrated the canopy of bright, green leaves illuminating three people standing within a glade. Julie's heart sank; she could see that the light clearly had the appearance of long pins and wondered how Cyril would perceive it. Losing a colleague as he had, murdered using a hatpin, had triggered his illness and now at the very moment that he seemed to have overcome the guilt and the trauma, he was faced with this. She could not believe it.

A line of light had been painted to fall directly on one of the three figures as if by an act of God. She watched as he stood back and admired the image. Ben discussed his technique and Cyril listened intently.

'This wasn't in the catalogue?' Cyril quizzed.

'No, sold one but this, in my opinion, is equally good but then I would say that wouldn't I!'

Cyril simply smiled. 'Sell when you can. I like that very much, Ben. It brings a friend to mind …'

Julie cringed and linked Cyril's arm.

'I heard a story, it may be apocryphal, but it suggested that the Ancient Egyptians built their pyramids after seeing the rays of light penetrate cloud in the form of an inverted 'V', not dissimilar to a pyramid. We've all seen it, I'm sure and it makes some sense. You've captured that; it's quite a heavenly and peaceful scene.' He paused for a moment and turned to look at Julie who returned his gaze and smiled. He saw the anxiety in her eyes. 'I'd like to buy it, Ben.' He put out his hand.

Ben was taken aback by the speed of the sale, but quickly shook Cyril's hand.

'Those pin-sharp depictions of white light sold it to me. Thank you. I'm sure it won't be the last I buy of yours, either.'

A red spot was added to the card description below the painting and Cyril was thrilled with his purchase. It was then that Julie noted the title, 'Pin-sharp Light.'

Never once did Cyril mention Liz throughout the whole evening. He seemed more relaxed and contented than at any other time since her murder and she was grateful to see the Cyril of old emerging from the darkness. He even talked openly about returning to work. They finished their meal and walked to the Cenotaph, sitting briefly. The traffic moved only in one direction as they chatted. It was like old times.

'Come on, time to get you home.'

Cyril and Julie climbed from the taxi and made their way up the path.

'Tempt you to a nightcap, Cyril Bennett, or have you something better planned?' She giggled as he pulled a face. 'Coffee and a little something?'

Cyril returned to the taxi and paid before joining Julie at the now-open door.

***

Cyril's phone vibrated and then rang, the old-style tone echoing around the bedroom. Initially he thought it part of a dream but then the constant ring brought a reality check. He answered. He felt Julie turn and rest a hand on his shoulder.

'Cyril, is that you? Oh, Jesus! The buggers have robbed the bloody gallery. Tonight of all bloody nights! I've sold a lot of the work and it's bloody gone.'

Cyril's head hurt as he checked his watch. The green luminous characters told him the time was ten past three.

'Simon I'm not in work, you know that. Have you dialled 999?'

'The alarm system is linked to a central watch; the coppers were here before me. Bloody hell, Bennett, the bloody Lowry paintings have gone, all of them and the Valette, one or two other odds and sods but that's only at first glance. Can you get down here? I'd be far happier than dealing with some heavy-handed bloody youth who doesn't know his arse from his elbow. These guys don't seem remotely bothered. Talk about laissez-faire they are definitely being bloody lazy and unfair!'

'The Ben Kelly paintings, what of the Kelly paintings?'

'Bugger off, Bennett, be serious, man. I need you here for Christ sake, I've got a fortune wrapped up in this place!'

'Stay there and I'll contact my partner, he'll handle it. It'll be thirty to forty-five minutes before he gets there. You should see Crime Scene Investigators arrive, don't interfere, let them do their job.'

He hung up before dialling Owen's number.

'Gallery robbed,' he whispered to Julie who simply turned over.

***

Owen's phone was on the bed, he had learned not to leave it amongst the mass of detritus that filled his bedside table. It shimmied across the sheet as it rang, slowly burying itself like a small mole under the duvet. A hand reached out blindly fumbling around until it was found.

'Owen.'

'Good morning, Owen, it's Cyril.'

'It's not good, Sir, and it's not morning, it's neither Saturday or Sunday, it's the middle of the bloody night ... Are you alright?'

'Nor, Owen. Neither nor, either or.'

'Sir?'

Cyril immediately sensed the anxiety in Owen's voice. 'Yes, yes. I'm not about to jump from a great height or do anything foolish. I'm fine. I need a favour. Can you get down to Montpellier Hill? There's been a break in at the Focus North Gallery, some valuable stuff has gone, too. You need to speak to Simon Posthumus. He knows you're coming. Please keep me informed.'

'Straight away, Sir. I was only sleeping anyway.'

Cyril smiled. 'Thanks. I owe you.'

Owen looked at the illuminated screen on his phone, it showed three twenty. He pulled the duvet over his head briefly and hollered one word, 'Shit!'

It made no difference to his mood, no difference at all.

***

Monica stirred as the light changed the whole ambience of the room again. The throb from her shattered arm pulsed down her left side. There was no real pain just this intense feeling of numbness. She watched the shoes approaching from her position on the floor. It was then that the stars and the agony struck again as the bar smashed onto her exposed ankle trapping it between the stone floor and the force of the strike. Myriad bones in the upper part of her foot were dislodged and moved as her foot broke free from the ankle joint stretching the skin taut. A figure knelt and injected anaesthetic above the damage.

'No time to sleep, Monica. Goodness me, no, whatever are you thinking?' The speaker knew that she could not hear him. Slowly she came to. The pain slowly drifted away and her eyes opened briefly.

'Now you're back with us, let me remind you of a little rhyme we used to sing. *The ankle bone is connected to the shin bone, the shin bone is connected to the knee bone …* You're not singing, Monica, but I think you understand where we're going with this. I can break probably five, maybe six more major bones before your body will scream enough is enough, but why go that far? I just need a name. Funny, we've now used the last of the anaesthetic too. Sad!'

Monica knew that as soon as she gave a name that would be the end, but then the end was going to come anyway after a good deal more agony. Why should she protect someone who had probably sold her down the river?

She whispered a name.

'Didn't catch that.' He knelt to her side before turning his ear towards her mouth. She whispered a name slowly again. He turned his face and smiled at her. 'Thank you.'

As soon as he had said the words she spat into his mouth. 'Now you can fuck off and leave me in peace!' She looked up and smiled, a last, brave act of defiance showed on her face but inside she was turning to jelly.

He stood slowly and spat the remnants of her saliva from his mouth onto her body before wiping his lips with his hand. He reached over and dragged the bar from the hands of the man standing next to him.

'May I?' He weighed it in his hands, all the while searching her features and hoping that she would plead for her life. She did not.

'People like you haven't got the balls.' She lifted her face higher. 'No balls and a small cock. In the forces, we used to say that you people had one forward gear and six reverse when it came to a fight.'

Not many people could get to him but she had found and pressed all of his buttons. 'Good night, Monica. I have to say, you're a brave girl. For your information, I'm Sicilian!'

The bar plunged from head height and hit Monica across the forehead, immediately crushing her skull against the stone-flagged floor. Blood and brains spattered the wall and those standing nearby. He struck twice more. She was already dead.

'Move this bag of shite, clean and sterilise it and then dump it where it'll be found quickly. I want a certain person to realise that we know. No trail, you hear, no trail.'

***

Owen saw the plethora of police vehicles as he drove down St Mary's Walk. The blue strobes illuminated the trees. The dark sky was just beginning to make way for the pending dawn. He parked and walked towards the taped-off gallery. He did not need to be introduced to Simon Posthumus. The portly gentleman pacing the pavement gave the appearance of someone who had just been relieved of a vast sum of money. Showing his warrant card, he made his way to the Crime Scene Manager.

'Whose shout?'

'DS Grimshaw, he's round the back. What are you doing here at this ungodly hour?'

Owen smiled. 'Special request!'

Owen walked down into Montpellier Street and then stopped at the Police tape. Dan Grimshaw was looking at the CCTV camera that was positioned to screen the back of the gallery. It was the dark, domed variety.

'Dan, sorry to tread on your toes but Cyril asked me to call. The owner is a friend of his, you know how it goes!' They shook hands. 'Anything?'

'We'll be checking this camera and those surrounding. Obviously, everything's been taken out of the back here. CSI are in there now and we should get a clearer picture once they're done. Bloody cheek though, opening night too!'

'What was the response time from alarm to arrival?'

'Ten, fifteen minutes at most. Looks as though it was triggered well after the robbery. We're not too sure but there was nothing when we arrived, just a flashing box.'

'Do you mind if I hang around and chat to Posthumus?'

'Be my guest! I'll not get to him for a while.'

Owen walked back towards Montpellier Hill, Posthumus was still pacing. The sky was much lighter, aided by a turquoise streak that had crept along the eastern end of the upper part of the hill, silhouetting the tip of the Cenotaph. Cigar smoke blossomed, white above Posthumus as he paced the edge of the grassy area.

'Mr Posthumus?' Owen didn't wait for a response. 'DS Owen. DCI Cyril Bennett asked me to pop down and have a word.'

'Bloody hell, man. Can't believe it. You can have nothing these days.' He puffed on the cigar, like a nervous father awaiting the delivery of his firstborn. 'Found anything, any clues?'

'They're still going over it, you'll have to be patient. There are others back at the station requesting and checking CCTV. You'll not get far nowadays without having one camera or another staring at you.'

Owen pointed down the road. 'We're on camera now. You had some security cameras at the back and in the shop. They'll offer clues, Mr Posthumus. It only takes one slip. Look at the Hatton Garden case.'

'Didn't get all the stuff back though, did they!'

'They never will either, the owners dare not share with the police what they had stashed there. What with Inland Revenue looking over their shoulders, it generated a lot of interest. Providing everything you had in there is legit and catalogued, it can't be sold. The difficulties arise when it's not disclosed, that's when you're in big trouble.'

As Owen spoke he noticed Posthumus draw more heavily on his cigar. His feet moved as if the pavement were now suddenly very hot.

'Bloody hell, been in the trade too long. Know the rules and know the pitfalls. Everything's legit, everything's legit.'

Owen noticed that now he had lost his bravado and he failed to keep eye contact. 'I'd go and get some sleep, that's my advice. You're going to have a busy day tomorrow.'

At that moment a reporter approached. He took a number of pictures of the gallery's façade, ensuring that the crime scene tape and an officer were in the shot. He then spotted Owen and Posthumus and hurriedly headed in their direction.

'Too late, Mr Posthumus, the sharks have already tasted blood. Your day will no longer be your own.'

'Detective Sergeant Owen?'

Owen turned and spread his chest in the hope that the reporter might not encroach too much within his personal space.

'Peter Bottomley, 'Harrogate Advertiser'. May I have a few minutes?'

Both Owen and Posthumus looked at the young lad who had so enthusiastically burst upon the early morning scene. His shirt was buttoned incorrectly and his jacket collar stuck up behind his left ear. Posthumus straightened it. Bottomley held a small Dictaphone and spoke into it before putting it to his ear.

'It's working!' he said as if to himself and a smile of success broke across his lips.

'There's very little to report, Peter. Scene of Crime people are in there now. We can tell you little about what has and what hasn't gone on. Early for you, Sunday at ...' Owen checked the time on his phone. '... 04:16. Out late too last night I suspect?'

Peter just nodded. 'I was told that the gallery held some very expensive paintings, Mr ... Mr ...' He looked at the person standing with Owen.

'Peter. Simon Posthumus.'

It was at this point that Owen decided to move away. He would catch up later. He dialled Cyril's number.

'What have you got?' Cyril sat in the kitchen. A coffee steamed on the counter and his electronic cigarette was not far from his lips.

'It appears that the alarm was triggered sometime after the robbery, possibly deliberately. Looking at CCTV at present. Dan Grimshaw's got the case. Is Posthumus legit. Sir?'

'Legit? In what way do you mean legit? He's been dealing in high-end art for years. Known him for years too.'

'Just had a funny feeling when we were chatting. You always say listen to those feelings.'

'Can we meet sometime today and we'll have a chat? There should be more to go on by then, too. Say Caffè Nero, by the Cenotaph at ...' Cyril looked at his watch. 'Say 12? I'll buy and I'll throw in a Panini.'

'Sunday, Sir. Not working, even God took one day off a week.'

'Good, then I'll see you at 12.' Cyril hung up.

***

The wooden crate was small considering the contents. It was clearly marked FRAGILE in red, block letters followed by the words, THIS WAY UP. The crate sat partially illuminated by the inefficient, Victorian-style steel lights that were sparsely dotted along the length of Swan Road. The container was perched on the top step resting against the doors of the Harrogate Mercer Art Gallery. It would be another two hours before it was spotted. A member of the hotel staff arriving at one of the many hotels that ran the length on the opposite side of Swan Road, noticed it. She mentioned it to the manager as she checked in for work.

Within fifteen minutes a police car was parked at the lower end of the road and two officers had approached within a safe distance. The Curator had been contacted but she knew nothing of the container assuring the police that when the gallery had been closed the previous evening, the steps had been clear. A further forty minutes had seen a sniffer dog move to the door. The container, according to the dog's sense of smell, held no explosives. Two SOCOs sealed off an area and began working the immediate vicinity along the front of the stone building. The dawn light had started to creep into every crevice and the streetlights switched off automatically. A temporary barrier had been placed across the bottom of the gallery steps; there were too many hotels opposite with too many guests watching from too many windows. It was only when the lid of the container was removed that they realised what they had.

***

52

The sun streamed through the blinds and the smell of toast and coffee made waking early at the weekend bearable.

'Smells wonderful, Cyril.' Julie yawned and stretched, the quilt slipping low off her shoulders.

'Looks fantastic!' Cyril responded.

'Was that Owen at some ungodly hour, I seem to vaguely recall hearing you nattering on. Problem with the gallery?'

'Not a good end to Simon's prestigious opening. They've been in and taken one or two items and I can guess which ones.'

'Surely the Lowry paintings were off the wall and locked away?'

Cyril just raised an eyebrow as he carried the tray towards the bed. 'Boiled egg and soldiers too. I just hope the Ben Kelly's still there.'

Julie just shook her head and looked at the egg. Cyril had drawn a smiley face on the shell and written the words 'Love you'. Julie started to weep.

Chapter Six

Caffè Nero on Cambridge Crescent was much busier than Cyril had expected. He sat by the window, a latte, the surface patterned with some kind of leaf, stared at him from an enormous, white cup. Fortunately it had a saucer but, disappointingly, it resembled bathroom porcelain rather than a bone china coffee can. It was another fine day and the tourists would be out in full force; it was one of the small drawbacks of living in such a magnificent town. He balanced it in his mind by recalling that even the Garden of Eden had a vile snake, smiled and sipped his coffee.

Cyril saw Owen arrive at the top of Montpellier Hill. He watched him check the traffic and then move towards the Cenotaph. It was then that he noticed Cyril sitting by the window and he waved. It was good to see the big man; how he had missed him, warts 'n' all.

Owen burst through the door. 'Great to see you, Sir. Looking really well,' he lied. Cyril still looked drawn, his complexion grey. He had lost weight and he had little to lose in the first place.

Owen sat whilst Cyril went to order.

'What news?'

Owen sipped some coffee. A small amount of milky foam settled on his upper lip, which he quickly removed with the back of his hand.

'All the Lowry paintings have gone, I think he said a Valette and a couple of others; it amounts to quite a haul. Posthumus is either furious one minute or morose the next. Can't make up his mind which emotion to hang his hat on. He's busy with the TV and radio, even Sky News is there so I don't know how Harrogate's own Stray FM will get on.'

'It's the best free advertising he'll get,' grumbled Cyril. 'If he over-eggs it they'll think he did it to get the publicity!'

'Do you think …'

A waitress brought over the Panini, breaking his train of thought.

Owen took a mouthful but it did not prevent him from continuing the conversation. Cyril knew what was coming from Owen's lips and sat back hoping that any food projectiles would not travel that far. He moved his coffee cup too just to be on the safe side.

'A body squashed into a wooden box was left on the steps of the Mercer Gallery last night too. What God takes with one hand he gives back with the other!' Owen's matter of fact tone played down the serious nature of the find and Cyril found himself doubting what he had just heard.

'What?' Cyril sat up and watched Owen finish the rest of the Panini. 'Whose body?'

'Long story.'

Owen went on to inform Cyril of Nathalie Gray's murder.

'So, we believe the body is that of the murderer, same build. As I say, the face has been totally destroyed.'

'Who's the medic?'

'Dr Caner. He's expecting me to be there for the post-mortem. Looking forward to it to be honest.'

Cyril watched as the final crumb was launched from Owen's bottom lip. It was time to go.

'SCO7 will no doubt be involved at some stage, of that I have no doubt!' Cyril pointed out. 'They have a small group which looks into art crime. They were at New Scotland Yard but with the cost savings and the closure, I think I read that they've been moved to Cobalt Square … anyway that's neither here nor there but someone will be in touch believe me.'

Owen just shrugged his shoulders, finished his coffee and followed Cyril to the door.

'Owen, I'm getting there, if I can help in any way … should be back in the next week or so.'

'I'd be happy if you came back now, this very minute. DI Claire's doing just fine, a good copper, takes no shit but it's not the same.'

Those few words were like music to Cyril's ears. He too felt the same way.

'Owen, tell Grimshaw there was a robbery in the Manchester area a few years back, very similar circumstances. Can't remember much as I wasn't collecting then. SCO7 will have the details. It's worth an ask.'

They shook hands.

***

Owen sat with Helen and Shakti as they went over the notes concerning the discovery of the body. Owen had received a call that morning from the Chief Constable and had taken charge of the case once it was believed that the body was linked to Nathalie Gray's murder.

'Why dump her on the steps of Harrogate's Art Gallery? Don't tell me there's a link between Nathalie's career in the fine art field and the gallery, other than it holds paintings?'

Owen said nothing.

'We've interviewed employees and guests working and staying in the hotels opposite. Other than two people going to work on the breakfast shift, nobody saw or heard anything. People returned to their hotels on Saturday up until one in the morning, but none could be sure as to whether the box was already there. If it were it was probably in the shadows. We've also been to see the Mercer Gallery staff, they were thrilled to be rudely awakened on a Sunday morning! None had seen nor knew Nathalie Gray, apart from one, who thought she recognised her. Another knew Dr Darwin Green. He'd been in the gallery sometime last year looking at an …' Shakti looked at her notes. '… an Atkinson Grimshaw painting. I need to talk to the Curator.'

Stuart Park popped his head round the door. 'Ma'am, a guy saw our request on Facebook and dropped a flash memory card from his dash camera. It was taken over two days, the date of the murder and the previous day. It's interesting to say the least.'

Stuart slipped the card into the side of the large screen fixed to the far wall. They watched as the car drove down familiar roads. The sky was dark and dull.

'You see here he pulls over to pass a runner.' He put the video into slow motion, then he changed back to normal speed. 'As we turn this bend up ahead what do we see?'

'Another runner?'

'Watch! The car pulls out, the headlights again highlight the runner.' Stuart paused the shot. 'She's wearing the same gear as seen on Nathalie Gray when she left the hotel on the day that she was killed. Did you notice the reflective strip on the second runner's shoes? That most definitely is Nathalie Gray, so who is the chaser, who is that first runner? I bet when they analyse that runner's gait we'll discover it's our murderer. She's been tracking Gray … it was well planned and executed. Now look at this! The video was obviously taken from the same car but this time the day was brighter. The sky was clear and the sun was just beginning to appear.'

The camera struggled for clarity, blinded by the near horizontal rays. Occasionally, as objects along the roadside masked the sun, the view ahead became clear.

'Here, coming up!' They could make out a runner, again, it was Nathalie Gray, the same clothes. The car passed her and rounded a bend. The road ahead stretched long and straight. The sun was now blinding and the car's speed was adjusted accordingly.

'In a minute you'll see the car move to the right and it will slow.'

Stuart paused it. Ahead they could discern the silhouette of a parked car. 'One of the lads wears an anorak marked, *car spotter* and he tells me that it's our Lexus.'

Helen was the first to speak.

'So no other runner?'

'No, we've gone through it all. Maybe the other runner was now a driver.'

'So she was deliberately hunted and killed? All we have to do is discover why. The hunter then became the hunted.' She turned to Stuart. 'Interview the owner of the camera and see if he saw anything on the previous day.'

'I have and he did. Saw the runners for four days he thinks. There are no images as the camera loops and has overwritten those days, so, as I said, had the pursuer now moved to the car? Once the deed was done she just jogged back into town.'

The story was definitely plausible and the physical evidence certainly supported the hypothesis.

***

The smell of bleach permeated the room killing any smell of turpentine. The stone floor had been disinfected and hosed down in the hope of destroying any trace of DNA. Every item of clothing had been bagged before the three people left the room. The bags would be incinerated, leaving no trace that Monica had ever been in the place. Their full attention would now focus on the name Monica had revealed. Hopefully they would receive a little more cooperation.

***

Owen stood in the kitchen; he was sipping tea from his mug whilst staring at Cyril's cup and saucer.

'Penny for them?' Dan Grimshaw asked.

'Just wishing Cyril was back. How are you faring with the robbery? Do you have a relative who paints?'

'Decorates houses, yes. Why?'

'Bloody hell, no, pictures and the like.'

Dan shook his head.

'In the Harrogate Mercer Gallery there's a painting by an Atkinson Grimshaw, thought he might be one of yours.'

'Never heard of him.'

'You have now. What have you got for me?'

'Give us a minute to make a brew, bloody hell it's clever, I'll show you. Just a tick.'

Owen looked at the computer screen.

'CCTV images. Clear? Montpellier Hill?'

Owen nodded his understanding. Suddenly, for a few seconds, the screen turned white before reverting to the street scene, then it happened again and again.

'Laser pen. It's been set up to target the public camera. The pen is placed somewhere off to the side. Probably they planned the position at some time in the last week during all the building work. Now look at this interior shot. This camera momentarily goes blank, like the blink of an eye, before returning to the standard image. Only now, that is a camera looking at a looped image. There are three cameras in the shop and each had been set up to loop the previous hour so what you're seeing is not what went on. If you had the time to look on camera three, you'd see the same car's lights strike the wall every hour.'

'Do you know the names of all the contractors and the individuals working on the development?'

'Yes, and they'll be interviewed, but it may well be an outside hacking job, possibly even done from abroad. Someone has taken control of the security system remotely, it's an expensive and sophisticated system and all that complexity has an Achilles' heel, of that I have no doubt. The technical boys are being brought in alongside the manufacturer's technicians. The same goes for the cameras positioned to pick up the rear door. The only way they could attack the public cameras was by pen, but these …'

'What about the CCTV in Montpellier Street and Mews?'

'Nothing. This was well planned and well executed.'

The five words made Owen stand up.

'What did you just say?'

'Well planned and well executed. Something wrong?'

'No, no, nothing … Good man … Thanks.' He tapped Dan on the shoulder and smiled. 'I'll tell you later, it could be nothing.'

Owen rushed back through to the Incident Room. Helen was still there but Shakti had gone to the second crime scene. He picked up a marker and wrote on the white board, *Well planned and well executed.* 'Where have you heard that today, Ma'am?' He stood with the pen to his lips as if willing the answer from her.

'Stuart Park said it when we were watching the video.'

'Bingo! I've just been looking at some CCTV of the Focus North Gallery break in. That's what Grimshaw said about the robbery.' Owen tapped the board. 'Word perfect. Art, and we're talking a lot of money.'

'Enough for a double murder?' Helen suddenly sat up as she spoke.

'People have been murdered for their watches in the past. If you've killed one person, what does it matter if it becomes three or four?'

***

There was nothing to see at the Mercer Gallery. Shakti stood and looked up the road to The Swan Hotel at the junction of York Road. The vehicle dropping off the case containing the body could have come from any of three routes but then, once the case had been deposited, the opportunities offered to leave the scene were open-ended. If nothing were to be seen on CCTV, then the vehicle must have taken the route away from the town centre. Once on York Road, the choice increased, like branches from a tree, each branch bringing more options.

She crossed the road and walked up the front path of one of the hotels, once a grand Victorian terrace. Some of the houses higher up the road were still maintained as private homes. She sat on one of the benches positioned in the garden, staring at the gallery. The trees to the left of the building were lush and dark, the Crescent Gardens running gently downhill towards the main road.

'If you kill someone, why would you put their body in a box and deliver it to an art gallery in the middle of town, when really you should be concealing the crime not broadcasting it?' She spoke out loud as if to someone sitting opposite before answering her own question.

'To set an example? To intimidate someone? To taunt the police? To demonstrate that nobody is safe?' She quickly ran out of ideas. Resting her elbows on the table, she steepled her fingers under her chin. 'Murderer is murdered. Did they get the wrong target? Did they fail to fulfil their role in some other way?'

'Are you alright?' The Hotel Manager had observed her for the fifteen minutes that she had been sitting at one of the tables. 'May I get you something? Tea or coffee?'

Shakti smiled. 'No thanks.' She showed her warrant card.

'From all the fuss I can assume it was serious and not somebody just fly-tipping?'

Shakti said nothing about the case's contents. 'What I can't understand is that nobody witnessed anything. A box appears, sits on a step of a municipal building for hours and nobody notices.'

'Maybe, with respect, you should look to your own. Very few foot patrols now, coppers zoom here and there in cars, often missing the subtlety of the daily happenings in the town's quiet corners, they miss the minor crimes. If we have a problem that requires police assistance, let's say a car is damaged, no one's interested. It can take days to get a response then suddenly, a wooden box is dumped on the municipal steps, there …' He pointed across the road. '… and we're inundated with the police and their entourage, the press and all the other parasites blue flashing lights attract.'

'It was a serious crime … and with crimes of this nature we always seek the help of the general public.' She felt her hackles rise and started to move towards the road. She had come to think, not to get into a one-sided debate about modern policing.

'This road has many hotels and other tourist accommodation. People arrive at all hours. It looks like a quiet road but you'll see some traffic each hour for the full twenty-four. Besides, what's that famous adage, if you want to hide something, hide it under their noses!'

Shakti simply smiled. 'Thanks for the use of your bench.' She glanced at the name badge on his jacket lapel, Mr MacParland. 'Your comments are duly noted.' She turned and walked back towards her car. She just wanted to scream.

Chapter Seven

DI Claire sat looking at the screen, waiting for the conference call to begin. She checked her watch against the clock on the wall, there was a discrepancy, but only a minute or so. SCO7 had organised the call. A DI Ian Thirsk appeared, taking a seat. Helen Claire watched him settle and arrange his papers. He adjusted the camera and smiled at seeing his Harrogate colleague on his screen.

'Never bloody get used to these. Can you hear me?'

Helen instinctively leaned forward and answered in the affirmative.

'It's a big loss for a gallery of that size. Mr Posthumus and his galleries are known to us. He's been trading over a long period and although he's suffered two previous robberies, neither was on this scale, couple of grand at most. What's significant is the sophisticated way in which the security system has been tampered with; they certainly used it to their own advantage. They could have allowed the alarm to remain silent. The break-in would then have only been discovered, say, twelve hours later, but they triggered the alarm when they were safely away. Arrogance, pure arrogance.'

'Or they simply cocked up!'

'In what way?'

'They hoped the alarm would be nullified, but no, we're immediately giving credit where it might not be due, if they'd got it wrong. It could have gone off when they were still in there, so instead of arrogance and skill, you could read bloody luck!'

There was a pause and both looked at each other over the ether, an unreal, clinical, silence grew. Helen could see on his face that he had accepted her point. She was determined to have her say.

'You're aware, I take it, of the case that's running parallel, the double murder?' She watched Ian Thirsk look away from his notes again and directly at the screen. 'We've no clear evidence link, just supposition, but the fact that the first woman murdered had worked within the fine art trade for a number of years is significant, yet we can't find any link to her and Focus North Gallery, or in fact Posthumus. She may well have a link to the missing paintings, but as yet, we cannot say.' She watched him rub his chin and sit forward. For the first time he smiled.

'Let me tell you what we know so that we can start looking for similarities with other cold cases. Just over ten years ago, a gallery, again a newly opened one situated on the outskirts of Manchester, was the target of an attack. Significantly, the robbery occurred after the opening night and not, as you might think, before it. All the paintings were to remain on show until after the exhibition so even though many would sell prior to or on the night, they would remain in the gallery. This leads us to the conclusion that an expert within the criminal group assessed the targeted works to determine whether they were authentic and therefore worth the risk. This was either done on, or shortly after the opening of the exhibition. Witnesses stated that they saw two men looking at the gallery catalogue on the night of the robbery, maybe memorising the ones to take, who knows? I'll come back to that assessment later. What is again significant, Helen, is that the majority of the paintings were by L S Lowry; other important paintings were by a Helen Bradley and David Hockney. At today's prices you'd be looking at three million plus. It doesn't end there, three years prior to that, a gallery in Wales, again specialising in northern art, suffered a similar fate. This time it wasn't predominantly, Lowry.'

'So, there's evidence to suggest that some member of the group came to the gallery and inspected the paintings? Wouldn't that have been noted? If they'd gone, let's say, to all the Lowry works, then the other paintings? Surely the person showing the work would have some knowledge of that person and what about the security cameras?'

'Ten years ago there were no cameras, the iPhone had just been released. We forget how technology has moved on in such a short period of time. The majority of people attending the opening night at the Harrogate show would mainly have gone to view the most expensive paintings, it's the nature of the beast. They can't afford one, but then, as the saying goes, a cat can look at a king. So, the owner or staff speak to maybe a hundred or more people, faces become just that … faces. You and I both know that if you drive a car past a group of people and then ask them the make and colour of the car, you'll get conflicting answers. People as witnesses are unreliable, cameras are not. Although in the case of your robbery, the system was corrupted, Forensics may well be in a position to retrieve the earlier images.'

'And the stolen paintings from the previous cases?'

'Never seen again, and unless we're really lucky, neither will Posthumus's paintings grace another gallery wall. Let's hope that he had adequate insurance. As far as we know, Helen, the stolen work has never hit any market. Besides, as you're aware they're all now on the Art Loss Register and will be on every worldwide art loss database. Once there, they'll never resurface, they cannot be sold on the open market but if they were stolen to order then they'll be in some private house, or yacht. Most likely they'll be used as collateral by the criminal fraternity, they'll be given a value and drugs or people will be traded against them.'

'We're now monitoring everything regarding this case and the murder case, all on HOLMES and we look forward to your full support. Thank you.' Helen smiled and closed her folder.

After a few courtesies Helen sat back and the call ended.

***

Owen found himself on the same mezzanine floor looking at the same autopsy table but on this occasion the corpse looked less alien and more human. He noted the vents around the periphery of the table. He had been fascinated after his previous visit and looked them up on Google. Air would be drawn into them protecting those working during the procedure; it was known as a downdraft table. Doctor Caner proceeded methodically, the assistants worked without instruction, it was just one of many such operations, appearing to run like clockwork.

'Sergeant, severe damage to the left humerus.' The voice seemed strange coming from a different location from the man below. The speaker was just above Owen's head. 'Multi-compound fracture with some bone loss resulting from severe blunt-force trauma causing contusion and to a lesser degree abrasion. There's evidence that it was some kind of metal bar, we'll know for sure once the samples of the fragmented bone have been analysed. The forehead has received the hardest blow resulting in a diagonal compression and lacerations, causing extensive distortion and disruption to the facial features.'

After five more minutes of photographing and careful study, during which small particles were removed, the commentary continued. 'Still with me, Sergeant? I've known Bennett leave well before now! If you begin to feel a bit queasy rise up and down on your toes, that sometimes helps.' He turned and looked up as if checking that Owen was following his instructions.

Owen raised a hand and smiled. 'The purple around the lower part of the body?'

'Where the blood settles after death, remember the heart has stopped and so too has the circulation. The blood pools with gravity, it's known as livor mortis. It gives us a clear indication of the position of the body after death.'

Caner went on to describe the other injuries, with particular reference to the bruising and minor lacerations to the area just above the elbows.

'Electrician's ties, wide ones, too. She was bound well before and at the time of death so we can safely say this young lady was murdered, after she was sadistically beaten. We'll check the internal organs and see if there's anything untoward. The toxicology results should be available soon. Staying for the cutting and sawing?' He looked up and smiled.

Owen realised that he had seen and heard enough. The murder he understood ... but the beating?

***

Four easels stood at the far end of the room, on each was placed a painting; they varied in size but none was large. Even to the uneducated eye, two paintings would be easily identified by the general public; the colours used and the stylised figures facing in all directions on the canvas, the children and the mills that were just visible in the background were easy clues. The others, less so, but all four were painted by the same man. To their left, leaning against the wall, were five more paintings of various sizes.

'Take those and burn them then go fishing and scatter the ashes in the Nidd and make sure it's done thoroughly!'

The same hands that had brought the bar down onto Monica Mac's arm and foot picked up the paintings as if they were about to explode.

'Bloody hell, Willis, they'll not fucking bite you!'

Within half an hour the flames from a garden bin incinerator licked well above the rim. He stood and watched as the framed paintings were swallowed into the flames one at a time and although he was little interested in art, he felt a degree of sadness. The last painting he held was small, about six inches by four inches. Although the frame was new, the painting looked old, the colours subdued. He looked on the back, there was a small, brown label. The title was handwritten but the rest printed and damaged. All he could make out was:

Tib Lane Galle
Oxford Street, Ma.
Adolphe Vale

He looked again at the fire and back to the small painting. He took out a knife and carefully cut the tape at the back of the frame, then removed the staples. He pushed out the painting before dropping the frame into the fire. Glancing round, he wrapped the painting in plastic bags before nipping into the out-building to conceal it. If he were careful, no one would ever know. Within two hours, he was sitting on the banks of the river, fishing and scattering the ashes along with the ground bait, into the water. He watched them disperse in the fast flow of clear but peaty-brown water; nobody would be any the wiser. As for the painting, that was now safely stashed away. He sat and fished until the sun had set, enjoying the solitude. For some strange reason he thought about the girl … *she was one of ours,* he reflected, and, as if on cue, a breeze rippled the transparent brown as if something or someone was moving below the surface. A chill ran down his neck. It was certainly time to leave. A fish broke the water's skin causing a splash and his heart leapt with it. The time just after a murder was always the worst. It was then that he felt at his most vulnerable.

***

Cyril had watched the sky turn from blue to turquoise and then streak with the various blends of yellow and red. He sat on the bench looking westward across The Stray. A few people were walking in the far distance but apart from them, he was alone with his musings.

'Beautiful, Liz. Let's hope that these are the worst of our days.' He looked straight ahead and his thoughts turned to the gallery robbery and the murders. 'Why murder the murderer, Liz? What would be the point unless …' A dog ran towards him, all wagging tail and lolloping strides. He leaned forward in welcome. The whole of the dog's back end seemed to sway like a boat on a bobbing sea before it turned itself in circles. He loved Airedale Terriers and this one seemed to like Cyril.

'Sorry, he's an old fuss pot, sorry to disturb you. Come on Jasper.'

Cyril waved and the dog bounded away looking for another victim to win over. He stood and returned to the road before passing through the snicket that led to Robert Street and home.

Cyril sipped through the frothy head of the Black Sheep beer as he stared at the computer screen. He was reading a news article about a similar heist. Lowry paintings and drawings had been stolen a decade previously from a gallery in the Manchester area. He smiled as he read the quote from a DCI Sarah Reed of the Greater Manchester CID.

We believe it to be a targeted attack by thieves who knew just what they were looking for and where to find it.

He muttered something about having a degree in the bleeding obvious but he never finished the last word. He sat back and inhaled on his electronic cigarette. Why kill someone and then take a laptop? Why then suffer a similar fate? He grabbed his phone.

'Owen.'

'Rather abrupt welcome, Owen.'

Owen just shook his head. 'Sir?'

'Owen. You mentioned in the café that the girl whom you believed to be the murderer left the hotel. With a laptop? Has that been found?'

'Yes to the first question and no to the second. Sir, you're on sick leave.'

'Humour an old, sick man with mental issues. What if the laptop didn't contain the information that she was supposed to collect, what if she got the wrong one?'

'Freshman told us that it was a MacBook Pro, even a Luddite can easily identify one. The images we have of the computer being carried by the girl leaving the hotel show it to be that model.'

The word *Luddite* emanating from Owen's lips shocked Cyril into a moment's silence. 'Precisely and Owen, you're missing my point. With any other laptop you'd have to stop and check … if it were a Dell or an HP you'd have to identify the logo, they don't all look the same, but a Mac, they're so easy to spot. She wouldn't have checked the room to see if Nathalie Gray had two computers, a business one and one for personal use. As soon as she entered the room she knew that was what she needed and she grabbed it. No matter how professional she is or was, she'd just committed murder, her senses would have been at an intensely heightened state. She'd have been conscious that one of her colleagues might just come along or might even be in the room. Boyfriend, Girlfriend?'

'She was having an affair with Dr Darwin Green but it wasn't information they shared with their colleagues and certainly not with their boss.'

'So, what laptop does Green use and what about the boss? Were they company property or personal? Come on, Owen, all these questions should have been answered!'

There was a sudden silence that seemed to expand. Cyril sensed that Owen was about to boil over and shout some obscenity down the phone.

'Sorry, Owen! I'm out of order. Maybe I need longer than I thought. I'm sorry! Forgive me.' He hung up.

Owen's anger showed in the force he exerted in tapping his pencil on the rim of his stained mug. It was now more out of frustration than to create any rhythmic, soothing beat. He felt sweat run down the side of his chest from his armpit, wetting his shirt, one tell-tale tear of his increasing insecurity. Cyril was right, he should have thought that through immediately. He pressed the mouse and turned to his computer screen to check the notes made and collated after the house and property searches of Nathalie Gray's colleagues. The computer equipment found had been clearly noted and listed; they had either been removed or assessed on site, none showing any irregularities. Dr Green had a personal and a business laptop both matching the description, Freshman had no computer at home but there was a desktop system at his storage facility. Freshman had also confirmed that Lynn McGowen had a MacBook belonging to the firm, as did Nathalie Gray. He was also sure that she had a personal laptop but could not be certain as to the make or the model. He felt that he was no further ahead just a little deeper in a mire, a mire that seemed of his own making.

He dialled Cyril's home number. It rang three times before the familiar answer.

'Bennett',

It made Owen smile and then relax considering Cyril's earlier rebuff.

'Thanks, Sir, you were right to ring. Just gone through the records and all, apart from the boss, have identical company laptops, Green has two, one's his own. The other colleague, a Lynn McGowen, isn't due back until ...' Owen checked his notes. '... tomorrow and Freshman believes Gray has a personal machine.'

'Where's McGowen been?'

'Working holiday, somewhere in Germany. You have a theory, Sir, I can tell!' Owen started to doodle on the pad, a series of circles growing slightly larger.

'She took the wrong one, the wrong laptop. I don't know how or why but whoever killed Gray wanted her laptop. Why go to the messy business of killing? Why kill in that way? I don't know. Whatever was on the computer has some link to art, why else drop the body at the Mercer? I take it you've checked all the paintings within the Mercer Gallery, that you've eliminated any tenuous links? You've checked that our killers and thieves aren't communicating in some subtle way, Owen? Do you have a turf war brewing?'

Owen did not like the word *you*, he felt much more secure with the word *we*. 'Why would Gray keep sensitive info on a laptop, a laptop that could easily be lost or stolen? Why not store it in the Cloud or Dropbox or somewhere only she had access to?'

'You're more familiar with Satan's machines and technology than me, my friend. That's for you to discover. It's all beyond a man of my age, that's why we now employ hackers and the like still wearing short trousers and sucking lollipops!'

'We know that Green had been to the Mercer and someone believes that Gray had some connection but we've only just started chasing that lead.'

'It's linked, Owen. Mark my words, there's a connection.'

Owen thanked Cyril. If he thought he was in the mire before the call, he now felt as though he were up to his bloody neck! He had considered there to be a link with the gallery but it seemed nebulous at this stage and therefore the real implications were beyond his comprehension, his only reassurance being that someone was checking.

***

Brian Smirthwaite went through the forensic report on Nathalie Gray's car. A full search had discovered little. A DNA semen trace matching Green was found on the back seat. Two ticket receipts had been found under the driver's seat showing that she had parked in Harrogate and at the Trinity Car Park, Leeds. Both were dated. The Leeds ticket was dated nine days before her murder and showed a stay of twenty-four hours, the Harrogate ticket was from the previous year! He left a memo on Helen's computer and also added images of the tickets to the whiteboard. He then checked the map looking for hotels in the vicinity of the car park. There were three. Within fifteen minutes he had established that Nathalie Gray had checked into the Leeds Marriott on that date. He would clear it with Leeds and pay them a visit.

***

Christopher Nelson walked his black Labrador, Lot, from Studley Roger along the arrow-straight driveway of Studley Royal Deer Park, a route he enjoyed most days no matter the weather. From the arched main gate the driveway ran directly to St Mary's Church. He only walked as far as the church unless the stags were rutting, then he kept to the paths as advised. He turned left off the tarmac driveway and headed over the hill between the trees towards the lake. Although there were deer in the park, Lot was more interested in the ball that was constantly being thrown.

They had quickly crossed the rise of high ground and were descending towards the narrow, quickly flowing run of the River Skell. They would soon arrive at the ornamental lake. The river, a rather grandiose title for the stream-like watercourse, had been used to create the waterways within the magnificent grounds and gardens of the now destroyed Studley Royal House and here it collected in a less artificial, more natural form. However, the garden folly, Fountains Abbey, and the Moon Ponds, still remained, an echo of its former, manicured magnificence.

Christopher watched Lot ford the narrow stretch of water and then follow along the course of the river on the opposite bank as it turned back on itself before disappearing into the trees. Lot, stopped constantly to either sniff or pee but soon vanished along with the Skell. Christopher was selfishly relieved; his arm ached from the constant throwing of the ball. No matter how many times he threw it, Lot would always want more. The park was quiet, even at the peak of summer there were times when he felt as though he were alone and at eight in the evening, the majority of tourists had gone leaving the place an oasis of calm. Two cars remained in the car park a few hundred yards away.

Following the footpath took him further away from the lake. He crossed the second footbridge over the Skell. Pausing to search the sky, he admired the swallows in their constant, on-the-wing forage for food. It was a moment of magic but in a heartbeat, it changed. It was then that he sensed it, the sudden stillness of The Dell, the silence, when to Christopher, even the ripple of the shallow water tumbling across stones, seemed to have ceased. He turned to look back along the path that he had taken and his heart rate accelerated, it skipped as he considered his future plans. On the first bridge stood a man, a man he was expecting. He remained motionless as if not wanting to intrude.

'Lot!' Christopher called hoping that his companion would soon be ready for home. 'Lot!' Christopher's voice was now direct and commanding as he scanned the trees for the dog, but he neither saw nor heard anything. The stillness remained. The shadows in the copse seemed darker as they lengthened. He tried to look more deeply, to penetrate the growing opacity beneath the leaves and then laughed inwardly at the thought of looking for a black dog in a dark wood. It made him realise the futility of his action. He cupped his hands to his mouth and called again. To his relief he heard sounds from within the woodland, only faint but they were there and he tried to focus his eyes in the direction of the noise.

Chapter Eight

DI Claire checked her watch. The briefing would be in an hour. She had two officers working on the Mercer Gallery inventory and an officer waiting for Lynn McGowen to arrive at the airport. She was due at 07:55. Helen moved to her computer screen. Lime green and pink Post-it notes were attached, they were from Owen and Brian respectively. She had seen the copies of the parking ticket stubs on the white boards and would await his comments after visiting the hotel. Owen's seemed more urgent and not a little intriguing.

Check your emails! *Received this information late last night. Worth a read*!

Checking her mail was usually the first thing she did on arrival but that morning in the Incident Room and the find in Nathalie's car had been the greater draw. She looked at her mail, thirty-four! Her heart sank. She scanned down for Owen's and it simply stated, READ THIS! She opened the attachment and read it through twice. It gave a clear description of a gallery robbery a decade previously. It was a combination of police reports, news cuttings and an up to the minute interview with the gallery owner. It was expertly crafted and a good deal of time had gone into the research. She picked up her phone.

'Owen.'

'Where from?'

'Morning, Ma'am. You've read it?'

'Obviously. Where from?'

'Can't say at the moment, Ma'am, but you can bet your weekly wage it's right. What I want you to see is the number of similarities between that heist and the Harrogate robbery. Happened just after the opening … many of the paintings had been sold in the days leading up to the opening night and on the night itself. Although security wasn't the same back then, the alarm was still monitored by the police and a central watch station. The police were somewhat tardy in getting to the scene after the break-in, inefficiency, maybe. There were other circumstances, which again could have been the reason why the robbery took place then and not later. Those committing the crime could be heard shouting to each other that they had time to get one more picture! It was timed, calmly ordered and calculated, very much like this new robbery.

'Ten years ago the gallery had no CCTV, apart from the coverage that had recently been installed by the council to the road outside. However, although the cameras were up, they were never connected, the installer simply vanished the week before the robbery. The council, having already paid most of the cost, was left with red faces and in the embarrassing position of having to chase the fictitious firm. Again, there's a modern-day equivalent here with the computerised security system.'

'We've nearly completed interviews with the company who installed the security system at Focus North Gallery. Similar circumstances, and amazingly, one of the installers has gone walk about! Only northern art was taken in the first robbery, a number of Lowry paintings and sketches plus others, thirteen works in all. You could say, unlucky for the owner, as they've never surfaced even though the insurer offered a reward of £50,000. The entry to the gallery, as you've read, appeared to be amateurish, but everything points to it being a well-ordered and organised robbery. By the way, Posthumus mentioned a reward is being offered here too after discussion with the Insurance Loss Assessor. How does £100,000 grab you?'

'So, Owen, you believe it's the same criminal group behind these two even considering the time gap?'

'Ruling nothing out. Probably not, but one might have been an influence. There was a time when rewards were given knowing that the paintings would be returned, worked like a ransom payment. Trouble was it just encouraged more robberies so that was quickly halted. Insurers, and as you know, the police at this present time, don't do deals with criminals. You also have to realise that nobody will grass for that amount of money. We already have two corpses and if, and I say if, there's a connection, we might discover that they were a weak link, considered as possible informers.'

'Is this Cyril's research, Owen?'

'Careless talk, Ma'am. We just have to assess its relevance.'

'By the way, DNA results on the body dumped at the Mercer confirm it to be that of a Monica Mac, ex-military and one of the first female medics in a front-line role. A full DNA match. The toxicology results show positive traces of anaesthetic found within her system, full name on the report but I'd only be able to pronounce it after a pint or two! Apparently they shattered her bones and then took away the pain in preparation for further beatings. Nice!'

'And when she told them what she knew, they finished the job! What else do we know about her?'

'Left the army with an excellent record and was head-hunted by Key Gate Security. They specialise in close protection to the rich and famous. A female with her training and skills would be in great demand. Stayed for two years and then set up her own smaller enterprise but the big boys just wouldn't let her play. Disappeared from the system with a few large debts. One GBH against her name. Some youth who tried to get too close to a starlet received a broken nose and lost a tooth. The report stated that the amount of force used was totally disproportionate!'

***

Christopher Nelson leaned against the tree realising that, as usual, he would have to wait, Lot would come when Lot was ready. No matter how much calling he did it would make no difference, just as long as he had not found something disgusting to eat or roll in. He would enjoy the moment, as from today he would not know what the future held. It could be a long time before he might experience this type of freedom again.

He turned to see the man approaching. At that moment he heard Lot rummaging at the edge of the woodland before emerging into the light. He watched as he dropped into the stream. He sensed the person next to him.

'He'll have a roll in the water and then climb out, it's his way.'

As if on cue, Lot climbed the bank and shook himself violently. A cascade of water droplets showered the area. He then casually approached, all wagging tail and lolling tongue. Nelson handed over the lead and the ball to Gregory, bent and stroked the dog before whispering into his ear, 'Now you stay!' The dog's tail wagged even more furiously.

'Two days and then release him.'

Nelson stood and quickly walked back the way he had come but then turned towards the two cars and the car park. Gregory maintained a firm grip on Lot's collar.

***

The black Labrador limped across the grassland before finally meeting the straight driveway leading to the arched gateway and home. He paused to lick the vicious wound that ran down his left flank, but then carried on. Within ten minutes, Lot had pushed through the hedge bordering the cottage that sat on the outskirts of the village. Even more slowly, the dog made his way round to the back of the house. He drank from the bowl of water that was always there before staring in at the French windows, his breath and wet nose marking the glass. He was noticed immediately and the door was quickly slid open.

'Are you messing up my windows, young man? Now just where have you left him this time, Lot?' Gwendolyn Nelson checked to see if her husband was close behind. There was no sign of him so she slid the door closed.

Lot was always the first home, the thought of a biscuit treat was just enough to encourage his enthusiastic final run. She bent to stroke him but then noticed first the clotting and then the warm matting of fresh blood from the long gash that ran along his side. The dog panted and lay down, his eyes turned to look at Gwen, those same sad, soulful eyes he used when he needed just that bit more attention.

'The vet for you, my man!'

Lot's ears pricked up momentarily as if he fully understood the significance of her words and then he fell back. Now there was a sudden, understandable reluctance to move.

'Now where's your Dad?'

Gwen moved back through the French windows and looked across the drive and down the road. There was still no sign of him; she would wait another ten minutes, as always, he was probably chatting. She checked her watch, it was now after nine. A slight breeze moved across the tops of the rose bushes that flanked either edge of the path, helping to release a mild perfume, an immediate reassurance. She wrapped her arms across her chest and looked towards the eastern sky; it was already darkening. She then felt the chill of the late evening breeze a marked contrast after the heat of the day. Her intuition told her that things were just not right. She returned inside. Lot was as she had left him. His tail wagged automatically as she came in. She went to the phone.

'Paula, it's your mum. Lot's returned from a walk, he's badly cut and needs to go to the vet but your dad's not come back yet and I'm worried. They could have been attacked by a stag or hit by a car. You know how the youths come up here to use the driveway as a racetrack.' She felt her voice weaken with the emotional turmoil.

'We're on our way. I'll call the vet from here to come and see to Lot at home. I'll stay with you and Seb will go looking for dad. You know him, he'll be chatting or simply watching the final moments of the setting sun. You know he's always loved Turner's sunsets ... *everyone should admire the fiery closing of a summer's day,* he always used to say when we were kids. If I had a pound for every one I've seen ...' She tried to make light of it, but she could not remember the last time her mother had sounded so anxious.

***

Owen carried two mugs of coffee, one for his boss, a mug that had started out on the journey enthusiastically over-filled. The coffee dribbled from the base of the mug as he hurried along to the briefing. By the time he had arrived, the brown liquid had settled to a more manageable level.

DI Claire looked at the murky offering and then at Owen.

'Two sugars, Ma'am. Nescafe Gold. Can't guarantee the state of the milk.'

He sniffed the contents of his own mug and pulled a face that seemed to convey that it smelled sour. Helen found herself leaning over the mug to smell for herself and then noted a smile appear on Owen's lips. Was he winding her up? She was not sure.

He dropped the files that had been trapped under his arm onto the table and sat next to her. There was a growing mutual respect. Owen, for one, realised that he needed support on this one and if he could not have Cyril by his side then Helen Claire would have to fit the bill.

The room fell silent as Helen went through the details of her interview with SCO7 and then the details offered by Owen. 'They're all in your files, read them and cross reference, please. What of the Mercer Gallery?' She looked around the room until her eyes fell on DC Harry Nixon.

'Ma'am, thank you! We've gone through the inventory of the paintings held and we have referenced one ...'

'Harry, Harry ... in English, please!'

'Ma'am. Nathalie Gray was employed two years ago to repair damage to one of the exhibits, but that's not all. She also entered one of her own works in the annual Harrogate painting competition that was held at the gallery last year. It's known as The Harrogate Open. Artists submit work by a certain date and it's then exhibited. Interestingly, the general public judge the work and the piece receiving the most votes by a certain date is the winner.'

There was a pause.

'Well?'

'She didn't win.'

Helen briefly put her head in her hands. 'Harry, I don't care if she won an Olympic gold in découpage, what of the contracted work?'

There was a bit of laughter but it soon stopped when Helen looked round.

Harry Nixon blushed. He knew that Cyril would never embarrass a junior colleague in a briefing and immediately a thin veneer of resentment could be heard in his voice when he answered.

'A painting was damaged by a member of the public. They apparently scratched the word, 'FAKE' across it and she repaired it.' He looked across and realised that more was required. 'It was a large work by an artist called Brian Shields, more commonly known as Braaq, the details for that are here.' He waved a few sheets of A4. 'I'll put them on the board after. He was an artist who, although born in Liverpool, came to fame whilst living here in Harrogate. His paintings are, I'm told, worth a lot. The Curator said that in certain circles he was known as the Harrogate Lowry.'

His last two words made Owen and Helen turn to each other and then back at Nixon.

'Say that again please, Harry,' requested Owen who had seen the change in his colleague's demeanour after Helen's pointed words. He had added the please deliberately.

'He was known as the Harrogate Lowry, Sir. Have I said something wrong?'

The chatter in the room increased.

'No, on the contrary, you've said something very right! Do we have a photograph of the work, Harry?'

Harry took a pen drive from his pocket and pushed it into the side of the large screen. Within a second the North Yorkshire Police Badge that normally occupied the space had been replaced by two photographs. 'I didn't have time to print them, Ma'am. They're being done now. As you can see there's a before and an after image. Nathalie Gray did a cracking job.'

Everyone stared at the images.

Brian Smirthwaite was the first to comment. 'Do we know where that's supposed to be?'

'The title's on the back, *Don't you dare put bloody tadpoles in my wellies*! The artist always gave his scene funny and sometimes rude titles as well as depicting himself in the painting, usually wearing a red and white striped jumper, an early 'Where's Wally'! The Curator thinks that Braaq made up the image with a huge dollop of artist's licence so it could be somewhere local or somewhere that doesn't exist, somewhere totally fictitious. The damage was reported but nobody was arrested.'

'Did the Curator believe it to be a fake?'

'No Ma'am, funny you should ask that. There are a few people who believe that the paintings were a huge, money-generating exercise. The Curator went on at length about the artist, suggesting that he couldn't possibly have painted so many pictures in the time before his early death ... something about dates ... It's all here.'

Again Helen looked at Owen.

'She intimated, but asked me not to quote her, that the painter was known to be a controversial figure, particularly with many experts in the northern art field, considering the value of his paintings. The record price set at auction for one of his works is over £50,000 and when you take costs into consideration you are looking at about £68,000. She also said, that like many artists, there are some dealers who have serious concerns about the work.'

A low whistle erupted from Smirthwaite's lips. '£68,000 for something like that!' He shook his head in disbelief.

'Thank you, Nixon. Please ensure that the notes are circulated and uplifted.'

He simply nodded.

'Shakti will be interviewing the missing member of Freshman's team as we speak so more of that when it comes in.'

Brian Smirthwaite just waved a hand. 'Ma'am, Nathalie Gray stayed one night at the Marriott in Leeds parking her car at the Trinity Car Park, the closest secure parking to the hotel. Checked in at 15:35 and left at 10:22 the next day. We've checked CCTV but none of the others were seen on camera, no Freshman nor Green. I've a list of other guests staying at the time and we'll whittle our way through them to see if there's any connection. However, it's a busy hotel, people come and go. Gray did leave at 17:05 and she returned at 23:10. We're checking city centre CCTV to see if we can find out where she went. We do know that her car didn't move during the time she was resident at the hotel.'

***

Lynn McGowen sat facing Shakti with an expression suggesting that she was tired and wanted to get home.

'This shouldn't take long, Ms McGowen. Whilst you were away one of your associate colleagues was murdered and certain items of her possessions were removed. Are you aware of this?'

'I received a call from Freeman Freshman. He was devastated. I know Nathalie, but only as a colleague when I'm working for Freshman's Fine Art.'

'When was the last time you worked for them and what was the nature of that work?'

'About a month ago. They call me in when they buy a painting that they believe to be a 'sleeper' and it either has missing provenance or none at all. I'm paid to research the painting. You do know that I'm freelance and you do understand the term, 'sleeper'?'

Shakti just nodded. 'The paintings you were investigating?'

'A small Lowry oil and a rare work by Mary Feddon.'

'Didn't Nathalie Gray also do that kind of work?'

'Yes, sometimes, but she was more on the cataloguing and conservation side. Re-framed the works too. Believe me, she was one of the best. I saw her renovate an extremely rare, signed print by Julian Trevelyan. It had been seriously water-damaged, all brown tide lines. It was bought at auction for a song with a collection of tat. When she'd finished you'd have thought it was new. Freshman also sold her services to a number of galleries and museums. He'll be lost without her.'

Shakti noted the final sentence and underlined it. It carried a lot of weight in his defence.

***

DI Claire was just about to leave when Owen approached her.

'You might be interested in this, Ma'am, thrown up on HOLMES. It may be nothing but there are too many coincidences to ignore.' Owen's discomfort clearly showed not only in his face, but in the way he quickly returned to the Incident Room.

'Missing person reported last night. Out walking in Studley Deer Park, near Ripon. The dog returned seriously hurt but his master didn't come home at all. Initially they thought that the dog might have got a little too close to one of the stags that roam freely, but it appears the injury was caused by barbed wire. The dog's owner has not been seen since.'

'Coincidences, you mentioned coincidences?'

'Missing person is Christopher Nelson, sixty-eight. He owned the Ripon-based auctioneers, Nelson and Steel Fine Art and Antiques, based in an old primary school building on Coltsgate Hill. Moved there when the school took over new premises in 1981. Nelson sold the business eighteen months ago. Apparently he got planning permission for the site so you can imagine the value. Sold immediately after a bit of a bidding war, apparently. The business was started by his father, originally as a cattle mart but as trade began to slow they moved into farm machinery and then household furnishings before specialising in fine art. They also ran an estate agency but that was managed by a Clive Steel.'

'So what's the state of play right now?'

'Police dogs did an initial run last night and tracked to the lake, well just past it but then nothing. A full search is taking place now; a number of locals and the Mountain Rescue are also involved. Both the area, the deer park and Fountains Abbey are remaining open to the public. The decision was taken to keep it open as the more eyes we can get on the ground the better. There's a large wooded area with ditches and dells, anyone going missing could take days to find. It's a very popular area for dog walkers and that may turn up something. Police are handing out photographs and there's already been a news alert across all media but up until now, nothing.'

Owen's phone rang.

'Owen.' He listened and held his finger towards Helen. 'A minute,' he said into the phone before covering the mouth piece.' They've found blood on the ground a few hundred yards from the lake within an area of trees. SOCOs are on their way.'

'So, Owen, we have a conservator dead, an art specialist, a murderer, and now an auctioneer is missing. Tie that to a major art robbery, we're gathering more and more pieces that seem to fit the same jigsaw. Why is it all coming to a head now?'

An officer brought a photograph through of Christopher Nelson and tagged it to a fresh board adding times and dates. Owen turned and studied it before looking back at Helen. He hesitated, turning to look at the photograph again. He walked over to it cocking his head to the side.

'I've seen him before somewhere.' He stood back and stared at it. 'No, maybe not.' Smiling at Helen, he turned to take his leave.

'Owen, anything from the interview with Gray's parents?'

'All on file, as you instructed.' He wanted to say, *if you make the bloody rules have the courtesy to follow them*, but he thought better of it.

Chapter Nine

Cyril could not remember the last time he had been accompanied to a Doctor's appointment and he felt foolish. It had been agreed after a fairly strong debate, during which Julie had offered a very convincing and professional argument for having two pairs of ears in the room.

'I see it all the time when I bring news to relatives, Cyril, they only hear what they want to hear. The bad stuff they seem to block out, it's natural. When they leave they've forgotten or misheard or ignored certain key facts. So, Mr Bennett, I should like to accompany you, chaperone you if you like, so that I can answer any medical questions you may have after the visit.'

Cyril knew all along that it was the most sensible thing to do and he was lucky to have someone who truly cared, but it still rankled. The final visit to Caroline had been critical to his being able to return to work and how passionately did he want that approval. To his delight she had agreed that the time was right.

They decided to walk from Robert Street and left plenty of time. He did not want to walk along Otley Road as that was his normal route to work, so they went via Harlow Moor Drive. Although most of the journey was completed in contented silence, Julie could sense Cyril's increasing anxiety the nearer they came to the Police Welfare Centre. Cyril had been quiet as he conducted a mental conversation with Liz and as they turned onto Harlow Moor Road, Julie was surprised to hear Cyril laugh out loud. She squeezed his hand.

'Cyril? You'll be fine, you're through to the other end.'

'Liz has said exactly the same thing, Julie. I'm fine.'

Julie frowned and pulled away.

The building held a familiarity that put Cyril at ease yet had the opposite effect on Julie. There was something clinical and cold, probably due to the increased anxiety she now felt. She knew Cyril to be mentally stable and was, until he had burst out laughing after ten minutes of total silence, convinced that he was so close to winning his personal battle against his depressive state. She reflected on his comment, *Liz has said exactly the same thing.* That statement released a flood of nerves which bombarded her senses. All she could do now was to hope that the correct professional judgement was made.

The Welfare Officer welcomed Cyril into his room. Cyril held the door to allow Julie to enter first. They sat.

'Well, Cyril, you've made some very positive strides. The report I've read clearly gives you the dominant hand and I congratulate you, not only on the progress you've made, but also on your patience and determination. However, ...'

Julie's heart sank and the pause seemed to last a lifetime.

'... only one person knows if you feel ready to face the daily responsibilities your job entails, if you still feel as though you have the same drive and the commitment. I want you to remember that taking more time will not be considered a weakness, but as far as your professional support programme shows, you are capable of making that decision. I shall fully support your wishes but then, as you know, it will be up to your GP.'

Cyril turned to look at Julie and he smiled. He leaned over and whispered in her ear, 'Don't worry about, Liz, it's just a phase I have to go through. Trust me!'

Julie felt the tension leave her shoulders and she began to relax, she was now convinced that he was in control of his mental state. Cyril stood and leaned across the desk, proffering his hand. 'Thank you very much for everything. I couldn't have asked for a more supportive and dedicated team of professionals behind me. I'm more than ready to return to work. Shall I contact my GP?'

'No, Cyril, that will be my pleasure. One thing you must promise me.' He looked at both Cyril and Julie hoping to get her support. 'If the Doctor continues to prescribe, then that's fine, you may still work, but the medication must be taken.'

Cyril smiled and nodded.

'He'll be in touch in the next twenty-four hours.'

Within twenty-four minutes they were sitting on the terrace of The Fat Badger. Cyril was already half way down a pint of Black Sheep. Julie ran her finger around the rim of her glass. Cyril watched predicting the question that he knew she would ask. 'One thing I need to know Cyril …'

He leaned over and put a finger to her lips. 'Don't worry about, Liz.' He smiled and tapped the side of his head. 'For thinking …' then he pointed to his shoes, but instead of finishing the saying, he simply finished the pint.

***

The news travelled quickly around the station that Bennett was back.

'Cyril Bennett, you do look, well a little thin, mind but you're a sight for sore eyes, let me tell you!' The Chief Constable's secretary stood, came from behind her desk and kissed him on his cheek. You've been missed I can tell you that. You may go straight in. 'He's hiding behind the Eiger!' They both laughed.

Cyril could not help but smile as he looked at the desk. It was a good job that the rest of the force had a more ordered filing system.

'Didn't expect you back so soon, Cyril, but I have to say, I'm thrilled. We have a case running at the moment that has your prints all over it. DI Helen Claire's been covering, bloody good copper too, but somehow it seems to be getting away from her. There are two cases that may be connected. Has Owen kept in touch?'

Cyril just shook his head. 'I know DI Claire.'

'She'll be here in a minute. I've ordered coffee, delicate moments these and we have to handle them carefully, you know how it is with professional bodies and the like! I want her here for another week, liaise, and then you should be fully up to speed. You will, however, take over the lead role in both cases. You're up to that I take it?'

Cyril raised an eyebrow.

Within twenty minutes, Cyril and Helen were in his office. She sat next to him as they progressed through the evidence of both cases on screen. Cyril made notes that seemed to take the form of Venn diagrams. He pointed within the connecting area of two circles. 'There are no reports here from the interviews with Nathalie Gray's parents yet it's noted as being done.'

Helen could not recall whether it had been sanctioned. She flicked through the various tabs on the screen and began to frown. 'I know family support was sanctioned and I feel sure we …' She blushed slightly. 'If it's not on here then it's been missed.' She cross-referenced the date and time. 'There was a serious police incident on that day, bomb threat at the National Railway Museum. However, it should have been followed up the day after but seems to have slipped through the net, Sir.'

'Is Nun Monkton your neck of the woods, Helen?'

'Know it well.' She felt relieved by the way he quickly moved on from the operational error and was grateful. She could see why he was so popular.

'Nathalie's parents, what are their occupations? Dates of birth? History?'

Helen flicked through more tabs. 'Mother, Bernadette, forty-nine, maiden name, Delmas, born Sedan, northern France. Married Paul Gray, fifty-three, in 1987. Moved to York in 1989, the year of their daughter's birth. Bernadette is an artist and illustrator, he's in publishing, that's how they met. They worked for Liberté Publishing specialising in modern, comic-style books for adults, always popular in France, but steadily growing in popularity here too now. They moved to the UK and established their own business, Fine Line Books.'

This was what he wanted to hear, sound information. 'Good, that's excellent.' It was the first opportunity that he had to praise her and he took it.

'Helen, I'd be happier if you could see them personally but check with the Support Officer first and see how Nathalie's parents are before you go in on your own. If the situation is sensitive, take the Officer with you but we need answers from them by tomorrow if that's possible.'

Helen left the room and Cyril straightened the items on his desk. He needed to get everything ordered in his head, a virtual timeline with everything tagged and in place, then and only then would he see the gaps.

'It's just you and me for the minute, Liz,' he said out loud. His mobile phone announced that he had a message. He checked it. It was from Julie. *Ring me if you have time. Hope all's well! xx.* Cyril smiled and replied with a single letter x. He then looked at the file that he had requested regarding the robbery and read through the interviews with Simon Posthumus.

***

The shadow of Owen in the doorway killed the light in the room and it brought a smile to Cyril's face. 'Bloody hell, Owen, things don't change no matter how long I'm away. You're blocking the light, man ... Come and sit! Do we have the full inventory of all the items stolen from Focus North Gallery?'

'Sir, good to have you back. Yes, in the file there.' Owen pointed to the thick folder that was open on Cyril's desk. 'However, we might have a breakthrough. Forensics stripped down the case that Monica Mac's body was dumped in. Concealed in one of the joints was a computer pen drive, bloody small one too, no bigger than my thumb end. You really need to come and see this.'

Cyril's smile turned to an inquisitive frown. 'In the case?'

'A small hole had been drilled into the joint of the wood, into one of the thicker reinforcing pieces. It was only when they stripped it down that it was discovered. Thank God they're fussy buggers.'

'So we can assume that it was meant to be found?'

Owen just raised his shoulders and they walked quickly to the Incident Room.

'Otherwise, Owen, why put it there in the first place?'

***

DC Park and DC Nixon stood in the lounge of Long View House. Nixon stared through the French windows at the view that stretched towards Ripon Cathedral two miles away. He noted the paintings on the walls and the quality of the furnishings. Framed, family photographs sat in groups on a baby grand piano.

Paula and Gwendolyn Nelson sat on the settee. Lot was down on the rug, looking more choirboy than dog, the Buster collar concealing most of his head and a blue medical shirt covering and protecting the recently stitched wound.

'So your husband walks the dog every evening up through the park?'

'Morning and evening. You can set your clock by him unless he gets chatting. Never likes to miss a sunset.'

'Has he mentioned anything recently about seeing anything unusual or talking to strangers in the village or the park?'

'Detective ... What do I call you?'

'Please, Harry, it makes conversations easier and this is Stuart.'

'Harry, he talks to anyone, he'd talk to the trees if he couldn't find a human being. Comes from living out here.'

'What made Mr Nelson sell the business?'

Paula laughed and gave her mother a squeeze. 'Age, Harry, age. My father used to say that old age comes at the most inconvenient time in your life. He'd built the business and when it was at its most successful he didn't have the energy nor the drive to maintain it. Neither I, nor my husband, has any interest, so, after careful consideration he decided to sell. The auction building proved to be a very good investment and selling it to a local builder means that my parents can have an extremely comfortable retirement.'

'Did anyone resent the fact that the old school was going to be redeveloped?'

'Whenever there's change you'll always have someone who will fight against it. You're not suggesting that my father's disappearance has anything to do with that, surely?'

There was a silence before Stuart Park changed the subject.

'I see your father loved collecting art work,' Stuart said, pointing to a large oil painting of a ship in full sail.

'Nelson's flag ship, painted by the Yorkshire artist, John Bentham-Dinsdale. One of his relatives, he used to say … Nelson not Dinsdale you understand?'

Stuart smiled. 'Has Mr Nelson been acting differently recently, going out more, on the phone or receiving calls?'

Paula looked at her mother who pulled a face and bit her bottom lip. All eyes focussed on her.

***

DI Helen Claire turned off the A59 York Road and onto Pool Lane, the only road into Nun Monkton. Helen knew the village well having enjoyed a number of weekend lunches at the village pub, The Alice Hawthorn. The village was idyllic with its may pole, village green and the Buttery Pond. She quickly checked the dashboard clock, she was on time as she pulled up outside a large, detached property. Two cars were in the driveway and one that she believed to be that of the Police Liaison Officer, was parked on the green.

After brief introductions and her expression of condolence, Helen began her questions, a difficult job at the best of times. It became clear that Nathalie had led her own life and had rarely come back to visit. On leaving university she had made her own way in life.

'So the last time you saw her was?'

Mr Gray seemed to take the lead answering for them both. 'March, my birthday. We had dinner across the way at the pub. The fact that she doesn't call much doesn't mean this is a dysfunctional family, on the contrary, we communicate by other means as many people with busy lives do these days. Besides, Nun Monkton isn't the centre of the art world, and believe me, Nathalie's world is art. It's an isolated if not idyllic spot but for the twenty-first century it has poor Internet and dreadful public transport.'

'You came to live here, when?'

Paul looked across at Bernadette for clarification and pulled a thinker's face. '2011, yes, 11. Nathalie never called this home. When will her body be released? It's the waiting.'

It was Helen's turn to look at the Liaison Officer. 'I'm afraid it will be after the investigation ... I know that it's difficult but we need the time to collect all the evidence. That's all I can say, and I know it's no consolation, but the case is very complex.'

Paul put his arm round his wife and drew her closer before kissing the side of her head. 'We understand fully, Inspector. We understand the position you're in.'

Helen was surprised to see Bernadette pull away.

'Did your daughter ever leave anything or receive anything whilst she was here with you?'

Paul just lifted his shoulders and pulled in his chin. 'She always likes to use the front bedroom, the one looking over the green when she comes. No one else has used it since her last stay. Feel free to look if you believe it will help.'

Helen stood and Paul showed her to the room.

'May I do a quick search?' She slipped on a pair of nitrile gloves.

'Your colleagues looked over the house a couple of days after Nathalie's death but Bernadette was in too much of a state to be interviewed and then when they were supposed to call, your people had some emergency, bomb hoax, I believe.'

***

Owen stood next to Cyril in the Incident Room and stared at the Police logo on the large, blue screen. Owen nodded and the DC using a remote control pressed '*Play*'.

The screen initially turned black and then an image came into view. It was of a mahogany case. Cyril leaned on the chair back that was in front of him. The still image began to move as the box was lifted up to reveal a model of a fat, moustachioed mannequin of a policeman. A gloved hand appeared from the side and an old penny was held on the edge between a thumb and finger. It slowly came into focus. Britannia was clear and so too was the date, 1967. The camera followed the hand as the penny was dropped into a slot and then panned to the policeman in the box. Immediately the figure rocked backwards and forwards as the policeman's booming laughter filled the Incident Room. Within two minutes, it was back in the position from which it had started and all was silent.

'Keep looking at its face!' Owen instructed.

The mannequin's right eye opened and closed as if it were winking, then the box was lowered over the policeman and the screen went black. Nobody spoke.

'Coppers!'

'Sir?'

'Old pennies, Owen. They were always referred to as coppers. If you had a few coppers you had brown coins, pennies and ha'pennies when they were legal tender. Whoever produced this wanted us to make a note of the date on the penny, it's significant! Birth dates of anyone involved ... how old would they be today if they were born in 1967?'

'Fifty, yes, a round half century.'

***

Gwendolyn looked at her daughter before she spoke. 'Over the last few weeks he's been to Harrogate more times than usual, said he was meeting old colleagues from the auction trade. You know they have a good auction house in Harrogate?' It was more a rhetorical question as she simply continued. 'He stayed over a couple of times, said he was having dinner and a drink and wouldn't drive after having alcohol. That was fine. Now I come to think of it he also received a lot more calls or text messages. He was always checking his phone. It was like that when he was selling the business but then afterwards he hardly received any calls. Often said he didn't know why he had the thing.'

'Did he have the phone with him the evening he disappeared?'

'He must have. I've not seen it in the house and it's not rung.'

'You've tried ringing him?' Harry hardly dared ask, thinking it was such an obvious question. It was and he received a quick, angry response.

'My mother may be old, but she's not stupid. Of course, she's tried to ring him and so did the two police officers who came out, as did my husband when he went searching for him.'

Harry just held up his hand as if in surrender and apology. 'We'll obviously check through his telephone records and see if that can throw any light on the recent calls. Last question and then we'll leave you in peace. Has anyone called at the door or sent a parcel or a letter to your husband that was different from the regular callers or mail?'

Gwendolyn shook her head. 'No nothing, sorry.'

Harry and Stuart stood. Lot wagged his tail and tried to look round the huge conical collar but then gave up.

'If you think of anything, anything at all, no matter how small, please call us. Some people think they'll be wasting our time but it's the small things that matter in cases like this.' He smiled and turned to leave.

As he got to the door he heard Mrs Nelson whisper to her daughter.

'What about the summerhouse?'

Harry turned. 'Anything?'

Paula answered. 'The other morning, before my father disappeared they woke to see the summerhouse door open. They both believed it to be locked but they put it down to forgetfulness.'

'Was anything disturbed other than the door being open?' Harry asked.

'We checked and so did the police on the night dad went missing but no, everything seemed to be in order.'

'May we take a look?'

Harry and Stuart were shown to the summerhouse and were left to look around.

***

Helen completed the search but she found nothing and returned downstairs. Bernadette had moved to her small studio at the far end of the garden. Paul was preparing some soft drinks.

'Go down to her. Bernadette knows you're coming, your colleague is with her. I'll bring the drinks. Just before you do, a private word.'

Helen stopped and closed the door.

'After Nathalie was born, Bernadette suffered dreadfully from post-natal depression. It was also something deeper as if she resented her daughter for destroying her ability to work. It took a while for her to not only accept the child but also to work again.'

Helen put her hand on Paul's arm.

'Thank you! The bouts of depression haven't gone away, you know, no, and she's always refused to seek medical help. She's a determined woman as you can see, she's out there working in her garden studio, even after the news. It was ever thus!'

Helen entered the studio through the folding glass doors that filled the north wall. The room was large, angled tables ran down either side and lamps were positioned above the surfaces. The walls were covered with drawings and photographs.

'Helen, look at these, they're part of Nathalie's early university work.'

Three sketches were handed to Helen.

'The draftsmanship is amazing. The intricate detail is astonishing.'

'She's watched me from being a little girl. My work involves fine, accurate lines. She's inherited her mother's artistic eye, I feel.'

Helen glanced around the walls as she sipped her ice-cold lemonade. There were a couple of family photographs, one of Nathalie and a few friends. She looked closely.

'It's Nat at university, some kind of fancy dress party.'

'Do you know any of the others?'

Bernadette came over and pointed to the different people in the photograph. 'There are some I can't name.'

'May I take a picture of this?' She was already getting out her phone.

'Please, if it might help you.'

Those words brought back a realisation that she was investigating a murder and here she was looking at artwork and drinking lemonade. It seemed wrong somehow. Recovering her composure, she noticed a small painting. 'Is that a Lowry?' She pointed to a shelf.

Bernadette laughed. 'If only! No, I painted it a few years ago as an exercise, a bit of fun, a challenge from Nathalie. She did one too. Five colours, that's all you could have. That's supposedly all he used.'

It seemed incongruous that someone who could draw so beautifully would turn their hand to something that to her untrained eye, seemed so crude.

Paul interrupted her train of thought. 'March was not the last time I saw Nat. Just remembered that she popped by in early June, a kind of flying visit. Bernadette was in France; some freelance work with her old publisher she gets on a regular basis, keeps the wolf from the door. Nat called here briefly with a colleague, I think his name was Green … Gray and Green … I can sing a rainbow!' He smiled at his own joke but then pulled a face as if to offer an apology. 'Even in her relationships she seems attracted to colours! They had a coffee and blew. They were heading for Newcastle or somewhere north east to do with work and she wanted to show him the village.'

'Do you know much about him, this Mr Green?'

'Boyfriend I guess by the way they held hands as they walked down to the pond. Seemed a nice enough guy. They were only here an hour at the most.'

Within forty minutes Helen was heading back to Harrogate.

***

Harry sat on the flower-patterned sofa in the Nelsons' summerhouse. 'Nothing. There's no sign of forced entry. They must have left the door open.'

Stuart ran his hand round the lip where the timber sides joined the roof. There was nothing. He stared at the picture on the wall, a print of Turner's 'Fighting Temeraire'. He stood back and admired it.

'Bloody beautiful! Christ you look at the crap that was stolen from that gallery and then you look at this. Now he could paint. The Temeraire, you know, had a distinguished career at the Battle of Trafalgar, one of the ships of the line. They broke it up can you believe. Vandalism? Probably still part of the roof rafters in some stately home! Loved sunsets, Turner, never missed one, allegedly.'

Harry jumped from the sofa and went to the picture before removing it from the wall. Taped to the back was a small, computer pen drive.

'Never missed a sunset! Well bugger me! What have we here?'

Chapter Ten

The file on the robbery was complete. Cyril checked the fifteen stolen items and compared them with the Loss Adjuster's assessment. A low whistle erupted from his lips. It was certainly some loss. He had flicked through the images of all the stolen works to reassure himself that the painting he had purchased was not on the list; he was pleased to see that it had not been taken and he sighed softly. He organised an appointment to see Posthumus in the gallery the following day.

The Incident Room was fairly quiet. Cyril looked at the framed print leaning up against the wall, his head to one side.

'Forensics have double checked it, the only prints on the tape and the memory stick are Nelson's, they can assure us that he stuck it there,' Owen announced looking across to the three officers who were admiring it. He yawned. 'So why there? Why stick the pen drive there?'

'Fighting Temeraire, painted 1838, fantastic piece of art work don't you think, Owen?' Cyril said turning to look at his partner, hoping to see a glimmer of artistic enthusiasm, only to see him glance at his watch. 'I don't mean the bloody time, man, the date, 1838 that was the year Turner painted … never mind … Pearls and swine!'

Owen simply raised his shoulders and moved away. Cyril was sure that he detected a smile on his lips as he turned. He was convinced that he reacted like this to wind him up.

'What's on the stick?'

Owen slipped it into the side of the big screen. 'I must warn you that we've been here before …'

The screen went black and then the image re-focussed on a wooden crate. Cyril looked across at Owen and then at the others in the room. They watched as the case was lifted to reveal the same rotund, moustachioed mannequin trapped within glass. Again, as in the previous video, a gloved hand appeared holding a copper penny. The camera focussed on the date, 1961.

'Pause it! It's not the same video as before, the date on the penny is different.' He went to the relevant area of the white board. 'First video the penny was dated 1967. Open mind everyone, please. Continue!'

The rest of the video was just as before and when the laughing policeman stopped rocking and laughing, it winked directly at the camera before the screen slowly dimmed.

'Owen, a minute!' Cyril took Owen to one side. 'Do you recall a conversation we had a while back regarding the computer taken from Gray's hotel?'

Owen nodded.

'What if someone had been there before ... what if they'd swapped the machines and what if the one that was left and therefore the one stolen, only held a video of the laughing policeman and not the information Monica Mac had been paid to retrieve? What do you think?'

'That's an awful lot of what ifs, with respect, Sir. Grasping at straws I'd have to say. Sorry!' Owen stared at Cyril and wondered if he had returned too soon but he recognised the old enthusiasm, the tension and determination.

Cyril and Owen moved back to the group. 'Your thoughts, please.' Cyril sat at the table and beckoned the others to follow whilst holding the chair next to him for Helen. There was silence.

Owen was the first to speak. 'We believe that this was either left in the summerhouse at Christopher Nelson's or it might have been delivered some other way. We know that Nelson's behaviour had changed over the last few weeks, he was spending more time in Harrogate and more time on his phone. Remember that the previous video was left for us to discover, it was for our eyes. So, with each new discovery we have either a body or a missing person. My thoughts, for what they are worth at this stage.' He paused and looked directly at Cyril. 'If they each received one, did Nathalie Gray also get a pen drive containing the jolly copper and if so, where is it now? Or did someone swap the computers leaving an identical laptop containing our fat friend before she had chance to see it? Question. Have we been looking for the right clues?'

Cyril looked at Owen and frowned. He had believed that his comments had fallen on stony ground. He then smiled inwardly to himself but said nothing.

Owen looked across at Helen as if to give her the cue to speak.

'There was nothing at her apartment. All IT equipment found was checked. Don't forget we weren't the first there, so those who combed through the place after her death could have taken it. I also checked the room she always used when staying with her parents in Nun Monkton. There was nothing. However, look at the dimensions of those things, they could be concealed anywhere. This might not seem relevant but has everyone read my report of the meeting with the Grays, particularly Paul Gray's reference to Bernadette's mental instability?'

A number of voices suggested that they had but it seemed that her point was lost in the moment.

DC Dave Jones leaned from behind a computer screen. 'Why hide it behind a picture? Why in fact, keep it? If it caused him to change his behaviour, why not destroy it, unless, of course, if anything were to happen to him, then it would be discovered.'

'Good point, Dave, thanks. Harry, we need to collect any IT equipment from the house. Have we checked his phone records?'

'Yes, but there appears to be no change in his mobile phone behaviour so let's assume that he had an alternative, disposable phone. His wife wouldn't know one from the other so she wouldn't realise that he had two phones. Do we know where he went in Harrogate and where he stayed?'

Cyril quickly responded. 'I checked with his friends in the auction trade and he does meet with them now and again. They commented that he seemed to be his old self the last time they met.' Cyril checked his notes. 'The last meeting was a dinner the evening before Nathalie's death. Stayed at the same hotel, the Grand Hotel, they believe.'

'That's where I saw him. Bugger!' Owen called out, slapping the palm of his hand onto his forehead as he stood and collected the photograph from the white board. 'He was in the lounge area of the foyer when we went to check the CCTV at the hotel. He was reading a paper. He looked like one of those actor types. I thought I recognised him from the TV so I looked at him until he went back behind the broadsheet!'

'Stuart, do we still have the copy of the footage from the hotel foyer? See if you can spot him and then ask if the hotel still holds footage from before Nathalie's arrival until the day he disappeared. Please do it now. Helen, call Nathalie's parents and ask if they have seen a pen drive like these, both are identical. Send an image too and then get someone to check names of distributors for them and also sales outlets. Initially work outwards from here. You know the drill.'

Helen went to leave as Owen replaced the photograph. 'Sir, have they tracked the missing technician who was involved in the installation of the security system at the gallery?'

'Nothing and that's a piece of jigsaw we really need to find but it seems he's worked under a false identity for the last six months. Only they know how many systems have been compromised and obviously they're not saying!' He smiled at Helen and raised his eyebrows.

'The system installed before that of the gallery, might he have been caught on their cameras as they were tested or the security firm's offices?'

'No, it's obviously a professional job! All we have is the image they used for his security pass. It's being run through Europol but no luck so far.'

Brian Smirthwaite popped his head round the door. 'Thought I'd seen the name Nelson before; when I checked the names of those staying at the Leeds Marriott, he checked in the same day as Nathalie Gray. Checking for CCTV now. Interestingly, if you look again at the case files, you'll see that he was booked in to stay that night at The Grand, Harrogate so we'll only know the truth of the matter when we see the footage!'

Cyril smiled. 'Let us know as soon as, Brian. Pleased the brain is still as sharp as ever. Thank you.'

Brian smiled, stuck his thumb in the air and left.

'I want to run something past you all and I want you to keep an open mind and fire back any thoughts.' He tapped the side of the large screen. 'Remember what you've just seen.' He moved across to an empty, freestanding whiteboard and picked up a red marker pen.

Owen pulled up a chair and sat down, the others in the room followed suit. He could tell from Cyril's demeanour that they might be there for a while.

'Let's assume that we have two groups with vested interests in this case.' He drew one circle. 'Let's call these the Montagues.' He then drew a second circle which slightly linked the first, another Venn diagram. 'These are then the Capulets. I said when I was discussing this with Owen earlier that this case has many common features; evidence probably indicates that we're witnessing the start of a turf war. As Shakespeare said, these families are, "*both alike in dignity*"'. He tapped each name on the board. 'One, however, has over-stepped the mark, one group's encroached on the other's trade and for that simple reason, there's a price to pay and we're now seeing the bill. Here we have, Nathalie Gray, a Montague.' He put her initials in the corresponding circle. 'Here, Monica Mac.' He placed her within the intersection of both circles. 'She belonged to neither group, she was contracted, paid. Now we have Christopher Nelson, also a Montague, but how can I assume that to be the case?'

The only answer came in the form of an electrical buzz and some embarrassed shuffling of feet. Cyril waited before looking individually at those around the room.

It was Shakti who spoke first. 'Surely the key as to who's with which family is based on the stolen, missing computer and the videos that we've seen?' Her comment was expressed more as a question, she was also unsure that she was on the right track.

'Expand your thoughts, Shakti, please.'

'Gray, we believe, was murdered for the laptop and iPad that went missing. The murderer, Mac, was killed either because she knew too much and had achieved her objective, or that she'd failed in her mission. Let's assume that the laptop was not the desired one. She'd one chance of getting it but Freshman pre-empted that by notifying the police so quickly after Gray went missing. There was no chance of a second search. On the other hand, a Capulet swapped the laptop knowing the situation. But my guess is, it was someone from neither camp, someone who was deliberately acting as an agent provocateur.'

'So how do you explain our laughing policeman friend?'

'Our 'agent' set it up. Why? How? I've no idea. I'm just thinking out loud.'

'Is there another group? What if it's a lone person seeking revenge for something that happened in the past?' It was Owen's turn to think on his feet.

'So person X, who might be Nelson, aware that his activities were compromised, took the evidence and ran, knowing that there was nothing that could be done for Gray?'

'Sir, in a nutshell, yes.'

'He would have to be safe in the knowledge that they didn't know him but then we find he too is missing.'

'Or simply done a runner. Business was sold months ago, the money's already in the bank. He could just disappear and if he were involved in the gallery robbery … he might be sitting on more cash.'

'So, you're suggesting that Nelson took the laptop to keep whatever it contained safe? That he knew that Gray was being watched or targeted?'

'Or he had an inkling that she'd decided to spill the beans. We know Nelson had started to become more active after a quiet period, his wife confirmed that. We know that he was in the same hotel in Leeds with Gray when he was supposedly in Harrogate. He was also seen at the hotel the day Gray was murdered. Possible affair or the end of a business understanding as well as an affair?'

'So why do we have the video in the box and in the summerhouse?'

'Nelson produced both, one for us to find in the coffin crate and he left one taped in the summerhouse to make people believe that he's been kidnapped and possibly murdered too.'

Cyril paused. 'Are you suggesting Nelson had Gray murdered and then murdered, Mac?'

'Yes, or someone linked to him and they were working together.'

'If he's not taking the lead in all of this, then very soon we might be finding another body.'

Cyril picked a cloth and wiped off the diagram. 'Facts, we need cold and clear facts.'

***

Christopher Nelson paced the room. There was no window, only the low light emanating from a fluorescent tube that was securely built into the cornice of the ceiling behind a metal frame. The wired glass gave it an austere look. His coat was hung on the back of the only piece of furniture in the room, a bent wooden chair. A toilet in one corner made the room appear more like a cell. He had neither seen nor called anyone since his arrival. He picked up a bottle from the shelf and drank the water. His anxiety continued to grow.

***

Cyril sipped a latte and stared at the photographs of the missing gallery artwork. His electronic cigarette was poised to his lips. Posthumus blew a smoke ring after drawing on his cigar.

'Bloody hell, Cyril. How do they do it? You know how much that security system cost me, Jesus! Let me tell you, more than one of these and one of these!' He pointed to his arm and his leg.

'The bastards employed a fucking crook, did a bloody runner after infecting my fucking system. Is nobody honest these days?'

Cyril handed Simon two images, one was of Nathalie Gray, the second was of Monica Mac, a picture they had received from her time working in security.

'Take a look at these two. Have you ever seen them before?' Cyril could see that he was in no mood to look. 'Simon, look at these. Do you know them or have you seen them before?'

Simon reluctantly spun them round before picking each one up. He began to shake his head. 'No, can't recall. Who are they? She looks a hard bitch.' He tapped his finger on the image of Monica Mac.

'You're sure?' Cyril moved the picture of Gray closer to him. She's in the art game.'

He took a pair of glasses from his pocket and looked more closely.

Cyril just shook his head. 'Vanity!'

'No. Pretty girl. Who is she?'

'She was, Simon, she was. She was murdered by, we think ...' Cyril's finger dropped onto Monica's image ... 'Her.'

'Said she looked a callous cow. Nasty piece of work in my opinion.'

Cyril returned the two photographs to his pocket. 'What's gone has gone, Simon. I'm going to ask you a question and I need you to look me in the eye and tell me the truth. Was this it, the total number of paintings stolen?' Cyril flicked the photographs he held on to the table.

Posthumus frowned and now shuffled the images. 'Off the record?'

Cyril said nothing but stared at him as if willing the truth from him. He knew that he had struck his old friend below the belt.

Posthumus moved his head and coughed.

Cyril remained silent.

Posthumus shook his head. 'Shit no, Cyril.' He paused and fumbled with his cigar. 'There were others that weren't official.'

'How many others?'

'Four, four Lowry paintings. They weren't insured but that's not my only problem. Those, those there,' he pointed to four photographs, 'they weren't solely owned by me. To get the funding for them, a number of, shall we call them, associates to be polite, put money in. You know what it's like when they come to market, you have to act quickly.'

'Apart from your unofficial paintings, what's the problem? The others were insured?'

Posthumus nodded. 'I was insured, yes, for those on display. I've been kindly informed by the assessor that there's small print within the policy.'

'How small?'

'Bloody wrinkles, wrinkles that defy description. They'll ruin me, you'll see! They tell me that the percentage of the paintings not owned by me wasn't covered under the terms and if I'd read the small print I would have been fully aware of the fact!. Now that cost is down to me so, quite frankly, my friend, I have to pay them back their share and I don't have it. It's all tied up here, lock stock and mortgaged up to the bloody hilt not to mention the bloody barrel.'

'The partners, they're in the trade I take it and will have taken out insurance?'

The silence was palpable. Simon's words flooded back into Cyril's head. *Is nobody honest these days?*

Cyril just hung his head. Before resting his forehead in the palm of his hand. 'Oh, Jesus! One of those partners could be the person who robbed you. What have you done?'

***

Christopher Nelson went over to the toilet and relieved himself. The sound of the flushing water echoed around the empty room. He slipped on his coat before moving to the door. He opened it and left. He did not know when he would return but what he did know was that when he did, he would not be alone.

***

Stuart stared at the footage from the CCTV at the Marriott. Although the images were not as sharp as he had hoped, they clearly showed Christopher Nelson walking down a corridor with Nathalie Gray. Both looked deep in conversation. The next image showed the Reception area. Here Nathalie was alone. He checked the other security cameras but Nelson was on none. He fast-forwarded the Reception camera video until it showed a time difference of twenty minutes and there he was, moving into the Reception before he took a seat away from the mahogany Reception desk. He was just in view. Stuart paused the recording and captured a screen shot. He posted it to his system at Harrogate Police Station.

'Now what are you waiting for, Christopher Nelson?' he whispered to himself.

He re-started the video and watched Nelson move away from the lounge area choosing an area even further from the camera, as another figure appeared to move in his direction.

'Bingo!' Stuart whispered as he watched as the two people shook hands. All he now had to do was capture a clear view of this stranger's face.

Chapter Eleven

Cyril would be the first to admit that he was not the picture of elegance as he stood dressed in his shirt and tie, boxer shorts, socks and slippers whilst ironing the creases into his suit trousers; a regular ritual. The pressing cloth steamed as he ran the iron along the length of the trouser leg. The radio was playing in the background and his mind danced around memories of Liz; he felt neither sadness nor joy. He draped the trousers over the back of the chair and cleared away the board and the iron, finished his coffee and within fifteen minutes he was ready, as immaculate as ever. It had often been said by his colleagues that the criminals could tell he was a copper by the shine to his shoes. He looked down and smiled.

Closing the front door of his house on Robert Street, he breathed the morning air. The sky was a clear duck-egg blue. Three workmen were setting cones to one side of the road. He nodded and smiled as he passed, their enthusiasm was noteworthy. He headed for the footway that would take him through to the A61 and The Stray.

The early morning shower had left a smell of freshness in the air. The leaves had been washed clean of their summer coating of dust and now glowed green in the morning light. He stood and admired his surroundings. How different his life was now from that of his earlier career, an apprenticeship and period that had formed many of his prejudices, his work ethic and his flawed attitude to loving, personal relationships. He seldom dredged the resentment from the depth of his years to the surface like this, so why should he do so today, particularly on such a blameless morning? It confused him. Maybe it was Liz helping him to realise just how lucky he was at this moment to simply be alive. 'Morning, Liz,' he whispered before inhaling a quantity of menthol vapour.

He turned up Otley Road, his usual route to work. Traffic was just building as he checked his watch. He shook his wrist and checked again. It was 07:15. He deliberately turned away from looking at the needle point of Trinity Methodist Church, his imagination was still too raw. In thirty minutes he would have collected a newspaper, some electronic cigarette fluid and he would be at his desk. It was so good to be back where he felt he truly belonged.

**

The large estate car belonging to Freeman Freshman turned off North Road, Ripon and drove along Ure Bank before pulling right onto Ure Bank Top. He drove half-way along the steep incline before pulling up and parking. The row of terraced houses stretched the full length of the left of the road. They were not overlooked. He scanned the address written on a padded envelope resting on the passenger seat before glancing at the numbers on the doors. He removed the key from the envelope and left the car before walking back down the road until he had located the correct number. He tried the key in the front door and he was rewarded with a satisfying click. He had to admit to being both excited and nervous, a cocktail that brought a slight feeling of nausea to the pit of his stomach. This, if it were like the previous occasions, would prove to be a very profitable morning.

Although the day was bright, the small front room of the house was dark and much colder than he had anticipated considering the warmth of the day. It was devoid of all furnishings as were the other rooms. There was a damp, musty aroma that seemed to permeate the place, quickly filling his nostrils. He sniffed again and the work that had taken place in the house added its redolence to the atmosphere. He knew that it had been unoccupied for some time but the smell of turpentine was clearly discernible. That could only mean one thing, oil paint. His excitement grew.

He moved through to the kitchen at the back of the building and looked out of the window. The garden ran to a row of trees that closed any view of the river but it also ensured that the garden remained private. He smiled when he saw the remains of the brick outside toilet and coal storage building at the far end of what would have once been a yard when the houses had been built. He noticed a blackened, garden incinerator tucked to the side of the wall. All of the other properties had had the outbuildings removed years ago but in this house they remained, a historical anomaly.

The door to the cellar was beneath the stairs, a simple wooden door with a latch. Pinned to it was another envelope on which the initials FF were clearly written. He prised away the drawing pin and collected the package. He slid his finger into the flap and tore it open. It contained a small, computer pen drive. He turned it over in his hand and frowned, He then noticed the message:

Look at only what you have come to see. Please leave everything untouched. That way is best for you!

It was just as the time before. He smiled at the familiarity before he lifted the latch and opened the door to what he knew to be the cellar. It was here that the smell of turpentine was at its strongest. He flicked the switch to the left of the door, a low voltage light to the side of the steps responded immediately and he slowly descended excited at what might be awaiting him.

***

Cyril hung up his jacket, straightened his desk before plugging a battery for his electronic cigarette into the wall socket. It hung limply, a single, red neon light showing that it was now charging. He checked his mail and then moved through to the Interview Room. If he expected every one of his team to check the white boards daily, then he should be seen doing just that.

Shakti was sitting looking through three files.

'Morning. Anything from your side?'

Shakti looked up and smiled. 'Looking again through the files on Freshman's employees. Wanted to know more about Darwin Green. Never really showed any emotion after Nathalie died, seemed somehow too cool, too relaxed. Read his statement again and again and I feel there's something that he's keeping to himself.'

'Bring him in and interview him again if you have any doubts, that's what we should be good at, responding to these instincts. You could also take Owen and interview him at his place.'

Shakti nodded and returned to reading the file.

It was a note on the second white board that brought Cyril up short. He stuck his e-cigarette between his lips and read it, looking at the still images captured from the Harrogate Grand Hotel CCTV.

'Christopher Nelson has been busy. Three days before Nathalie Gray's death, the day of her death, but we know he stayed as he had an ex-colleagues' function, if I recall, but then he's back two days later and now he's missing. Have we put a check on ports and airports and has his image been broadcast?'

'Yes, and nothing as yet. Have a feeling that he may not be going far from his current position if you get my drift, Sir.'

'Indeed I do and I feel the same way. Somebody is going to smell him before they see him!'

It was unusual for Cyril to seem so cold and it did not go unnoticed. Shakti could not help but pull a face. He left the Incident Room and went to DC Stuart Park's desk. Stuart was just uploading his findings.

'Sir, not added this to the wall yet but it's really interesting. Nelson might have been seeing another woman as well. Not only does Gray appear in the footage but also another, a more mature lady. Significantly, both not at the same time!' He winked at Cyril. 'A ménage?'

He brought up three screen capture images. Clearly Christopher Nelson was in conversation with another woman, one shot even captured an embrace.

'Do we know who she is?'

'She certainly didn't check in personally at the hotel. There's no footage of her in the bedroom corridors, only in the Reception area as you see here. It was possibly a meeting of some kind.'

'Difficult to ménage in the hotel lobby, Stuart or am I just getting old?' It was Cyril's turn to wink. 'Was she also in Leeds?'

Stuart shook his head.

'So, there's a chance that Nelson wasn't seeing Nathalie during his stop overs in Harrogate, maybe this mystery lady?'

***

At the bottom of the steps, Freshman paused. A shiver ran up his neck. The stone-flagged floor of the cellar seemed to bring its own chill to the room. Once away from the steps there was little light. He felt along the wall for a switch but there was none. He looked to his left and in the centre of the room was a large stone, slab-topped table; originally the cellar would have been the place to keep food cool and fresh. Many of the properties had converted this lower, subterranean level into a kitchen area that led directly to the garden but not this one.

The smell of turpentine was now much stronger. His eyes gradually grew more accustomed to the dark and slowly the room and the far wall became clearer. There, placed upon a stone shelf were four small easels, an unframed painting sat on each. Freshman's excitement grew as he eagerly removed his mobile phone and flicked the screen to locate the torch. Immediately the camera flashlight illuminated the area in a cold, white light. He stood and admired the four paintings that he had been told were available at a bargain price. He studied each with care but he was also conscious of the battery life remaining in his phone. He liked what he saw. He stood and breathed deeply, now able to relax for the first time since putting the key in the door. He was surely onto a winner again.

He recalled the instructions he had received. *If you want the paintings they are available but only as a set of four, if not, look no further, say nothing to anyone, return the key. Thank you for viewing.*

He turned off the torch and immediately his night vision deserted him. He made his way to the light emanating from the bottom of the steps, fumbling his way around the table. His foot caught on something and he stumbled falling to his hands and knees. His phone clattered on the stone floor.

'Shit and fucking derision!' he growled as he fondled the floor to find the phone. He grabbed it and the screen illuminated but a large crack was now visible across the screen and fine flakes of glass had broken from the edge.

'Fuck me!'

He flicked the torch back on and raised himself to his knees before turning to see what he had tripped over. An iron bar protruded about a foot from beneath the table.

***

Shakti rang both Dr Darwin Green's landline and his mobile phone. Both immediately went to answer phone. She rang Owen.

'I think we need to speak to Dr Green again. Flash suggests we see him at his place. I've tried ringing, but there's no response.'

'With Nelson's disappearance it's worth checking out, it's not too far. Give me ten minutes.'

Shakti felt relieved, she had a growing anxiety about Green. It was an itch that needed scratching.

Cyril ploughed through the growing links on HOLMES and noted two avenues that he wanted to pursue. After the scrutiny of Christopher Nelson's bank details, it was evident that he had been frequently drawing some large amounts of cash from two of his accounts, but since his disappearance there had been no further withdrawals. He looked at the amounts, swiftly totting them up and whistled to himself. The sums varied and there was no pattern to the removal of the cash but it totalled over £450,000. He needed to know the reason for the withdrawals and he sanctioned the action authorising the banks to release the full account details.

The second, and for him the more pressing matter, was to discover whether Nathalie Gray had done some conservation work for Manchester Galleries. He felt sure that Manchester had their own team of experts similar to that of Liverpool Museums and Galleries, but on researching he had read that a cost-cutting exercise two years previously had robbed them of this vital skills base. He picked up the phone.

***

Freshman slowly recovered his composure and got to his feet whilst steadying himself using the stone table top. Now, in the torchlight, he inspected his clothing for damage; there were dark stains on the knees of his trousers and his jacket sleeve was torn. 'Bloody clumsy oaf!' he said out loud. It was then that he noticed the door to the far side of the cellar. The torch flickered momentarily as he moved towards it. Curiosity got the better of him and he lifted the latch, surprised to see the door spring back towards him forced by the weight of an object that had been jammed into the small space behind it.

***

Cyril was put on hold whilst Felicity Tonge, the Duty Curator, was paged. He was pleased that they did not play music. He could only hear the echoing sounds of the gallery and the indiscernible chatter of visitors; it transmitted the gallery's atmosphere perfectly.

'DCI Bennett? Sorry to keep you, I was just ...' she paused '... you really don't want to hear my work-related tasks, sorry. How may I help you?'

'Some time ago the gallery employed a conservator by the name of Gray, a Nathalie Gray. We believe that she was employed through Freeman Freshman Fine Arts. Is that the case?'

'Nathalie? Yes, she's worked with us on occasions, maybe two or three, I think, but don't quote me. Her work is outstanding, believe me, the best I've seen in my career. Granted that's not very long!' She laughed.

'What exactly did she do?'

'The last work she did was to renovate a damaged oil by Adolphe Valette and before that … I think it was a Lowry that had been vandalised. Why anyone wants to add more figures using indelible coloured pens to such fabulous work is beyond me.'

'Both paintings are by northern, Manchester artists?'

'Nathalie's speciality, particularly, Valette. I know he's French but we class him as one of our own and Nathalie being French, she loved his stuff. Funnily enough, we had someone in last month studying his work and although he's an expert in this field, I'm pleased to say that he failed to detect the repair to one of the paintings he inspected and that was at close hand in a private viewing. That's how good she was.'

'You said was, past tense.'

'Is? Was? What does it matter? I didn't know that I was under scrutiny. She worked with us in the past, that's all I meant.'

Cyril sensed the sudden change of attitude and immediately regretted his abruptness. 'Sorry, once a copper. May I ask his name?'

'Dr Green.'

'Darwin Green?'

She heard the surprise in Cyril's voice. 'You know him? Is there a problem?' The same steeliness was reinforced in her voice.

Cyril could only reassure her that there was nothing untoward and thanked her, suggesting that he might need to speak with her again. He hung up immediately regretting his blunt questioning. It was not like him. 'Bloody hell, Liz. Made a right dog's breakfast of that!'

Why would Green look at Gray's work? To reassure his partner that her work was up to scratch? He thought not. So why travel to Manchester and inspect her work? He scribbled an aide-memoire and underlined it twice.

***

The door flew back crashing against the wall and for the second time within ten minutes, Freshman found himself on the floor, but this time his backside had taken the brunt of the fall as his head glanced the edge of the stone-slab table. He momentarily passed out; at least on this occasion he had held on to the phone. As he opened his eyes, he could see the light from his phone bounce off the ceiling giving a strange, white glow to the room. After a few moments, he could feel a weight across his legs and he bent at the waist, propping himself on one elbow to see what it might be. He shone the phone towards his feet only to see the naked, male torso spread face down trapping his lower legs. His uncontrolled scream filled the room as he kicked and struggled to release his trapped limbs from beneath the body. He quickly slid away on his behind until his back found a wall.

Once under control, he stood slowly. His hand shook as he focussed on the prostrate form. The head seemed wrong, somehow, it was totally distorted; it seemed to have been crushed. He moved around the room avoiding the body until he came to the steps. Even with legs that felt like jelly, he quickly climbed the stairs and left the cellar. Once in the kitchen he checked his clothing again. He looked as though he had been in a pub brawl. He switched off the torch and headed for the front door. The sooner he was in his car and away, the better. Within seconds of leaving the house and turning the key, the next-door neighbour stopped him. A petite woman holding a small dog across her bosom simply stared at him.

'Is she selling it then? About bloody time if you ask me! Christ, we'll have rats and all sorts of vermin if she doesn't get it cleaned up, finished and sold. Workmen in and out never staying for long must be robbing her of a fortune. We told her last time she was here, didn't we, Mr Biggles, but she didn't listen, just told me to mind my own business.' The dog barked on hearing its name as if on cue. 'You a workman?'

Freshman simply looked at her. Her make up seemed heavy and the scarf covering what seemed like a head full of curlers transferred her, in his mind, to another era. It took all his willpower to stop himself from telling her simply to disappear. He had had enough for one day and the last thing he wanted was to converse with an interfering busybody. He must, however, remain calm. The last thing he wanted was to draw attention to himself.

'I've inspected it and I fully understand your concerns, Mrs ...?'

'Higginbottom. And this is Mr Biggles.'

It yapped again.

'Yes, Mrs Higginbottom ... Mr Biggles. Good to meet you,' he lied. How could she be anything else other than an outright arse-hole he thought? 'I've given it a full inspection as you can see from my clothing. It's passed and I'm pleased to inform you that it will go on the market within the month.' He smiled and pushed past her.

'Miss, not Mrs ... and you are?'

He wracked his brains for a quick name. 'Tennant, Paul Tennant. Good day!' He waved a hand as he walked towards his car. He neither cared nor worried if she saw the car or could identify him. He simply had to get away. Within minutes he was heading towards the centre of Ripon. His phone rang and *unknown number* appeared beneath the cracked screen. His heart sank and his stomach tightened as he pulled up. He knew just who it was. He didn't answer it. He quickly opened the car door, leaned out and vomited.

***

Shakti pointed to the gates as Owen pulled up to the kerb.

'You expecting him to be in?' Owen tapped the wheel as if some tune was going round his head. Occasionally he made the sound of a cymbal crashing.

Shakti rang the house number. After three rings it was answered. She smiled and turned the phone off. 'He's expecting us.' She smiled cynically. 'Ever thought of playing the steering wheel professionally?'

Owen just raised his eyebrows.

She had not gone three steps up the drive when her mobile rang. 'It's Flash.'

Owen pulled a face.

'Just arrived, Sir.' She listened and Owen watched her facial expression change during the conversation. He also noticed Dr Green appearing at the door.

Owen moved towards Green and fished his warrant card from his inside pocket.

'Dr Green? DS Owen and this is my colleague DC Shakti Misra. We need a little of your time. She won't be a minute. It's a busy day! May I?' He made his way in, not waiting for a reply and Green was in no mood to stop him. Owen was impressed with the layout of the main hallway. The grey painted bookshelves stretched down to the stairs.

'Have you read all of these?' Owen, who had never really considered books to be an essential part of life, asked the question in all innocence.

'Every one and some many times over. Sorry what was your name?'

'Detective Sergeant Owen and this is DC Misra.'

Shakti moved down the hallway. 'We'd like to ask you a few more questions about your partner, Nathalie Gray.'

As she spoke, the sound of someone dropping something in the kitchen made them all turn in the direction of the disturbance.

'I have an old friend staying for a few days. He'll never make a juggler!' He laughed at his own joke but Shakti simply looked at Owen and Owen read her mind.

'May I offer you tea or coffee?'

'Just fifteen minutes of your time will be sufficient. You obviously have plans for the day.'

Although during the questioning, Green seemed comfortable, Shakti still had this nag in her stomach.

'As I've said before, it's really hard to come to terms with not only a colleague's death, but also that of a very close friend.' Those words clearly resonated with Owen as he considered just how Liz's death had affected him but then, Green could have done nothing to prevent Gray from being murdered.

'She was a friend and not a lover, is that right?'

'Let's say we had a sexual understanding and that's where I shall leave it. We must all deal with mortality in any way that we can and fortunately I have many friends who have rallied round and of course I have my work. As you can see from these walls, I truly love that side of my life.' He pointed to the myriad pictures.

Shakti stood and proffered her hand. 'Thank you. We've intruded on your time enough.' She smiled and looked at Owen who responded.

'Yes, thank you. I don't usually like paintings, Dr Green, can't really see the point but I like that one.' Owen indicated the painting to which he referred.

'The Brian Shields. Strangely, one of the other policeman who called liked that one too. He was known as Braaq and if you look carefully …'

'Where's Wally … It was Brian, one of our lads, who told me about this artist recently.' He smiled. 'They're fun. I like that.' Owen's smile was genuine.

Green seemed to relax and Shakti now saw her opportunity to share the information she had received from Cyril during the phone call. She had been saving it for just such a moment and she watched his expression with care as she popped the question.

'I believe that you were in the Manchester Art Gallery on 16 July. Can you tell us the reason for your private visit?'

Owen was quick to note that Shakti did not take her eyes off Green and he too looked at him before moving a step closer. Initially, Green blushed, and his expression clearly indicated that he was surprised by the direct nature of the question. The soft-edged tones of Shakti's voice had been replaced by a short, staccato timbre that seemed threatening and somewhat intimidating. There was a pause whilst he regained a degree of his original composure.

'Adolphe Valette. I was studying the Manchester works of Valette. Why? What has that to do with Nathalie Gray?'

'We were hoping that you'd be able to tell us that, Dr Green.'

Shakti and Owen simply stared at Green, neither taking their eyes off him.

'May I offer anyone a drink?' A new voice entered the conversation.

Owen turned immediately to identify the voice. A tall, thin man stood in the doorway, a broad smile on his face, a face he recalled seeing on one of the whiteboards. The name escaped him.

'Just made fresh coffee. Can I tempt anyone?'

Owen just turned to Green with his hand pointing at the stranger in the doorway. 'Who's this?'

'Paul, come and say hello. DS Owen and DC?...' Shakti nodded. 'I was right, DC Misra. This is Paul Gray, Nathalie's father.'

Owen looked at Shakti and then at Paul Gray. It was their turn to be wrong-footed. Gray's entrance was perfectly timed.

'Sorry for the intrusion.' Gray moved back towards the kitchen.

'May we resume? I think we have more to talk about.' Owen sat as he was making the request.

***

Within two hours, Freshman was home. He poured a large brandy and drank it with the ease of a condemned man and then poured a second before moving through to the conservatory. He could still taste the vomit on his breath, even after the brandy. The acidic aroma clung to his nostrils intensifying his constant feeling of fear. He dug his hand into his jacket pocket for the envelope and the computer pen drive. Once removed from the packet he tumbled it in his hand as if weighing it.

'What have you done, Freeman, you bloody fool? Just what kind of Pandora's box has your greed opened?'

He drank more from the glass, the warmth of the brandy seemed to soothe him and he felt a little calmer. If only he had a computer at home he could take a look. He popped the pen drive on the table and went to pour another drink. He would look the following day that would be soon enough. He checked the locks on the doors for the second time.

Just as he was settling, his phone rang again and he rooted for it in his jacket. Again, *'caller unknown'* appeared beneath the broken screen. His heart rate increased and he felt the taste of nausea erupt from his stomach. Had they discovered what he had disturbed? He tried to control his breathing and tossed the phone onto the table next to the pen drive.

***

Shakti stared at Green. 'How long have you known Paul Gray?'

'Nathalie took me to their home in the village of Nun Monkton earlier this year. It was only a brief visit, we were heading up to Newcastle, for separate appointments, but we travelled together. She suggested that I should meet her parents, surprise them and at the same time she could show me her home village. It was spontaneous, we just made the visit to coincide with a business trip we were taking. Sadly, only Paul, her father, was home, her mother was in France working, something she does more and more. It helps to keep the business in York afloat.'

'So what's he doing here now?' Shakti's internal nag was growing and she could not quite keep her burgeoning distrust of the man from her voice.

'We've both lost someone very close to us and we're sharing the grief, if you share it, you halve it, yes?' His brief smile was like a slap of insincerity to Shakti.

She wanted to return the blow. 'So who's sharing her mother's grief, Dr Green or does she just have to manage that alone?'

There was a palpable pause. Owen did not take his eyes off Green. He could almost see his brain working to counter her last comment.

'Maybe I'm more qualified to answer that than Darwin. May I?' Paul Gray emerged from the kitchen and pointed to an empty chair.

The timing was again perfect; this metaphorical bell saved Green for the second time when he was clearly against the ropes.

Owen simply pointed to the chair and Gray sat before looking at Green with an expression that conveyed that all was well.

***

Christopher Nelson sat in the small café in York, a toasted teacake had just been delivered and the butter ran onto the plate. He dabbed the warm liquid with his finger and then licked it; the slippery, salty, sweetness clung to his lips. He had booked into a small guesthouse on the previous day, having planned for this eventuality. A case and clothing had been stored in what he knew as his den in readiness. He checked his watch. Time for the next few days would be unimportant. All he had to do, even today when cameras and facial recognition software were so active, was to stay lost, to remain missing. He had seen the initial reports of his disappearance on the local news and in the press, but like all things, news quickly moves on to other more pressing issues, fed to the general public by the so-called free press in manageable chunks. He just had to be careful and careful he most certainly was. He had shaved his goatee, something he had sported for years and his appearance was now quite different; he believed that he looked younger. He had withdrawn sizeable chunks of cash over a period of months, he had a bolt hole and he had a plan. What he now needed was patience and time. God provided him with one, the other was for him to control and at his age he found that relatively easy.

Chapter Twelve

Cyril did not usually interview people in his office but he made an exception for Simon Posthumus. He even had coffee and biscuits ready.

'It's quite straightforward, Simon. You hand over all of your accounts and the details of all sales and purchases and included in those will be the under the counter transactions.'

Simon Posthumus resembled a child who had been caught stealing apples. It was as if he were digesting each of Cyril's words individually.

'Surely my legitimate accounts will suffice. I don't want to claim for those not catalogued, only these here.' He removed the photographs of the legitimate, stolen art works. 'You and I both know that they're never coming back.'

'I need names and addresses of everyone from whom you purchased, where each of these came from. I want their provenance, Simon, and I want it ASAP. We're not just covering your robbery. Two people have been killed and another is missing and the longer there's no trace of him, the greater the chance we'll find a body. I also want to know about the other pieces, the unofficial works you've handled over the last twelve months. Those, providing we get everything else, can be our secret for the time being but no promises for the long term.'

Simon nodded. 'I'll have all the details with you by tomorrow. The paintings not catalogued …?'

Cyril sat up.

'I respond to phone calls. Started a few years ago, usually with an artist who's beginning to show strongly on the art market, mostly northern artists. Isherwood is a prime example, you know him, Christ, we've had many a discussion about his work. Started with him. I'd buy one or two and they'd sell very well through the galleries, particularly the Manchester shop. However, with popularity came the fakers, no provenance, false stories, but with Isherwood they seldom had provenance anyway so, after a while, I left them alone. Braaq was the next big thing. Over two years his prices started to climb very rapidly, so I was buying his work whenever I could. Don't forget, Cyril, I was also picking up the odd Lowry sketch and small oil as there was a ready and growing market. Here, of course, you're dealing with a lot of money so you have to have a history, an unbroken record of ownership that goes, if possible, all the way to the artist or one of the galleries that represented him. Having a full provenance will bring the highest price, without it, you're on treacherously thin ice.'

'Go back to the Braaq paintings,' Cyril requested.

'I'd get a call to go to a house and look at a painting. It was usually on the wall. There might be some history with it and I might decide to buy or not. Strangely, the price was always well below what was expected, maybe half of the real market value.'

'Was the call always from the same person?'

Simon fiddled with his cigar and shook his head. 'No, funnily enough when I went to some of the houses and believe me, Cyril, some homes looked as though the owners or tenants didn't have a pot to piss in, there might be other paintings on the walls. One I went to had a Braaq, a Harold Riley and a Valette. Couldn't believe my eyes.'

'All for sale?'

'No, just the Braaq. I asked about the others but they weren't for selling.'

'Fakes?'

'I bought the Braaq, sold it the same week turning a good profit. As far as I could see it was right and that, my dear friend, is all that I can go on. Christ, I'm supposed to be an expert and my reputation always rests on the last painting I sell. I can't take risks, I have to be sure, the provenance has to be right otherwise I don't buy and I certainly don't advise others to buy. Surely you know that from your first-hand experience, my friend?'

'Indeed! So what of the four you had here?'

'Bought over a period of two years, similar way to how I've described. Over the last twelve months I've been buying Lowry prints too. I think I told you on the opening night that a year ago they were selling at a third of the price they are now. Trouble is, unsigned prints that are worth very little can suddenly acquire a pencil signature and with that an inflated price ... I leave them alone now too.'

'So let's get on to the Lowry paintings.'

'They're all small and are real gems ... were! One came from a house in Wigan along with an Isherwood, one from Lytham. That's ...'

'Bloody hell, Simon, I know where Lytham is and Wigan for that matter, get on with it, man!'

'Sorry, just thought that I was being helpful ... and a pair from Keighley. That house had a number of interesting pieces. Small terraced house but goodness me, a veritable Aladdin's cave. He showed me receipts from the artists for all of them, must have had five classy pieces, all small, but great quality. He told me that he sold art supplies in the fifties and sixties and so he got to meet a number of artists. Like artists today, they were always scrounging bits and bobs. Probably swapped paintings and drawings for materials, that's how it worked in those days.'

'That's how it seems to work today! So how come you're the man in their little black address books?'

'Other than the fact that I have two well-known galleries dealing in this kind of art and that I advertise regularly in the local and national press, I do regular leaflet drops in areas and specify that I pay cash for original art work, I've no idea. Some would say that they had others interested, particularly the guy from Keighley. He drove a bloody hard bargain, but whether that were true I can't say, couldn't take the risk. They were gems. You get one chance in most cases.'

'Receipts for the cash? I take it, Simon, that it was always cash?'

'Cash is king, my friend, when dealing like that, the best bargaining chip in the world. Bring out a bundle of notes and you have them just where you want them.'

'You have the addresses and the names and possibly the telephone numbers?' Cyril was beginning to lose his patience. He felt that Simon was being deliberately obtuse.

'I could find maybe one house but not sure. Kept a couple of numbers. No need to ask, Cyril, as I've tried ringing them to see if they wanted to sell another painting but the numbers, usually mobile, were no longer available. People change their phones and their numbers more regularly than they change their underwear nowadays.'

'So, what you're saying in a nutshell is that you have no records.'

'There was the provenance. The name of the chap from Keighley and I think the guy from Wigan were written on the letters and receipts. The Isherwood was originally bought from a sale at Wigan Town Hall and he still had the bill of sale.'

'You have copies?'

'Given to the new owners.'

'You have their names and addresses?'

'Cash, Cyril. Cash is king.'

'Try this saying after me, Simon. The Inland Revenue rules.'

Simon could see from Cyril's expression that he was no longer in the mood for further prevarication.

'You have twenty-four hours to give me something to lead on otherwise our friendship ceases. I'll raise the game by involving the Inland Revenue and I'll also contact the Insurance Assessor; you were seriously under insured, my friend. The ball is in your court. I don't have the time to mess about any longer.'

Cyril stood and showed Simon to the door.

'Brian, please show this gentleman out.'

Cyril touched Simon's arm. 'Think on this, 'Twenty-four hours and not a minute longer.'

Simon hung his head but said nothing, he just obediently followed Brian.

***

Shakti and Owen stood in the Incident Room adding the details of their visit to the board. A new, red line stretched in a rather circuitous route from Dr Darwin Green's image to that of Paul Gray; an arrowhead was added to either end. The second line leading from Paul Gray to Nathalie had been broken with an annotated note. STEPFATHER! He also tagged on a short note about Bernadette's bouts of depression.

'I didn't see that coming! It was like a bloody bolt from the blue. Bernadette had Nathalie the year before she met Paul!' Owen wiped his finger through the line and added a question mark, this time in black. DNA will confirm that, it's organised. Still wonder why he was there ... as you said, you'd have thought he'd be with Bernadette, that she'd be the one needing the support.'

'So, do you believe that the first time they met was when he briefly paid a visit with Nathalie?' Shakti was still trying to undo the Gordian Knot that was trapped within her stomach and Owen knew it.

'Evidence, Shakti, evidence and not supposition. He's innocent until you can prove differently.' He tapped his finger next to the question mark. 'See, innocent but not to be believed until we have the proof. Something Cyril taught me. He used to say that gut feelings are fine but that's all they are, they'll keep you alert to the smallest of clues but don't let the feelings drive you into making a silly error. He also said that you either have them or you don't, Shakti. The good coppers do!'

She nodded, knowing that Owen was right and put her hand on his elbow, appreciative of his support.

Cyril had entered the Incident Room a few minutes earlier, a trail of vapour, like a small patch of white mist, followed. He listened but did not interrupt.

'Contact Bernadette Gray, I know she's in France, but we have the details of the company she's working for and her mobile number. See what she says. Do it now, it will help confirm it one way or the other,' Owen requested.

Shakti moved away to a desk. Owen watched as she dialled. She became quite animated as she spoke. He watched her hand draw patterns in the air and then she turned to face him and nodded. She mouthed, *It's true*! After a few more minutes she hung up.

'She broke down! Didn't think that it was anyone else's business. She's probably correct. She told me that the only way she can deal with Nathalie's death is through working. Sitting around at home wouldn't help and Paul has a business to run with commitments and deadlines to meet that often rely on her ability to produce the artwork.'

'Paul Gray didn't seem to be too concerned about deadlines to me! Is there a relationship there, him and Darwin?'

Shakti did not respond but did question the reason that Darwin had given for being in the gallery in Manchester. He had certainly had the opportunity to concoct something by the time Paul Gray had given them his life story. She moved across to Cyril and detailed the interview. They gave Cyril a brief résumé.

'So, according to Dr Green, he was in the gallery checking on her restoration work at Freeman Freshman's request whilst also taking the opportunity to make a detailed study of the Valette paintings held by the gallery. And his conclusion?'

'He said that Nathalie's work was second to none. The work she'd done on the Lowry was also exceptional.'

Cyril sat, his electronic cigarette in his mouth. 'Interestingly, Helen informed me that Bernadette Gray mentioned that she had produced a copy of a small Lowry as an exercise, some kind of competition with Nathalie. He was supposed to have only used five colours. Bernadette had no idea where Nathalie's picture ended up.'

'Five colours, right! From what I see, they are grey, grey, grey, white and black, Sir,' Shakti grumbled and looked at Owen.

Cyril smiled. 'No, Shakti, if you look a little more closely, I think you might see red, just as you did when you were discussing Green earlier! Open mind, please, keep the gut feeling but drop the prejudice. You'll do your job more effectively and be a better copper for it.' He looked at them both and left.

Owen tapped her arm. 'You're doing just fine.'

***

Freshman Freeman entered his storage unit and turned off the alarm before closing the door quickly behind him. He ensured that it was locked before moving through to his office. The computer eyed him as he fished the pen drive from his pocket. He was anxious, not only because of what he had witnessed the previous day, but also about what he might find hidden on this pen drive. The computer took a few moments to stir itself to life and as usual he cursed himself for not upgrading the machine. He slipped the drive into the USB port and waited. The small icon appeared. He enlarged it and pressed on the mouse to make it play.

Facing him, filling the screen, was the fat, moustachioed policeman trapped within the glass case. A hand appeared but did not linger, it simply dropped the coin into the slot. A light came on inside the box and the mechanical man started to rock and laugh. Freeman smiled and sat back uncertain as to the meaning of the video. Within two minutes the laughter had ceased and the model remained motionless apart from one blinking eye.

'That's the only thing wrong with that bloody machine, both eyes should blink three times at the end.' It was then that he realised that it was in fact his; as soon as the single eye had winked he had immediately recognised it. He entered the warehouse, passing a small mountain of brown furniture that now nobody wanted to buy, until he came to a number of old amusement house games. He stood and scanned the mahogany cases, chromium one-armed bandits alongside the odd pinball machine, but he could not see the box containing the laughing policeman. He quickly pulled some protective blankets off other cases but there was an empty gap, a space where he thought the machine should be. Perspiration began to bead his forehead and he dabbed it away with his handkerchief.

'Get a bloody grip man. It has to be here.'

He searched the building methodically, but he could not find it. He returned to the office and sat looking at the screen. At that moment his mobile phone rang, *'caller unknown'* was illuminated under the broken glass screen. He slid his finger to answer the call and listened.

'Mr Salvatore is not pleased, Freeman. Instructions are there to keep us all safe. Why, oh why didn't you follow them?' There was a pause but Freshman said nothing. 'You've broken the strict code that we established. He trusted you with the paintings and now they're gone. Other people were interested, people who can read and comprehend.' There was a pause. 'Mr Salvatore says goodbye for the moment, Freeman. You can throw away the key. Goodbye.'

The voice sounded cold and clinical. Freshman said nothing but continued to listen. The sound of the laughing policeman erupted from the earpiece and he tossed the mobile phone onto the desk, the now manic-style laughter still filling the office space. With a shaking hand he reached to grab it and ended the call. His stomach churned and his hands shook. He clasped them together trying to control his emotions.

After a few minutes, his hand searched for his wallet and he found the card passed to him by DI Claire. He needed to tell someone, tell them about the house and the body, but it would mean admitting to handling paintings in the past. He put it on the desk next to the phone and the pen drive, To Freeman they had become the satanic trinity. Suddenly he did not know which he feared the most.

Chapter Thirteen

Cyril turned his fork through the risotto; clearly his mind was elsewhere.

'Not to your liking?' Julie asked, knowing it to be one of his favourite meals.

'Perfect, as good as ever … thank you.' He smiled and she could tell he spoke the truth. 'I need to talk to you after dinner, it's work I'm afraid, I need to try to get a focus on some thoughts, get things into some kind of perspective, if that's OK?'

'Happy to listen, Cyril.'

Cyril loaded the last of the plates into the dishwasher before turning on the laptop. Julie settled beside him.

'I want to share some thoughts that have been nagging me since my conversation with Simon Posthumus, the gallery owner. I believed that he's always been above board until the discovery that the four paintings that were not catalogued may have dubious pasts. It appears that he's always, and I use his term, *dabbled in this way*. So, I started an Internet search looking at the history of art fraud. Nathalie Gray, the girl who was murdered, did some work at the Mercer Gallery. She repaired a Braaq painting that had been vandalised by having the word 'fake' scratched into the paint. With that and with Posthumus's possible shady dealing, I started to consider the idea that art fraud and the way fake paintings are introduced onto the market, may have a connection as a possible link to the two cases under investigation. Do you mind?'

'Please, go ahead. I don't know what I can contribute, but I have ears!' She put her hand on his knee.

'There have always been fakes, some better than others. An interesting fact I read was that up to forty per cent of works in the market place may be fake. Today, if you go on to on-line auction sites, they're full of them. Even to the uninitiated they're clearly not right. Look!' Cyril added the names of a number of artists and scrolled down. 'It's frightening and there must be buyers willing to pay otherwise this market would've dried up not long after it started. People are always looking for that lost treasure. Here are some Lowry drawings and sketches advertised right now.' He turned the screen. 'And here's some lost and now found Lowry oil … from a house clearance … right …! It clearly states that it's signed by the artist which is not a lie, misleading, but the seller's not telling an untruth!'

'Surely that's against the law?'

'No, because they say that there's no provenance and therefore they're selling the painting '*in the style of*' and that's their let-out clause. Christ, that's not even in the style of anyone but people still take the risk. £2,600 for absolute garbage! I spoke with a Manchester dealer and he assured me that there are no cheap Lowry paintings out there in car boot sales or on the net. If it's cheap it's ninety-nine point nine per cent wrong. People come into his gallery every week with a Lowry and he has to tell them that unless they like it and want to keep it, they've thrown their money away! As with all auctions, it's Caveat Emptor … let the buyer beware. '

'We're not talking about this type of art work though, Cyril. Simon wouldn't be fooled into buying any old picture from someone coming in off the street. He's been dealing for years and that's why people trust his judgement. You did!'

Cyril nodded and reflected for a moment.

'I daren't linger too long on that thought, Julie! Anyway, let me get back to this. Forgers can be one of three types of individual. Firstly, there's the person who paints the work and passes it off as the work of someone else. We all know of that one. Secondly, there's the person who discovers a piece and then attempts to pass it off as the work of another, maybe adds a signature and thirdly, someone who buys a piece, discovers that it's false and even having that knowledge passes it on as an original. All three are breaking the law.'

Julie pulled a face and nodded. 'So, if I bought something from you, discovered that it wasn't what you said it was, why not just give it back?'

'First of all you'd have to find me. If you buy from an auction house you have a limited time to tell them of your concerns. You have to remember that art fraud, like everything else, embraces modern technology, there's big money to be made if you get it right. Look at the past where people have eventually been caught after years of painting and passing their work off as someone else's. We are talking millions, not thousands of pounds.'

'Surely forensics, art forensics, must make it easy to detect what's authentic?'

'A good point, the legal side has some big guns. There's the Courtauld Institute of Art, the International Foundation for Art Research and as you've just rightly pointed out, there's the Forensic Science Research Unit. There's paint analysis and spectroscopy but what's good for one is good for the other. Gamekeepers can quickly become poachers when dealing with high value paintings.'

'Cyril, I'm sorry but you're losing me. Just what are you saying?'

'That simply buying a piece of art work is now never good enough. It needs a history, a provenance, a paper trail that, if possible, goes back to the artist and for that to happen you need documents; for fake art you need fake documents, invoices of sales, false page entries in old catalogues, fake auction and gallery stamps and labels, even placing fake documentation within gallery archives and the archives of the institutions. What's truly frightening, Julie, is the fact that it's been done! The art institutions have indicated that it will take years to identify and remove the false information that's been illegally and fraudulently stored within their systems.'

Julie went to make coffee and left Cyril flicking through other sites.

'If the major auction houses and their so-called experts have let things slip through the net, Cyril, then surely Posthumus wouldn't always be in a position to identify the good from the bad. Even in my job I get it wrong. All the evidence could point one way but actually the cause of death has been cleverly concealed. Don't forget we're human!'

'It's the way they're bought, Julie. It's greed. Human nature suggests that we always believe what we want to. The innocent, retired seller of the artwork, he's in his seventies with a fine collection of northern art, rare stuff and he's called you because he needs money for this or for that. You're flattered by the opportunity to buy something rare that's come to the open market for the first time in decades. There's a letter from the artist to this stranger showing that it was swapped for art materials. It's like finding the Holy Grail. His age, his circumstances, his humility suck you in and you see the other treasures on the walls that might one day come your way if you handle it well, forgetting the two famous words ... caveat emptor.'

'Surely he knows where the vendor lives?' Julie sipped her brandy.

'Julie, it's more complex and more selfish than that, he WANTS to believe. He can sell it and double maybe triple his money. Cash, no questions asked. It's as simple and as corrupt as that. They fish for the big boys and avarice brings them swimming to the bait.'

'If there's a doubt in his mind, why would he risk his reputation?'

Cyril didn't respond.

Julie continued, the wine and the brandy loosening her tongue. 'If what he says is true about the wrinkles in the insurance policy, then he stands to lose everything he's worked for. If he could get hold of two paintings right at this minute, no matter how dubious he feels them to be, then that would pay enough to get him out of this mess. Do you think he'd take the risk, Cyril? He's your friend, you've trusted him over the years with your cash.'

He thought of Simon. The robbery had affected him badly, but it was more than that, it was, for him, having to acknowledge out loud to a friend and a police officer, that his actions in the past might be suspect. Cyril knew that he had been looking at a broken man but only now, after talking it through with Julie, did he interpret his observations with a degree of clarity, free from emotional baggage.

Cyril responded to her stifled yawn and realised that he had monopolised the evening for far too long. He closed the laptop.

'One last thought. From what I've read, most of the good forgers were once conservators, like Nathalie Gray, so is that a coincidence?'

'It's a possibility, I grant you. By the way, Sherlock, the dates on the pennies seen in the videos you showed me match some dates on the paintings stolen from the gallery, but you knew that.'

Cyril just looked and then opened the laptop again before flicking through the images of the stolen paintings. How could he have missed that? He turned to look at her and shook his head. 'Thank you I'd not seen that. You're in the wrong job!'

Julie smiled, leaned across and kissed his forehead. 'No. My day job involves investigation too remember. Now, bed, where nobody will be producing any fakes!'

Cyril burst out laughing and Julie frowned.

'Cyril Bennett, you know what I meant.' She blushed slightly before slapping his arm.

***

Afraid of returning home, Freshman slept in the office. The warehouse was alarmed and he felt more secure. He woke early. At first, he questioned whether his experiences had been a stupid dream but then he noticed the pen drive. He made a coffee and after taking another look around the warehouse for the Fairground Policeman, he checked his sales inventory where it was listed as unsold. It had gone. He had seen it on the video. Obviously, he could not be certain that it was one and the same, the coincidence was too obvious. He stared at the card and the name DI Claire. He picked it up and dialled.

He was informed that DI Claire was unavailable, she had returned to duty in York, and he was asked if anyone else might assist.

'She had a Detective Sergeant with her, big bugger, don't know his name.'

Control took Freshman's number and asked him to stay on the line. After a few minutes the same female voice responded.

'Mr Freshman? The Sergeant you need to speak to is a DS Owen …'

'That's him, yes.'

'I've passed on your number and he'll make contact with you in the next hour. Please keep the phone with you at all times. Your call has been logged at …' She read the time, issued a log number and wished him good morning.

Owen was travelling in to the station when the call came through. He answered hands free.

'Owen.'

He listened carefully and asked to be patched through to the number. The line went momentarily silent and then he heard the ring tone. It rang twice before he heard Freshman's voice.

'DS Owen returning your call. How can I assist?'

'I've seen a body, I've been accused of taking paintings and someone's taken an arcade amusement from my warehouse. To be honest with you, I'm frightened shitless. Slept here last night. Felt more secure. What are you going to do?'

Owen pulled to the side of the road and flicked on his hazard lights.

'Do? Mr Freshman. What am I going to do?' He emphasised strongly the word, 'I'. 'In what order? Deal with the body, I think you said, look for a lost or stolen arcade amusement and paintings or deal with your fear?' Owen could not help but sound sarcastic. 'Did you take the paintings?'

'No, no. Christ man. Please, I need to see you or DI Claire, today, if possible … please.'

'What was the arcade amusement?'

'You're too young to remember them. It's a laughing policeman ...'

Owen did not wait for him to finish before requesting his address. He reminded him to keep the phone with him at all times and if he felt in danger, to remain in a secure place. He hung up and immediately contacted Cyril.

***

The drive down the A1M was relatively traffic-free, which was more than could be said for the M62. Their involvement within Greater Manchester had been officially sanctioned as they drove to meet Freshman. Cyril had requested a watch be put on the address just in case Freshman's worst fears were realised before they arrived. Once on the A627M, the navigation system informed them that ten minutes of their journey remained. Cyril checked the dash clock with his watch. He shook it and checked again.

Stakehill Industrial Estate was unimpressive; a collection of small, brick-built storage units ran down one side of the road. CCTV masts were positioned on every corner.

'See why he feels safe here.'

They pulled up at the security office and Cyril showed his ID and the address. The guard pointed directions and raised the barrier.

'There's already one of yours sitting in a patrol car, has been for a while now.' He then thought he heard the guard mumble something about a bobby's job but chose to ignore it. Once outside the warehouse unit and after relieving the officer, Cyril dialled Freshman's mobile number.

Within half an hour they were heading back to Freshman's house and after collecting some clothing, personal items and his passport, they were making their way back towards Harrogate. Cyril sat in the back and interviewed him throughout the journey. On arrival at Harrogate Police Station, Cyril had a clear understanding of how the investigation was going to proceed. Within the hour,

Freshman would be housed in secure custody. A warrant had been requested to search the house in Ripon. Freshman's phone, the envelope that held the key, which Cyril now had secured within a plastic bag, the pen drive and the note, were being couriered to Forensics. Two officers were stationed outside the house on Ure Bank Top, covering both the rear and front entrance to the property and, all being well, the SOCOs would also be on their way. Information about the house's owner was being sought.

After another ninety minutes, Cyril, Owen, Freshman and Shakti were already passing Wormald Green, closely followed by a back up team, which included two firearms officers. They were eight minutes away from Ure Bank Top.

It had been Cyril's idea to take Freshman. He could describe what he had seen whilst outside the building. He would not enter. To add his DNA would clearly compromise the scene, but he could watch on an iPad via a chest camera link and communicate with those inside. Cyril had already asked him to draw a plan of the interior, proving without doubt that he had been there at some time in the past. He would then only have to establish, when.

As they drove towards the parked police vehicle, Freshman could see the police tape across the door. Two females stood talking to the officer. He searched for Miss Higginbottom but he could not see her.

**

Christopher Nelson stood looking at the red Methodist chapel. It was tucked away from the busy tourist area but was still just outside the walls of the famous city. What could be agreed upon was that it was clearly a shadow of its former self, not only in its appearance, but also in its function. The only prayers now heard within the sanctuary of its four walls were those uttered at the end of each month in the hope that sales of the publications it produced would continue to rise and that cash flow would improve.

Taking the lease on the building had been a gamble but one that, in the initial years, had paid off. The work that Paul and Bernadette Gray produced was unusual, unique and of the highest quality. However, with quality came cost and there was the rub! People wanted the quality but did not want to pay for it and so slowly there were changes made. It was clear that the British appetite for this genre of book did not match their expectations. They had increasingly been forced to diversify, which to both of them, had been a great disappointment. However, the money was always there when bills needed to be paid, partly thanks to Bernadette's ability to work freelance.

Nelson watched as the white box van pulled up outside the chapel doors onto the 'Loading Only' bay. The driver looked across at Nelson and simply nodded.

Paul Gray was stacking boxes of books ready for collection as Nelson rang the bell positioned in the small, Reception lobby that had been built within the entrance hall. The opaque glass partition prevented visitors from looking directly into the studio. Gray stopped packing and went to the office before sliding open the glass window. He smiled at Nelson.

'Mr Gray?' He thrust his hand through the opening. 'John Gaunt, Educational Graphic Novels. I received a call to say my order was ready for collection.'

Gray took his hand and shook it. This commission had been a bolt out of the blue. Eight hundred copies was a good order to take during the spring ready for the summer publishing date.

'We were all thrilled by the quality of the art work, truly stunning. You came highly recommended.' Nelson knew that flattery always worked and watching Gray's face light up was proof that it was working a treat.

'I've just finished boxing the last of the order. The invoice is also ready. I would appreciate a quick payment, Mr Gaunt, as you can imagine there is an awful lot of outlay tied up here for a small business such as ours.'

Nelson nodded. 'It will be paid within the week. Cash as with the deposit or would you prefer a bank transfer? It matters little to me. I'll also be placing another large order within the month, but a somewhat different one.' He smiled and leaned towards the opening as if he were sharing a secret. 'It's again meant for the teenage market but like this vampire-inspired tale, the new book will include a good deal more intrigue. I take it your artist will be available? She signs herself 'Allumette' I believe.'

'Yes, my wife, she's French. She does all our graphics ... that's not strictly true ... but I'll ensure that she's responsible for your new project. She's in France at present working on a novel based on *Les Miserables*. The books are so much more popular over there than in the UK, but thanks to people like yourself, we're experiencing a steady improvement in sales. We are also unusual as a publisher in that we have our own 'in-house' artist.'

'Many of the schools to which we distribute are expressing that very sentiment, Mr Gray. That's why I can promise further orders. Shall we load? I have a van ready.'

***

Cyril and Owen had dressed appropriately before Owen slipped the key into the lock. They then stepped away from the door. The two firearms officers moved into the building. Cyril could hear their conversation on his headset as they checked and cleared each room. Within ten minutes the building was declared safe to enter. They moved to the rear to check the out buildings comprising the toilet and the coal storage.

Owen went first. As described, the room was free of furnishings and the amalgamated aroma of damp and turpentine was all-pervading, neither seemed the stronger, it was as if they were one.

They immediately moved through to the kitchen. Freshman and Shakti monitored their progress on the iPad from the images taken on Owen's chest camera. Cyril tried the light at the top of the cellar stairs. It worked and they descended into the cellar. A bulb, the first difference that Freshman noted, illuminated the whole area.

'That bulb didn't work, it was dark, that's why I used the torch on my phone.' Shakti made a note for Forensics to check the bulb for prints.

The stone-slab table was clearly visible but that was all, there were no easels, paintings, iron bar nor a body. The door from which the body had fallen according to Freshman was open. Everything, apart from the objects that could be moved was just as described. There was one more thing that Cyril wanted to confirm.

He returned to the kitchen and closed the cellar door, checked the painted wooden surface carefully and found the fine hole made by the drawing pin. The thought made him shiver as it suddenly brought Liz to mind.

'You OK, Sir.'

Cyril recovered his composure and simply nodded.

'Freshman described the note pinned to the cellar door. Here, look. One pin prick.'

Owen immediately understood his boss's sudden loss of control. They moved to the rear of the building. By this time a number of spectators had gathered, some clutching mugs of tea!

There was nothing in the coal storage area other than an old chair, a spade and some kindling. The toilet, however, took Owen back to his youth.

'Bloody hell, Sir. My Nan had a bog like this at her terraced house in Bradford. Even when they installed an inside bathroom, she kept the outside loo. She loved it. It had a paraffin lamp in it in winter and the spare toilet roll was stuck under the dress of a knitted doll! As a kid I was scared to use it, thought a rat might be lurking behind the pipe. Had a cistern like that and a chain with a pot handle on the end. Blue and white it were.'

Cyril could not imagine Owen being frightened of anything even as a child.

'Walls were painted in something called distemper. I originally thought it meant when you had the shits, like. Flaked everywhere. Often came back in with white marks all over my kecks.'

He noticed Cyril looking at him enquiringly.

'Trousers, Sir. Thought you'd know that coming from Yorkshire!'

'Pays not to presume, Owen. Trust me!'

Owen simply frowned and carried on the search.

'Stand on the bowl and look in the cistern,' Cyril requested as he looked into the toilet bowl. It was not, he thought, too dissimilar to Owen's drinking mug; it had the same dark stain marks. 'Seen that somewhere before, Owen. There must be millions of antibiotic type germs lurking in there; just like your Festival mug!'

Owen stared in. 'Bloody hell, that's disgraceful!'

Balancing his foot on the rim, he leaned up and peered into the empty water tank.

Cyril went outside and lifted the lid of the garden bin incinerator.

'Bugger me. Now what do we have here?' Owen called.

Cyril replaced the lid and stood in the toilet doorway as Owen retrieved what looked like a tightly bound supermarket bag.

***

Paul Gray and the driver each lifted the final two boxes and carried them to the vehicle. The driver nodded for Paul to go first. Paul smiled, grateful to be relieved of his burden and moved quickly to deposit it on the second layer of boxes. The driver did the same. Nelson stood looking into the van as the driver pointed into the corner. Paul's head turned to follow his hand. It was the right fist that he did not see, poised and waiting for his head to turn back as if questioning what he was supposed to be looking at. The blow struck him hard under the chin, crashing his jaw and teeth together. Fragments of tooth enamel shredded parts of his lips as his rapidly colliding teeth removed the very tip of his tongue. Blood quickly oozed through his incapacitated mouth and then sprayed a fine, red mist as he involuntarily exhaled as his collapsing body moved sideways towards the boxes. Before he crashed onto them, a second, more powerful blow, hit the other side of his head between his eye socket and temple. Paul neither felt the second blow nor the edge of the cardboard boxes digging into his collapsing frame.

'Bingo! You never lose the skills!'

The driver quickly pulled the unconscious body onto the floor, grabbed two large electrician's ties and bound his arms and legs. After removing his gloves, he jumped onto the rear lift platform before dropping the shutter door.

Nelson tapped his arm. 'Well done! That was a fine one, two, Sir. You were always the best porter I employed at the auction house.'

The driver simply grinned. 'Always a pleasure.'

Nelson removed what appeared to be a thin A4 file from the van's cab before walking back into the building. The door to the office was still open. He carefully laid three sheets on the empty artist's work surface, ensuring that they were straight and in the correct sequence. He picked up Paul Gray's keys from the desk before returning to the van. Within minutes, the van had pulled away from the loading bay and an hour later, Christopher Nelson and his guest were back in the cell.

***

Owen brought out a tightly wrapped package that seemed to comprise layers of plastic bags. He handed it to Cyril who weighed it in his hands. 'Forensics'. He brought out a large plastic bag dropping their find into it.

'Hold this!' He handed it back to Owen and returned to the incinerator. After lifting the lid, he carefully inspected the inside. 'What do you see, Owen?'

Owen peered in, pulling a face as if Cyril was asking a trick question. 'Nothing!'

Cyril nodded. 'Precisely. The bin has been well-used to burn rubbish but strangely there's no sign of any ash debris. Now, Owen, I find that extremely odd. Whatever was burned in here, the residue has been completely removed.'

***

Freshman stood by the car. The sun was high and the street was bathed in warmth. Three officers had questioned the onlookers who now drifted away. One of the officers jogged up the road towards the large collection of static caravan holiday homes.

'There are two neighbours in this row who own dogs. None owns a dog that you described and neither is called Mr Biggles. Also, there's no one by the name of Higginbottom as far as these people are aware. The lady living next door is eighty-one and as deaf as a post.' Cyril pointed to the house to the right. 'This couple who live to the other side have been, for the last ten days, and still are, on holiday. The description of the neighbour who stopped to speak with you matches no one who lives in this row, or over there …' Cyril pointed over the road to houses that were well out of view.

An officer approached and had a private word with Cyril before he pointed up the road.

'Apparently your mystery lady lives up yonder, enjoys a drink throughout the day, every day so we're told. Probably that's why she's not here now. I've sent for her to see if she recognises you.' Cyril just smiled.

Shakti's mobile rang and she walked away to the far side of the road.

Cyril watched Freshman, his face clearly demonstrated that he was as confused as they were.

'She stopped me right there, said she lived next door. Bloody furious she was. She never said she lived up there! Could she be caring for this old bird who lives here?'

'Freshman, I hardly think so, do you?'

'Sir, a word in private.'

Cyril walked across to Shakti.

'They've tracked the owner of the property …' She moved closer to Cyril so that no one else could hear. 'It's a Nathalie Gray.'

'What! Are they certain?'

'Certain.'

Cyril turned and looked back at Freshman. 'If he's lying about any of this then he's bloody good. Neighbours told us that they haven't seen the owner for a while, workmen, yes, sporadically, but not the woman. The house was in the process of being refurbished but to be honest there's not much work been done. Get a photograph sent through of Gray and show it to all the available neighbours. See if it's her.'

Cyril returned to Freshman and instructed him to get in the car.

'No paintings, no body, no iron bar. Why is that do you think, Mr Freshman?'

Freshman started to protest his innocence and blurted out a string of sentences clearly describing what he had experienced and what he had seen. 'The neighbour …' Cyril held up a finger, an indication that he should stop speaking. Freshman complied immediately.

'I believe that you've been in this house before; you knew its layout and its smell. How could anyone not notice that heady cocktail? I believe that you have examined paintings in this house before. I believe now that this Higginbottom woman startled you. I believe that there was, at some point, a drawing pin pushed into the cellar door, but as to a metal bar and a body, my jury is still out. Is that why I'm confused do you think, Mr Freshman? Why every ounce of my reasoning is screaming out that something just doesn't add up?'

Freshman was about to start protesting his innocence yet again when the same digit was raised. He stopped, but on this occasion, open-mouthed, and looked directly at Cyril.

'This building, this house, is, in fact, owned by one of your employees. Did you know that?'

Freshman's mouth opened a little more and a trickle of saliva ran over his lip and onto his chin. He shook his head.

'Strangely, neither did we, it didn't show on the initial search of Nathalie Gray's property. That's because the details held at the Land Registry Office show the owner to be a Natalie Grey. Strangely, both the Christian name and the surname are spelled differently from the woman we know. Natalie without the 'h' and even more oddly, Grey spelled with an 'e' and not the 'a'! So, it didn't show. Before you say anything, we are intelligent enough to know that there are many people with the same name as ourselves, Mr Freeman Freshman ...' Cyril paused, believing that the man next to him might be the exception. 'You might like this, however, to one of your hidden paintings, you know, the ones that carry the incorrect name in an auction catalogue, the ones that Dr Darwin Green likes to track down. I think that you said they were known as sleepers. Is that correct?'

'Yes, yes, sleepers but I don't see the connection!'

'Well, Sir, this is what we have here, a sleeper. Someone owns the house and they register it in their name but cleverly they, let's say, amend that name. What's special about a sleeper in your trade?'

Freshman took a moment. 'You register your collecting preferences on line with auction houses and places like The Saleroom, an internet site that details thousands of auctions worldwide. If one of your preferred artists comes to auction you are alerted to the fact. It suits the trade, particularly the seller, as it brings buyers to compete. A sleeper.'

'So, where the auction house has incorrectly spelled the artist's name in the catalogue allowing the error to slip through the net, it then isn't picked up, computers don't discern! I've read that some auction houses allegedly do this deliberately to protect a certain buyer from having to compete, keeps others potential bidders away.'

'I don't subscribe to that point of view, as I know from experience that the auction houses want to make as much commission as possible. Don't forget the power of the Internet has opened up all the auction houses to the world. Paintings that once were only seen locally or provincially and in some cases nationally are now seen by buyers from all countries so a sleeper can be an incredible discovery, making the finder in some cases an awful lot of money.'

'Right, that's what I thought. So, you see, Mr Freshman, we have a sleeper here. A secret place where a lot of money can be made.'

'I can assure you on my mother's grave that although I've been here before, I had no idea who owned it. I'd no idea that Nathalie had a property in Ripon.'

'Let's see what Forensics find shall we? Believe me, they will find more than you can ever imagine and until we have all the results we'll keep you safe.'

Cyril could feel Freshman's tension grow throughout the interview. He tapped on the rear window and Shakti opened the door. The child locks, deliberately employed, prevented his opening the door. Freshman stayed put.

The officer jogged back down and approached Cyril. 'Sir …' He took a moment to catch his breath. '… I've just been trying to have a word with Miss Higginbottom but she doesn't seem to know what day it is let alone identify someone from the past. At the moment, she'd be a very poor witness.'

Chapter Fourteen

Paul Gray tried to focus but his world was still rather cloudy. His perspective seemed skewed, as he looked sideways along the lines of the concrete floor. He tilted his head backwards and saw the bottom of the toilet bowl. He could not feel his hands, they were numb, the ties were tight and restricted the flow of blood. He looked down at the black plastic that bound his feet before rocking himself over. At the other side of the room, he noticed the bent wood chair, the shelf and then the door.

Running his tongue across his teeth, he felt the rough edges but the immediate stinging sensation from the tip of his tongue made him stop as the blood began to flow again. The warm, metallic taste made him aware of the injuries that he had sustained.

Why? Surely not for twenty boxes of books? he thought, finding it difficult to grasp fully his present predicament. The noise of the key turning in the door made him immediately curl into a foetal position. He closed his eyes pretending still to be unconscious.

'Mr Gray, I know that you're back in the land of the living and I'm aware that you're very confused and possibly in need of an explanation. My friend here, you met him in the van earlier, is about to remove the ties. I'm sure now that they're uncomfortable. However, before he does, I want you to think carefully about your reaction. Should you try to struggle and make an unnecessary fuss, then he'll remain with you and I'll leave and lock the door. What he does with you and to you is at his discretion. Do you understand me?'

Gray nodded and the blade sliced through the plastic. Rough hands lifted Paul's upper body off the ground allowing him to bring his arms to the front. The relief was palpable.

'Thank you.' He tried to rub feeling back into his numb hands.

'I'll bring you some tea shortly but there's water there if you need it.'

Paul Gray looked up at Nelson, his eyes begging the question; he did not need to utter a word.

'All in good time, Paul, all in good time. Fortunately for you, you have a good deal of that, the Lord made sure of it.' He smiled and nodded to the driver who backed away, his eyes never leaving Paul.

The door slammed shut and the key turned in the lock.

***

The Incident Room was busy as people checked the boards or mulled over the notes they had received. Owen stumbled through the door carrying his usual mug that always appeared to leak, and a cup and saucer. He placed them on the table.

'Anyone got a clean tissue?'

Three were kindly donated and he soaked up the surplus tea from Cyril's saucer. He lifted his own mug and sipped. Droplets from the base of the mug dribbled and soaked into his shirt. Cyril entered and the noise level diminished significantly.

'You're dribbling, Owen!'

Owen looked down and then raised his eyebrows. A number of new tissues were sent his way. He raised a hand in thanks as he tried to dab away the stains.

People quickly settled as Cyril checked his watch. Everyone waited for the ritualistic shake and review but today it did not happen. A number of faces smiled and one person handed a fiver to someone else. It did not go unnoticed and Cyril simply smiled and shook his head.

'Fool and his money, Tomkins!'

The brief moment of laughter soon faded.

'Right what do we have?'

Tomkins responded. 'The object found in the toilet cistern is a painting by a Pierre Adolphe Valette. Matched to one stolen from the Focus North Gallery. A number of finger prints were extracted from it but the interesting ones belong to a Derek Willis, forty-three years of age. Arrested for ABH (Actual Bodily Harm) in 2014, here in Harrogate, received a fine and a community order. Secondly, he was given a drunk and disorderly charge 23 August 2015. He was handed a Drinking Banning Order for three months from the town centre pubs and clubs. No problems since. Employed by Nelson and Steel Fine Art as a porter until the last offence. From all accounts moved to Manchester straight afterwards. We have no known address and he's not on the benefits system. It's likely that he dropped out and is now living rough. He's not registered with a doctor nor a medical centre.'

'Nelson and Steel, Ripon. There's that name again. I want Steel in for questioning. I wonder if our man Willis ever left Ripon?' Cyril tapped the e-cigarette on his teeth. 'Where's the painting from the house now?'

'In Forensic storage.'

'Clear it. I want it here today.' He looked round the room until he saw the officer he required. 'Brian, get Dr Darwin Green in here this afternoon, please. Explain to him that we need his expertise to identify and confirm that a painting is by Valette. Be tactful but he doesn't have an option, you know how it goes.'

Brian nodded.

'There's more from Forensics, Sir. Blood was found on the floor just outside the second door in the cellar and it's a DNA match for a Derek Willis. Skull fragments and brain tissue and part of the septum were also recovered, same match. From the fragments found it's been suggested that we're looking for a corpse. Glass also found is a match for Freeman Freshman's phone screen. Rust stains on the floor under the table suggest that a metal bar had been in situ for some time.'

'Where would we be without the boffins?'

'That's not all, Sir.' He smiled like a magician bringing rabbits from a hat. 'Blood and cloth fragments on the floor match Freshman's so it looks like his story holds up.'

'Anything from the incinerator?'

'I don't know how they do this but even though it'd been washed out, there were traces of gilt in the encrusted, solidified residue found on the bottom joint.'

'Frames, bloody hell they burned the frames and maybe some of the paintings.' Cyril made some notes. 'Get someone from Forensics to take samples from the gilt frames that remain in the Focus North Gallery and see if there's a match. I should imagine one gilt is very much like another.'

'That's our job, Sir, dealing with guilt!' Owen's face remained deadpan; there was not a flicker. Cyril had to smile.

'Anything on Christopher Nelson?' There was silence.

'We need to put out another missing person's shot. Shakti, work with the Corporate, Communications Team, please. Get it out again on social media, and local radio and TV. See if you can persuade Nelson's wife or daughter to go before the cameras, might help, particularly if he's done a runner with another woman. Seeing his loved one's emotional trauma might bring him to his senses. Oh! Get the dog on too if you can! Also get out a picture of Willis from his criminal record. Let's see if anyone can shed any light on where he might have been these last few years.'

***

Cyril contacted Simon Posthumus at Focus North Gallery to inform him that someone would be coming to take samples from the frames of the remaining paintings. He was pleased to hear that the gallery owner seemed a little more positive. All the publicity had brought a stream of people to the gallery and, in some cases, they had come to buy.

'People are taking pictures of themselves both in and outside of the shop. I believe it's also on Twitter and Facebook. Someone even asked if I'd stolen the pictures myself to get this amount of free publicity. Can you believe that, Bennett?'

'Yes, and did you?'

The phone went quiet … 'You know the answer to that. We've been friends too long for you to doubt me, Cyril Bennett. It's OK for them to come. Will they take away the whole frame?'

Cyril explained the procedure and hung up. He sat back and inhaled the mental vapour. *What will I do if the Valette turns out to be a fake?* He considered the question and thought of the paintings he had collected. *Forty per cent of paintings sold may well be fakes, forged, wrong*! His phone rang somewhat to Cyril's relief.

'Bennett.'

'Sir, Helen. How's it going?'

'The pieces are slowly coming together thanks to our friends in Forensics. It never ceases to amaze me what they can discover. We've another potential body to locate. What can I do for you?'

'Paul Gray hasn't been seen since yesterday afternoon. His publishing works were left unattended overnight. A PCSO noticed that there were no lights on in the building and yet the door was open. Everything seems in order apart from three pictures, well cartoons to be honest, that were on a drawing surface within the office.'

'Home? Phone? His wife?' His abruptness took Helen by surprise.

'Nothing. I've sent an officer to wait at the house just in case he does return home. I've left a message for his wife to contact me and we've secured the works premises.'

'Good. Keep me informed ...'

'Sir ... sorry to interrupt but the picture-type cartoons, I've sent them to you, you've obviously not had chance to view them. Please take a look. You'll see why I'm concerned. I'll hold.'

Cyril quickly logged in to his PC and looked at the last communication. He hung his head a little. 'What the ...?' He didn't finish the sentence.

He looked at the detailed cartoon clearly depicting the case containing the laughing policeman. It was so accurately drawn, the same moustachioed, chubby face, the same body position. He read the caption out loud to Helen.

'Very soon the last penny will hit the slot.'

The next sketch simply showed the policeman, head back, hands holding his fat belly and the words, 'Ha! Ha! Ha! Ho! Ho!

Ho! See how the copper laughs!' Cyril looked at the third page; it was a drawing of an empty container; the laughing policeman was gone and in its place was a drawing of a Lowry painting. Scratched clearly across the image was the word 'FAKE'. Cyril read the caption out again. 'No policeman's laughing now, I see.'

'Déjà bloody vu!' mumbled Cyril.

She did not wait for Cyril to continue. 'Sorry to interrupt but the original work from the Mercer Gallery was by Braaq, known as the Harrogate Lowry whereas here the artist has included a work by the real Manchester Lowry. Is this telling us something considering that the painting repaired by Nathalie Gray suffered exactly the same damage! Thought you should see this as soon as we became aware of it.'

'Too right!' He scribbled on a note pad on his desk ... *CHECK ALL GRAY'S PUBLISHED AND CONTRACTED WORK!!!* ... He continued to look at the three images, amazed at the quality of the draftsmanship. 'Are they original?'

'No, copies. They've gone for analysis. There's something else. The last order collected yesterday was by a John Gaunt from a company called, Education Graphic Novels. Checked it out and there's no such firm therefore no such representative and I can assume no John Gaunt! Before I go on, we don't know how the boxes were collected but considering the quantity of the order we assume some kind of van. Neither do we know a collection time so we've worked backwards from midnight last night checking the CCTV of the area around Gray's publishing works.'

Cyril knew what was coming.

'During the twenty-four hours for which we had details, there were a hundred and ninety-two vehicles that could be relevant. A hundred and five are local and have been put, for the moment at least, on hold. However, we have a box van that was on camera at 14:05. You'll notice that the registration plate is masked in some way, maybe by mud. What we do know is that it's a Ford Transit long wheelbase with a tail lift. It's gone to Traffic but I think it will have been stolen, and it will either be found a smoking wreck or concealed somewhere. As soon as we have anything …'

'Thanks. Keep me up to speed and make sure everything's written up. I take it Forensics are at the works?'

'Since first thing.'

Cyril printed the images and went to find Owen. He dropped them onto his desk. 'These have just come through. They were found at the publishing works belonging to Paul Gray, who surprisingly now has gone missing!'

Owen looked at them. 'Which came first, the chicken or the egg?'

Cyril pulled a face.

'The videos or these? Did one inspire the other?'

'Bloody good question, Owen. I wonder if these were used within one of their publications! Always said you were as keen as mustard. If it's these then we're into the final round, the end game. Call Helen and get her to check all of the artwork at Gray's works, paper and electronic.'

Owen made the call as Cyril took a note to DC Proctor. He wanted details of every conservation job that Nathalie Gray had be contracted to do for galleries, museums and private clients whilst working for Freeman Freshman.

'If needs be, you might have to liaise with Greater Manchester.'

Owen ambled over. 'Dr Darwin Green's here. Brian put him in Reception with a coffee. By all accounts he's not too happy!'

'Come down with me and bring those with you but please keep them covered.'

Owen slipped them into a file and picked up his tea.'

'Please, leave the tea, your Jackson Pollock-style shirt couldn't stand any more!'

Owen frowned and followed Cyril unsure as to whether the word Pollock was a derogatory term or not. He made a mental note to look it up later. Green was sitting, a laptop open on his knee, and he was deep in thought.

'No rest for the wicked, Dr Green!' Cyril announced as he came through the security door. 'You know DS Owen. Thank you for coming in. We appreciate your assistance.'

'Your chap didn't really give me much choice.'

'I'll have a word, my apologies. I'd like you to give me your opinion on two pieces of artwork. I'd like to record everything. Your first impressions through to the last will be vital to me and I hope also to you when we reflect on your thoughts later. May I say at this stage you're not in any way in trouble here, you're simply helping us out. Is that understood?'

Green closed his laptop. 'Well, I'm relieved to say, that's good to know, Detective Chief Inspector. I was feeling a little anxious I have to admit.'

Cyril led him into Interview Room Three. The painting was on the table. He checked the recording and the video quality before commencing.

'There's a painting under this cloth, study it carefully and tell me everything you know about it. Please speak your thoughts.'

Green removed the cover and immediately smiled. 'Pierre Adolphe Valette ... possibly.' He looked carefully moving it closer to the light. 'Manchester scene showing all the characteristics of one of the small paintings he did, en plein air about 1905 to 1910. Could be anywhere in Manchester there's no real landmark.' He brought the painting up to his nose and sniffed the edges of the board pulling a face as he moved it away. 'Some chemical aroma but not that of fresh paint.' He turned it in his hands and stared at the back. He smiled when he saw the label. 'First impressions, the back looks old and authentic. From Tib Lane, Manchester, one of the many that were sold by Valette's wife in the seventies through the gallery. Most small Manchester scenes you'll find have a connection with Tib Lane at some stage.'

Cyril and Owen just watched. Cyril was clearly mesmerised by observing an expert at work. Green brought out a jeweller's loop and studied the work carefully.

'Not too sure until I look further into its provenance. All I can do is offer you my first impressions.' He looked directly at Cyril.

'Please, Dr Green.'

'It's not right. If I have to commit now, I'd say it was a fake. In my job I've seen so many Valettes you get a feel, you have a sixth sense and this is just not there. Wouldn't stake my reputation on it until I'd done more research into its background, but first impressions … if you're thinking of buying it. Don't waste your money.'

Cyril laughed. 'No! It's just been recovered.'

Green just raised his eyebrows. 'Really? Focus North?'

'Couldn't say, Dr Green. Now we'd like you to look at these.'

Owen handed him the folder and Green pulled them out and laid them on the table.

***

Owing to his damaged mouth, Gray had declined to eat the sandwich brought in by the driver and only sipped the tea. The door opened again and the driver entered carrying another chair.

'Do you have a name other than, driver?'

He said nothing and left. After a few minutes Nelson came in and closed the door behind him.

'Firstly, Mr Gray, may I apologise for this. It is not you I seek. However, you do have information that will be of great interest to me. Please, during our conversations, call me Christopher. I'd like your time here to be as comfortable as possible but be under no illusion that should you fail me, then this small room will be the last place on this earth you will ever see. You will not see your wife, the blue sky nor feel the rain again and honestly, that would sadden me. Truly. Now, over the next few hours we'll have a conversation and should I be happy with your responses, then you will, in the near future, be released. Do you understand?'

Gray said nothing. He simply looked at Nelson. 'What could I have done to you to deserve this? I printed some books for fuck's sake. I didn't ruin your life!'

'True, very true, Paul. May I call you, Paul? No, you didn't but somebody did. Think on that. Somebody did and I believe that someone was very close to you.'

He stood. 'Now we fully appreciate where you stand in all of this, I'm going to ask you a question. How well did you know your daughter, Paul? That's it, simple question.' He turned and went, leaving the empty chair and Paul, whose mind was a maelstrom of confused thoughts and emotions.'

**

Green studied the three pages.

'You do know that they've come from a printer and that they're not originals?'

Cyril nodded but said nothing.

'Cartoons, illustrative, graphic art. Paul Gray would give you a far better critical appreciation, they're not my field but they're certainly his. The drawing is excellent, I can tell you that, but then it doesn't take a trained eye to appreciate the craftsmanship. The detail is incredible. You do know Nathalie Gray repaired a painting for the Mercer Art Gallery in Harrogate that was vandalised? The same damage as shown here?' He pointed to the last of the three cartoons.

Cyril was surprised that Green knew about the conservation work and mentally filed it away.' Dr Green, the drawings were discovered in Paul's office, in York.'

Green looked again. 'Discovered? Why discovered? Surely this might well be Nathalie's work. It has all the hallmarks.'

'Possibly, yes, but they were discovered by an officer who thought he'd found the Methodist Chapel version of the Marie Celeste. Looked as though people should be there and working but there was no one, it was deserted. It's where we discovered these.'

'That's what they do there! They produce this stuff. Bernadette's a graphic artist too. So where was Paul?'

'We wondered if you might know the answer to that?'

Chapter Fifteen

Clive Steel sat patiently in the Interview Room and smiled as Cyril entered. He politely stood and they shook hands. 'I'm grateful for your time, Mr Steel. Please, sit.'

Cyril explained that although he had attended the interview voluntarily, it would be recorded. He should be aware that he was not under suspicion nor was he under caution and that he was free to leave at any time. Steel nodded his understanding and acceptance.

'Happy to help in any way that I can. There's no news I take it?'

'Thanks, no, nothing as yet. Most of the questions, Mr Steel, are going to be centred on your relationship with Christopher Nelson. It might save time if you were just to talk through that history and I'll ask specific questions along the way if that's acceptable.'

'Not a problem. I met Christopher when we were both at a turning point in our careers. I was, and probably in loose terms I still am, a land and property valuer and auctioneer and Chris was working for his father. He'd gone through his apprenticeship with his father as his father had done before that and was learning on the job as well as attending college. Back then Nelson's Auctions was predominantly centred on the farming industry, live animal marts, agricultural equipment, dealing with farm closures. This was probably 1971. We met at a sale at Mickley, just outside …'

Cyril smiled. 'I'm aware of the geographical location, thanks.'

'A farmer had died and there was no one to carry on the farm. Nelson's were there on site selling off the contents and I'd gone along in the hope of buying an old pre-war MG that had been trapped in one of the barns for years. There's always a certain sadness in this type of auction as you see the person's history, all that he's experienced and worked for, pass under the auctioneer's hammer. It's cold and indiscriminate but that's life I'm afraid.'

Cyril immediately thought of Liz and had to take a deep breath to compose himself.

'Did Christopher take that auction?'

'Goodness me, no. His father controlled all elements of the business and I believe that even his father was there too, watching with great care to ensure that the best prices were reached. Three generations under one roof! No, Chris was a bit of a lackey in those days! That's why we met; we were both having a fag round the back as I looked at the car; the auction went on all day. It was from there that we got to know each other.'

'So, when did you become partners?'

'Maybe two years later. The animal market suffered after decimalisation and when we entered the European Union. Chris persuaded his father to diversify and so initially an estate agency was started in Ripon and I was asked to be a partner. Old man Nelson was a shrewd, old bugger, Inspector Bennett, wouldn't go alone into strange waters. I was asked to share the commitment and the financial risk and so Nelson and Steel was formed.'

'Tell me about the time when Christopher Nelson took the helm of the auction house.'

'Auctions were dismal places unless you were a specialist like Sotheby's or Bonham's. The small country auctions were dying on their feet and to stay afloat they had to branch out and move with the times. Nelson's did, moving into house clearances and then furnishing and eventually Fine Art. Their lifeline was the Internet and the growing number of antique and auction programmes on TV, you've seen them. *Flog It, Bargain Hunt*? They had an amazing effect on the trade.'

Cyril just nodded. 'So, were you both partners in each business?'

'The house market did really well in the eighties and nineties and its success was the exact opposite of the auction trade. It needed regular cash injections and the best way to support it was through an amalgamation with the estate agency. It more or less became one firm but we each looked after a separate business, if you see what I mean. It was a ten-year plan, after which we separated, neither owing the other money, but the titles, Nelson and Steel stayed above the doors. Both businesses were prospering until a few years ago.'

'What happened then?'

'All businesses go through difficult times. Chris moved to new premises, the old primary school and that was probably the most astute move he's made throughout his entire career. Its sale has made him a wealthy man and turned around his personal fortune. Without that, I can assure you that he'd now be destitute.'

Cyril stopped him after making a note. 'Broke?'

'Cash in the bank? Yes. Look, I don't know whether this is any of my business or yours for that matter and I wonder whether I should be telling you any of this. Maybe when Chris returns he can give you all the details, besides, everything has turned out well for him.'

'I suppose if you consider his probable kidnap and murder as turning out well, then yes.' Cyril watched Steel's expression and complexion change completely.

'You honestly think that he's been murdered?'

'He's not sitting opposite his wife at breakfast anymore, Mr Steel, and the dog goes out on fewer walks, no doubt. We have no trace of him since the evening he went missing. What I do know is that anything, anything at all that you can tell me might just be the one vital clue we need that allows us to find him.'

'I don't know the dates but he came under a lot of pressure from certain individuals, let's say clients. He sold paintings, high value works and then they came back. He was informed that they were fake and they demanded not only the return of the money, but also some compensation. He said that they threatened to ruin him at best and put his family in the ground at worst. Let's say that they were very persuasive. At that time, he was doing really well and should they have gone to the press, it could have impacted disastrously on the business. This happened on more than one occasion, even though he employed the services of a specialist who checked the provenance of the works that he accepted to sell.'

'Do you have the name of the expert?'

'Somewhere, probably. It was at this stage that he came to me for some financial support, support in the shape of £250,000.'

Cyril whistled. 'To pay back for the paintings?'

'Yes, and I was led to believe that was only a percentage of the cost. Mac Gail, Mc ... Mac something, the woman he employed, the expert ...'

'Lynn McGowen?'

'That's it, yes. She was the specialist. She was responsible for checking the history of the paintings.'

'What do you know of a Nathalie Gray?'

Steel just shook his head. 'Nothing, can't recall anyone of that name, not at the auction house anyway.'

'Could you have sold her a property?'

'Inspector we could have sold you a property, I don't see every client. Do you know how many properties go through the business either as rental or bought in any twelve-month period?'

'Tell me more about Nelson.'

'He was close to going bust, bankrupt. It has to be said that some of these paintings were sold outside of the auction house, on the quiet, cash sales. I warned him about it but he just told me that it was often done and that he needed to keep a particular wolf from his door.'

'Gambling, drinking or another woman?'

Steel just shrugged his shoulders. 'I know that he wasn't a drinker or a gambler but he did have an eye for the ladies. Whether he'd pick up sticks and leave is anyone's guess. Who knows what suddenly gaining a few bob has done to him which leads me on to the saving grace that came a couple of years ago when he decided to sell up. His daughter was keen to take over the business but he insisted that it be closed. Fortunately there was a bit of a bidding war for the site and he came away a wealthy man.'

'His daughter informed us that neither she nor her husband were interested in the business and that was one of the key factors in deciding to sell. She said that the business had become too popular and that Nelson was getting too old to keep up with all the technology.'

Steel just spread his hands. 'I'm just telling you what I know.'

'Did he pay back the money he owed?'

'As soon as the sale of the business had gone through as we'd agreed, yes. I don't have an axe to grind with Chris. I thought he was foolish, greedy and in many ways naïve, but he never did me nor my family any harm. I'm here now in the hope that I might be of help in finding him.'

Cyril stood and put out his hand. 'I'm grateful for your time, Mr Steel, and your honesty. I'd appreciate it if you could check to see whether this person has bought a property through you.' Cyril jotted down the name ensuring that the spelling was as it was shown on the Land Registry.

'I can do that, if you give me a minute, I'll phone through. That coffee would be nice now.' He smiled, removed his mobile and dialled. Cyril went for the coffees.

He brought back only one polystyrene cup of coffee, if it were not in a cup and saucer, then Cyril had no interest.

'We have a positive on the name. Bought a property in Ripon, on Ure Bank Top.'

'Is it possible you could send through all the details?'

Steel sipped his coffee. 'I don't see why not ... There's one other thing, now I come to think about it. When Chris was going through this difficult period, he employed some, how shall I put it, interesting characters as porters and as security. I do believe that he took the threats very seriously.'

***

Cyril had been in his office barely ten minutes when Shakti leaned round the door. 'Box van found burned out containing one body, Sir. Dr Julie Pritchett will be attending.'

'Is it Gray?'

She wanted to say that it was black, twisted and smoking but thought better of it; Owen might get away with it but she knew that she wouldn't.

Shakti just spread her arms. 'It's close to home. Dumped on Little Studley Road, Ripon.'

Cyril changed his mind about the possible victim as, on hearing the word Studley, Christopher Nelson immediately came to mind. 'I'm going out there. I want Lynn McGowen in again ASAP ... and by the way, she's no choice in the matter. Caution and arrest her if you have to. I also want her bank details, particularly any card transactions both from here and abroad that have been carried out over the last couple of months and get hold of her phone records. If she's culpable, I imagine that she's covered her tracks very well. And Shakti, we need to keep this burned-out van and body out of the press at least until the victim has been identified.'

'I'm on it.'

***

Cyril turned off Palace Road on to Little Studley Road. Very quickly the houses on either side of the road disappeared as the open countryside came into view, it also grew narrower until he came to the police tape spread across the track. An officer was standing close to a dilapidated, corrugated iron garage-type structure. He directed Cyril to park on a piece of wasteland just off the road. He noticed Julie's car.

Cyril showed his ID.

'Sir, becoming a habit.'

Cyril looked at the young man. 'You were up at Ure Bank the other day.'

'Yes, Sir. Wilkinson, Sir.' The young officer smiled proudly. 'I found the drunken lady in the holiday home. Not a pretty sight up yonder. This time we do have a body. The pathologist is there now and two Crime Scene Investigators.' He lifted the plastic tape and Cyril ducked beneath it.

'A tip, Wilkinson. Don't stand too close to that shed. It looks as though a breath of wind would have it down!'

Wilkinson looked and then immediately moved away before bringing his hand up as if in salute.

Cyril nodded and walked the hundred yards to the scene of the fire. A further tape was stretched from a tree to a gate post, behind which, part of the skeletal, burned remains of the van were visible. The foliage surrounding it was either burned or singed. The whole of the box section had melted leaving a twisted sculpture of charred metal. Solidified pools of aluminium had amalgamated with the internal wirework from the destroyed tyres. A temporary screen had been erected to conceal the cab. The Crime Scene Manager raised a hand to Cyril, his palm flat, requesting he go no further. After a couple of minutes he walked over. He quickly logged the date, time and collected Cyril's signature. Cyril put on overshoes and gloves before lifting the tape.

'The doctor's there but can give us little other than to confirm it's a male body.'

'What's all that?' Cyril pointed to what looked like grey, compressed card that was scattered on the area that was once the inside of the van. Occasionally, small fragments fluttered into the air as a fine filigree of ash before settling almost immediately.

'Compressed ash residue of what was, we think, books, boxes of books. Considering the heat, I'm amazed they haven't completely disappeared. If you touch them, they just crumble even though they're still wet.' He turned as Julie Pritchett came towards them, leaving Hannah Peters to continue photographing evidence. 'It's a match to the van used in the possible abduction of a man in York yesterday.'

'Books. Makes sense.'

Julie lowered her mask and let it dangle at her throat. 'I'll know more when I have the body back on the table.' She smiled at Cyril. As their relationship had grown more intimate, he always felt a little uncomfortable when meeting Julie professionally. He was fine providing that they were alone but when other officers were present, he just had this uneasy, edgy feeling. The one thing he prided himself on was his total commitment and professionalism and he knew that on these occasions people would be watching.

'You might like to ask Owen to attend. He seems to have the capacity to watch and interact, DCI Bennett.' She smiled as she signed herself off the scene. 'Hannah will be a few more minutes. I'll be in touch.' She grinned and puckered her lips as if she were about to blow him a kiss, then walked down the road thanking the CSM for his assistance. Cyril blushed and it did not go unnoticed. Fortunately, his phone rang.

'Bennett.'

He listened as Shakti explained that McGowen was in London and that she was still in the process of tracking her financial records.

'When's she due back?'

'She'll be there for another two days and will be available any time after that. She appeared to be more than happy to help, in fact, seemed very concerned that we hadn't found Nathalie's murderer.'

There was a moment's silence from Bennett.

'Sir are you still there?'

'Yes, sorry, great work, Shakti. Well done.'

***

Paul Gray sat on the more comfortable of the two chairs. He felt as though this time when he was left alone was deliberate, a ploy to frighten and unnerve him, it was working beautifully. At first, he refused to use the toilet in case someone came in. The thought of sitting there with his trousers round his ankles disgusted him, especially if it were the driver. However, desperation can weaken even the strongest man's will.

He thought of the question he's been left with, *how well do you know your daughter?* At first, he rejected it out of hand considering it both stupid and facile. *How well does any man know his daughter, particularly as they enter their teenage years? She'd become a stranger and an emotional monster.* He spent the hours reflecting on the memories he held of Nathalie from that first introduction when she was barely one year old to her difficult and arrogant adolescence. He remembered making the selfless decision to treat her as his own and those thoughts brought smiles as well as tears. He reflected on the special occasions watching her grow, times that had flowed by so quickly, the sand in the clock of life ran so very fast. It hardly seemed possible that now, that baby, that bubbly child, that truculent teen had blossomed into the talented, amazing adult that he dearly loved. The images were still so vivid in his mind's eye and yet, the hard truth was that she was now dead. The room suddenly seemed more hostile. He wrapped his arms across his chest and rocked slowly on the chair.

He thought of how she came through that teenage stage and how her mother nurtured her to blossom into a talented and creative human being, how Nathalie had developed the traits that mirrored those of her mother. That was the true prize, the true reward but also in the end, a curse.

His mood changed yet again as he thought of Bernadette, of her jealousy and her moods. It was, at times, as if she resented her own child, as if she had wanted to create someone in her own image but realised that she had failed. She had created not an equal, but someone better, someone more skilled, more dynamic.

He thought of the constant competitions set by Bernadette; at first they were fun, trivial, bringing much laughter. Silly games; who could create the best Christmas card, who could paint the most realistic dewdrop? Paul was always to be the judge and the jury. Even though he could see the competition grow more and more unhealthy as Nathalie's work grew marginally better, he had failed to stop it.

He remembered one particular challenge where they had to paint an oil in the likeness of one by Laurence Stephen Lowry. On that occasion it had been Nathalie's idea. They should take them to auction houses and the one that was accepted for sale was the winner. Bernadette thought it would be innocent fun until Nathalie's was accepted and sold and Bernadette's failed to sell. If he had to pinpoint the one critical moment that changed the mother–daughter relationship immeasurably, it would be the moment that Nathalie had rung to tell her mother the news and the moment that Nathalie had brought her mother's painting home, unsold, rejected. He closed his eyes and he could still see it on the shelf in her studio; a Nemesis that she refused to reject.

Paul heard the key in the lock. Nelson entered. He was alone. He took the chair that was empty and looked at Paul.

'I take it that you've had enough time to reflect on my question?'

***

Cyril tapped the white board in the Incident Room as he read that it was impossible to determine the source of the gilt found in the incinerator. He was certain that the frames had been destroyed there. A few heads looked at him but soon realised that he was deep in thought and so carried on with their tasks. Simon Posthumus was waiting in Interview Room One, to be confronted with the fake Valette. Owen was attending the autopsy of the body discovered in the van. Shakti was chasing information received from the requests for the public's help and was coordinating interviews.

Cyril walked down to see Posthumus and tossed the painting onto the table with total disregard to its alleged value.

'Bloody hell, Bennett, be careful!' He lifted the painting and looked at it. The frame's gone, bastards! Cyril just looked at Simon and shook his head.

'Where did this come from?' Cyril tapped the top of the painting with his pen.

'Bought it from an auction house in Cheshire, rare as bloody hen's teeth these and you know it! Lucky to get it for the price I did.'

'It's a fake.'

'The Manchester scenes are the mos … What?'

'It's a fake!'

Simon inspected it with greater intent whilst changing the angle to catch more light. 'I have the provenance, Tib Lane, then sold through Nelson and Steel's Auction house about six years ago by the initial owner; their expert verified it otherwise it wouldn't have sold.'

'Nelson and Steel Fine Art Auctioneers, Ripon? You have the details?'

'Yes! Who says it's fake?'

'A specialist had a close look and he was sure that although it was good, he was convinced that it was wrong.'

Simon Posthumus frowned, held it at arm's length and then tossed it as irreverently back onto the table as Cyril had previously done. 'Is that it? Can I go?'

Cyril just nodded. 'I'd like to see the documentary evidence for this painting, its provenance, I'll send an officer with you to collect it. Sorry to bring the bad news. I wonder how many other pieces you've handled or that you have that fall into the same category?' Cyril's facial expression made Posthumus lower his gaze.

'Some friend you're turning out to be. None I hope!'

***

Owen did not make the same mistakes twice. He knew on this occasion what he was looking at as he stared as Julie worked around the charred cadaver.

'Looking at the skull damage, he was killed by a severe blunt force trauma to the head. More than one blow.' She looked up through the protective visor and demonstrated with her hand across her own face.' Here and here. At this stage, it's impossible to say for sure what the weapon might be. Certainly metal and probably quite thin considering the compressions to the cranium. My guess is a long bar. It's clear from closer inspection of the lung tissue that he was dead before he was put into the van and therefore before the fire.'

'Do we have any idea who he is yet?'

'DNA results show him to be a Derek Willis, forty-three. From the records, I believe he's the gentleman who's been reported missing.'

'Another mystery solved, thank goodness for science!'

'Thank goodness for Franklin, Watson, Crick and Wilkins the people who won the Nobel Peace Prize for identifying DNA!' She looked up and smiled. 'Still feeling OK?' She stuck up a thumb.

Owen responded. 'Sounds like a shady law firm!'

Julie and Hannah laughed.

'DNA? Thought it was that guy they named the Forensic lab after.'

'Alec Jeffreys? No, he developed DNA fingerprinting and profiling. There was a horse before the cart. I suppose each is equally as important scientifically as the other. Our jobs have been made a lot simpler thanks to their genius.'

Chapter Sixteen

It was as if Paul Gray were turning the metaphorical pages of his daughter's life. The final chapter was the one that had the greatest effect on him, that of her cruel murder. He could not help but focus on Bernadette's lack of any sincere grief, he felt whatever sadness she had displayed was a façade. He tried to expunge the mother and daughter rivalry in the hope that he was giving his captors the information that would secure his release.

'Mr Gray, Mr Gray, please don't take me for a fool. For one, I'm so tired of it all and for two, I believe that I know the truth. Your wife, your daughter and possibly you are all culpable. What I want to know is to what extent each of you is guilty and if there are others involved. Should I allow the driver some time in here with you alone so that I may discover the truth? As I've said, I don't have all the time in the world.'

Gray's demeanour crumbled and he held up his hands. 'Right. All right!'

Gray explained the competition with the Lowry painting and how, as a family, the money it had generated at auction had genuinely astounded them all. They had been even more surprised that there had been no repercussions, no questions asked.

He described how a number of years after Nathalie had left home, their publishing business, that had been built on financial sand, had struggled to keep afloat. Even with Bernadette's freelance work, it was slowly sinking in a sea of debt. However, he revealed how Nathalie had started sending payments to him, payments that covered the debts. She insisted that he asked no questions and that he should tell no one. She said that the skills she had been taught were now allowing her to pay something back.

Nelson listened carefully. 'So where was this money coming from do you think?'

Gray shook his head. 'To be honest, I didn't want to think about it. I had a feeling that it wasn't through fair means but what do you do when the money is keeping things going? Probably from an extension of the silly game, probably more dubious paintings, I don't honestly know!'

'Believe me, I don't fully understand your moral dilemma. You knew exactly where the cash was generated and you allowed your moral compass to swing you completely off course! It was greed and desperation, you determine in which order.'

'Maybe and I regret that now. I might have prevented her premature death if I'd shown greater strength and acknowledged that the business was failing but you always hope that the next month will be better. The thought that I might have contributed to her death will haunt me for ever.' He glanced up at Nelson, a genuine sincerity flooding his eyes.

Nelson could see tears well in his lower lids but he continued with the inquisition. 'Tell me, did your daughter return home to see you both or was she selective in her visits? I believe that she only came to Nun Monkton or the publishing works when she knew that her mother wasn't at home or at work. The rift had grown so wide that the mutual distrust could not be healed, even with your caring, if not naïve, intervention. I think you knew that in here.' He tapped his chest.

Gray simply nodded. 'But how do you know these things?'

'When this is resolved, I'll explain, but until that time you must be patient. So, may I presume that you have the information, the details of all the paintings that were created, the photographic evidence, sizes, titles?'

There was a long pause. Paul Gray considered his options. If he were to hand over everything that Nathalie had stored, he would then be superfluous. Would the driver be given carte blanche to end it all and get rid of the human evidence or could it really be the end of this saga, where he'd be allowed to go free?

He bit his scarred lip until a trickle of blood ran onto his chin and the familiar taste flavoured his mouth.

'It's at the works, hidden, but it's definitely there. It's all on a hard drive.'

Nelson stared. 'Where exactly?'

'It's in the safe.'

'Thank you, Paul. As the police have been all over the building with a fine-tooth comb, let's hope that it's still there. We need you to reappear suddenly. We also need a firm understanding that you'll ensure that I receive the hard drive and nobody else. If you agree, then this is what you're going to do.'

***

It was only when Cyril returned to his office did the thought cross his mind. Why had he not asked Steel if Nelson had other property than the one in Studley Roger. He picked up the phone and was eventually put through. After a few minutes' conversation, Cyril had two addresses, one was his daughter's address. He tapped the sheet of paper with his finger. *This one,* he said to himself. *Some address*! There was a knock on the door.

'This is for you, Sir. It's marked 'Urgent'!'

Cyril slipped the letter opener across the top of the large, padded envelope. It was the provenance he'd requested from Posthumus. He quickly flicked through it and then returned it popping the envelope into the top drawer of his desk. For the time being it would have to wait.

***

The driver followed Gray as he walked into the light. Gray rubbed his eyes, the strength of the sunlight stung as he tried to look at his surroundings; he needed a moment to acclimatise to the bright daylight. A black Land Rover was parked on the track.

'Back seat, right side.' He felt a hand push him on the shoulder.

Paul turned and looked at the grass-covered building and frowned before climbing into the car. Nelson was sitting in the passenger side. The driver bolted and padlocked the door and climbed in. Within minutes they were heading towards the A1M.

***

'A munitions' bunker?' Owen looked across at Cyril who sat staring through the windscreen, a pair of Bausch and Lomb aviator sunglasses filled most of his face. 'Those sunglasses remind me of those guys who dropped the atomic bomb.' He started humming the tune, '*Enola Gay*'. He was clearly in the wrong key!

Cyril quickly reminded him of the fact that if you kept something for long enough that it would eventually come back into fashion rather than, as today's culture demands, throwing it away as the trends change.

'Nice!'

'Older than you, Owen, and in better condition I might add!' A smile came to Cyril's lips. 'Bought in '89 when I learned to fly.'

Owen's mouth dropped. 'You, Sir?'

'Me, Sir.'

'Right! Aeroplanes, like real ones?'

Cyril just smiled.

'Get little use in the UK, sunglasses, I guess, other than when you're flying above the clouds.'

Cyril remained quiet for the next ten minutes. Owen sat considering his boss with leather helmet and a scarf at right angles and the sunglasses. He could not help but chuckle. Now the tune to, *Top Gun*, whispered from his lips.

'According to Steel, Nelson bought it as part of some farm sale. Originally it was situated on the site of the disused Dalton Airfield. It was disbanded in 1954 and although some of the buildings were turned over to industry and storage, the majority was ploughed in and returned to agriculture. The bunker, as you can imagine, is situated well away from the main airfield and is partly subterranean.'

'I know Topcliffe and Dishforth Airfields but never heard of Dalton.'

'You haven't heard of many things pre-1980, Owen, so I'm not in the least surprised.'

Owen followed the A168 before turning right onto Dalton Road. At that moment, a black Land Rover sped past at well over the speed limit.

'Bloody hell, he was moving! Never a copper when you need one!' He turned to see if his joke had brought a smile to Cyril's lips, but he had failed.

'You need to turn right in a minute.' Cyril looked down at the map on his knee. He'd asked someone to check on Google Earth and mark the position on the map. 'Here, turn right!'

Owen swung the car sharply and Cyril felt his stomach turn more quickly than the car. He could never read maps in a moving vehicle without the feeling of nausea flooding his body. The first tell-tail signs beaded his forehead and he began to yawn.

'There, the track to the right. Pull up!'

Cyril quickly opened the door and let the fresh air flood his lungs.

'I was like that on a flight back from Nice once if you remember, Sir. I think you advised taking deep breaths.'

Cyril removed his glasses, took out a handkerchief and wiped the sweat away. 'Are you sure you're not related to Fangio, Owen?'

'If I knew who Fangio was I'd be able to give you an honest answer.'

Cyril just gave up and Owen smiled and walked round to stand next to him.

'Throw up in the hedge, you'll feel tons better.' He knew that Cyril had an acute aversion to body fluids, particularly his own.

'Your bedside manner's not one of your more admirable traits, Owen, but I appreciate your obvious concern. It's there, look! That's it, the mound to the left of this track.' Cyril pointed whilst peering over the hedge. 'Originally this road would have been the perimeter track of the airfield. All the ammunition dumps would have been dug on its outside for obvious reasons. There are few such structures remaining intact. Some have been destroyed but others were utilised by farmers for storage, which probably depended on how dry they were and how accessible as to whether they survived, I guess. Come on. I'll walk, I need the air. You follow in the car.'

The lane was edged with overgrown and gnarled hawthorn bushes that seemed alive with birds. Cyril looked at the track. The concrete was crumbling but it was a manageable surface in both wet and dry conditions. After a hundred yards the bunker's entrance became visible, even though it was partly concealed beneath a grassy, earth mound. Two weather-worn, concrete arms protruded from either side exposing a light blue, steel door. Graffiti had been sprayed over the steel. The ban the bomb sign made Cyril smile. He inspected the locks that were attached to the door in three places. All looked relatively new. He bent and looked at the ground. No grass grew up to nor along the base of the opening door.

'It's been used recently. Call control and get SOCOs here. I also want this opening and I want it doing within the hour.'

***

The Land Rover pulled up two hundred yards from Paul's publishing works. Nelson climbed out and spoke to the driver, tapping the glove box as he did so. Nelson walked round the rear of the car and opened Paul's door.

'I'm here to help you, Paul. I know you feel under threat but you really have to trust me.'

The Land Rover pulled away and Paul felt a sudden relief that he had the opportunity to run or shout, but for some inexplicable reason he decided to comply with Nelson's request.

'Your daughter's innocent. You'll have to trust me on that, Paul. I need an hour or so with you in your publishing works and then I need to call the police.'

The statement staggered Paul. 'What? You've bloody knocked me about, kidnapped me, held me against my will and you want to call the police?'

'When I find everything I need, yes. It will help you find closure and it will certainly help me.'

They walked in silence. York was busy and on more than one occasion they became separated but Nelson was relaxed, he just continued to walk towards the Methodist Chapel that was the home of Fine Line Books. Nelson took the keys that he had picked up and handed them to Paul.

'The front door will have been secured by the police so we need to use an alternative entrance.'

Nelson stopped at the same spot in which he had looked at the building the first time. There was no police presence outside the main entrance but the door had been secured.

'The door's around the side.' Paul pointed.

They crossed the busy road and made their way down the side of the chapel.

***

Cyril watched the two police vehicles trundle up the track. A burly female officer opened the rear door of the van and approached. She smiled.

'Sir.' She looked at Cyril and then at Owen, nodding at each. 'Lovely morning.'

All the while she was looking beyond them at the door.

'This?'

'If that's possible.'

She returned to the van and brought a large pair of bolt cutters.

'The best tungsten, high tensile centre bolt. It'll be like a knife through butter,' she announced proudly as she approached the first of the three locks. The resounding 'click' of the jaws meeting and the snap of the shackle made her turn and smile proudly. Seconds later the other two had yielded and the door was ready to be opened.

'Owen!' Cyril pointed to the door.

He tentatively swung it open and moved inside. Three powerful LED lights came on, startling him until he realised they were on a sensor. He looked around the large, concrete room. There were two beds, a table with a camping stove and chairs. It was then that he saw the bank of batteries and a cable leading to a portable generator.

'It's clear!'

Within half an hour the SOCO team was checking both rooms and Cyril and Owen were heading back to Harrogate.

'A tenner says that's where he's been since his disappearance.'

Cyril turned, his green sunglasses framing his face. 'Think you're spot on. That's too easy. However, a tenner says you can't say where he is now.'

Owen thought for a moment and scratched his chin. 'He's in Yorkshire, Sir. You're on.'

Cyril slumped in the seat realising he'd left himself wide open to that. 'He has to be alive, that's the only stipulation!' He raised his e-cigarette and inhaled as he considered the corner he had just boxed himself into.

'Fine. That's just fine.' Owen hummed the *Top Gun* tune again much to Cyril's annoyance.

***

The alarm to Paul's works was still off. Fortunately, the sun streaming through the tall, leaded windows offered enough light in all areas to work by.

'The hard drive?'

Paul went to the safe and retrieved the small black box. He plugged the USB into the Apple computer that was positioned on the desk. Two dated files appeared. Paul flicked the mouse and clicked. Five rows of file icons appeared. He clicked on the first. It showed a small oil painting, giving details of its dimensions, title and its provenance with clear sub files showing copies of the various documents that supported the painting. There was also an image showing the reverse. It stated to whom it was sold and for what price. It also tracked the next sale price.

'Thank goodness for this, Paul. Each of these is a fake that's been passed on through different outlets for considerable sums of money.'

They scanned through the others and Paul was trying to total the amounts as they were going through.

'Bloody hell, Nathalie was busy!' Paul whispered.

'Remember this is over a period of years. This has been going on ever since that first dabble at the auction. They're certainly not all by Nathalie, not by a long chalk! Not all Lowry either and produced in a variety of media. I don't think that they were all logged.' He looked at Paul watching the information sink in. 'Please remove it and keep it with you.'

Paul did as instructed. 'Now, can you find me a number of professional graphic works that Bernadette has produced?'

'That's nearly all of the drawings here. We've been supported by other graphic artists when we were pushed to meet deadlines and Nathalie helped initially when she could.'

He brought over four files. 'We always work large and reduce the images for publication, that way the detail is more concentrated.' He spread the work out along the design table. 'This is all Bernadette's work. I've brought a cross section from when we first started to the last thing she worked on just to show the consistency of her work.'

Nelson spread them carefully and looked at each one.

'Now those by others artists, including Nathalie, please Paul.'

Paul turned as he was heading to the store. 'May I ask your name?'

'In good time, my friend, all in good time. Remember, as I've always said, you'll hopefully have lots of it and in my case, enough of it.'

The contrast in styles was quite marked. 'These, I can tell are by Nathalie?'

Paul just nodded.

'What's this all about?'

Nelson took out more copies of the three drawings that he had left when Paul was taken. 'Look carefully at these, they were drawn by Nathalie.'

'I've seen these before, she sent them here after she'd just completed the repair to some painting. They came with a note about the police being useless at catching the person who did it, said they just weren't interested. The only copper who ever did anything, she said, was this one ...' He pointed to the drawing of the bobby in the box. '... and even then, only after money had changed hands; a copper to help a copper, she had joked. This laughing chap, I believe, belonged to her boss at the time.'

'Freshman Freeman?'

'She was actually telling you something, Paul, but you weren't to know. The clue is in the drawing rather than the image. Look carefully.'

'Did Freshman put her up to all of this? Did he put her in harm's way?'

Nelson just looked. 'I think you know who's done that, if not, the answer is staring you in the face and has been for some time.'

Paul studied all three and then looked at other of Nathalie's drawings. It was as if the penny suddenly dropped. He brought his hand up to his face. 'Shit!'

'You see, she was hinting. She drew a penny being dropped into the machine ... and so, what do you see?'

'No signature. Nathalie always signed her work with a small thought bubble containing a candle in the shape of a cross ... a monogram ...'

Nelson interrupted him. 'Her name, the name Nathalie means, 'birthday', doesn't it? Christ's birthday to be accurate. It was her signature from when she was a child. In fact, the Lowry painting that sold through auction had such a monogram but it still sold.'

Paul stood open mouthed. How on earth ...?'

***

Cyril had collected the Valette's provenance sent by Posthumus and was crunching his way up the pea-gravel drive. He removed his sunglasses before pressing the bell. He rang it a second time and stood back from the door to study the house. He noticed the small camera facing him. The door swung open and Dr Darwin Green smiled.

'DCI Bennett this is a surprise. You're not here to arrest me I hope?'

Bennett smiled. 'I'd just like more of your time and your expertise if you have a moment?'

Cyril entered and was immediately impressed by the bookcases that ran down the sides of the hall. He was also drawn to the painting set within the books.

'Please.'

Green walked half way down the hall before pulling one of the bookcases towards him revealing a door. 'My dungeon.' He turned and smiled before opening the smaller door. 'It's a bit tight at first and mind the steps!'

Cyril immediately thought of Liz when he heard the word dungeon, bringing a small shiver to his flesh, but he was totally intrigued by the clever concealment of the stairs. Once at the bottom, the room was bright and modern. Desks and filing cabinets lapped the perimeter and the walls were covered in whiteboards and photographs.

'An owner in the late fifties was an American stationed at Menwith Hill, during the time of the Cold War. I think he reasoned that if the Russians were going to drop bombs anywhere it would be on Harrogate because of the listening station, so he had the cellars converted into a nuclear bunker suitable for his family. I think he knew that he'd be safe at the station. There's a toilet and an air filter system and it had its own generator, long since gone, as have the steel, air-tight doors that were at the bottom and top of the stairs. The next owners slowly removed some of the features. I've kept it as I hold many valuable resources down here and occasionally, very valuable works of art; my life's work really is here. If anyone breaks into the house it will be unlikely that they'd find this place. It's cosy too, Detective Chief Inspector.'

Cyril checked his phone.

'There's a booster so you'll still be in touch with your colleagues. It's where I do all of my research, away from distractions. How may I help you?'

Cyril handed him the padded envelope and explained.

***

Paul Gray stared at Nelson. 'You know a great deal, Mr ...?'

'Now is as good a time as any. My name is Christopher Nelson. For years I owned a Fine Art Auction House in Ripon, I handled a number of these fake paintings. At first, it was unintentional, but I'm embarrassed to say my greed got the better of me. More of that later when we speak to the police. I can also let you know that I spoke with Nathalie Gray at a hotel in Leeds before her untimely death. She did some work for me, renovating a painting. It was whilst she was there that she saw another painting in the catalogue that I was about to sell. She inspected it and said that in her opinion it wasn't right, it was a fake. She also told me that she knew just who had painted it. You now know that many of the fake drawings and paintings created were in the style of Lowry. Knowing that, please take a look at the way your wife signs her work.'

Paul did not need to look. 'Allumette'. It was a light-bulb moment as he said it and he hung his head. 'Matchstick bloody men! She only started to use it after the competition with Nathalie. It was her little joke.'

'Allumette, French for matchstick.' Nelson leaned back against the table and folded his arms. 'What do you think now, Paul, considering your wife's long absences in France, the anonymous donations, the donations you were convinced came from your daughter?'

Paul said nothing for a good few minutes, he just leaned forward, palms flat on the work surface staring at the drawings. Suddenly, he swept his hand across them sending many of them fluttering to the floor. 'The bitch!' He turned to look at Nelson, there was, for the first time since their meeting a fire in his eyes. 'I know she was jealous of Nat but Christ not enough to see her dead.'

'Don't jump to conclusions too quickly. I have the benefit of having tried to put this puzzle together for a while and at some personal and a good deal of financial cost. Apart from the first few paintings, your daughter was not guilty of the fraud that has been perpetrated, in fact, it was only seeing the painting at my auction house that made her ask questions. She only then began checking past auction and gallery sales on the net and recording all those paintings that she thought were fake. You have to remember she had both the skill and the knowledge of where to look. She told me that once she had enough evidence she could confront Bernadette in the hope of stopping her, otherwise she said that she'd informed her that she'd pass it all to the police.'

'I don't know when Nathalie confronted her mother but it seems that someone else discovered what she'd been investigating and if that information were to surface, there would be some very embarrassed experts in galleries and auction houses. We now know that I wasn't the only one chasing this information and that's the major reason we need to go to the police. The fact that someone has discovered her research leaves us with little time and I don't need to tell you the consequences of that discovery; it won't be long before they come knocking on your door, they've already found me!'

Paul crashed his fist on the table. 'Why didn't she just come to me?'

'She did, Paul. She handed you that.' He pointed to the hard drive. 'In some ways, she was saying that you were the only one she could trust. Who would have thought that they'd resort to murder?'

Paul broke down, unsure as to whether it was all making sense.

'Do I fear you or hug you, Christopher Nelson?'

'I just want to ensure that the information Nathalie worked so hard to compile gets into the right hands. We can walk into the police station tomorrow. You need more time, a good meal and a night's sleep, that might help you to make up your mind. Just make sure that you keep that safe. Without it, we have nothing.'

Chapter Seventeen

Cyril had arrived back in Harrogate as Christopher Nelson and Paul Gray checked into a hotel. Now that they had established a degree of trust, it had been decided that they should consider everything before confronting the police. Paul was eager to learn more about his daughter as the next day they would walk into the local police station, both fully aware of the facts and therefore, the consequences. Both had something to gain but they had both broken the law.

***

A memo from DI Ian Thirsk, SCO7, was marked *Urgent*. It was obvious that he had been following the progress of the investigation and was curious about the recovery of one of the paintings. Cyril made the call and briefed Thirsk, assuring him that with the discovery of the painting, they had a greater understanding of the case. It was not a totally accurate résumé but it would give Cyril more time before he would start demanding more involvement in the case.

Cyril left the station for his usual walk home. He had hoped to hear from Dr Green before he left but then patience was not his strong suit! The late afternoon was mild and he carried only a small umbrella. Once off Otley Road, Cyril crossed The Stray finding an empty bench half way across. He sat and allowed the cooling breeze to wash over him as he considered the progress they had made. It had been a particularly full day, one that seemed to offer promise but that had failed to fulfil his aspirations. *Another disappointing day,* he muttered to himself. If he only had a pound for the number of days that had ended like this during his career, he would be retired by now. He reflected on that thought too but quickly cast it from his mind; what on earth would he do if he retired? He looked at a young lady performing yoga and felt himself stretch as she leaned backwards and forwards. He was fascinated by her flexibility. *Maybe I could learn to do that*! He then noticed a brown and white bulldog sitting near her.

'Come on, Freddie!' she called.

The dog ran and positioned itself directly in front of her mat and copied her as she went into a downward facing dog pose. It barked once before lowering itself, its front paws outstretched, its tail end high in the air. They both held the position and Cyril laughed out loud; he had seen everything now! *I could always get a dog!* he thought. He then realised that he had laughed spontaneously for the first time that he could recall since Liz's murder. He also noted that Liz was not around as often.

He strolled down towards the Coach and Horses and within minutes the worries about his retirement and the day's proceedings had vanished. He stared at the pint of Fernandes, 'Murderer's Yard' session ale recommended by the landlord who had assured him that it was a good pint. He inhaled the minty vapour from his e-cigarette. What better way to end a working day? *May these be the worst of our days, Liz*, he said to himself as he held the glass up. *Where are you now, I wonder?*

Happily, the landlord was right!

***

The driver turned on to Pearl Street and parked. He slammed the Land Rover door and entered the terrace house. His rented home was cluttered and dirty. He headed straight for the fridge, removed a six pack of Stella and opened the back door before sitting on the step. The yard seemed no cleaner than the house but at least here the sun shone. He opened the can and sank it in one go, crushed it and tossed it into the far corner before opening a second. He moved to the brick shed at the bottom of the yard, kicking the recently thrown can against the wall. He threw his arms up as if victorious and shouted, 'Goal!' splashing beer across his head. 'Shit!'

He unlocked the shed, dragged open the sticking door and peered inside into the gloom. The four paintings were still leaning against the wall, a thin layer of bubble-wrap protecting each one. He took a gulp of lager and shoved the protesting door closed. Within the hour there were six crushed cans in the corner and he was heading out to find more.

***

Nelson sat in the bar. They had showered but were still in the same clothes; neither cared.

'So, who's the animal you brought with you, the driver, as he's called?'

'He used to work with me at the auction house, great porter, could move anything. He was also good if you had any, let's say, difficult customers. Helps me out at home, garden and odd jobs. He also works as a porter at the International Centre when they have exhibitions and fairs.'

'Looks more like a bouncer and acts like one too!' Paul sipped his beer.

'He does that too. Many talents has our Mr Gregory.'

Paul just raised his eyebrows. 'Can you trust him?'

'He's always been very loyal.'

***

Freshman sat in the Interview Room. He wore a blue jacket, a matching blue shirt and a bow tie. The shine to his shoes was a match for Cyril's brogues. His hands were clasped in front of him on the table. Cyril and Owen observed him on camera.

'Doesn't give the impression of a guilty man, Owen. Not yet anyway. Shall we make his morning and see what rabbits he tries to bring out of his hat?'

Owen just smiled.

Freshman stood when they walked in.

'Please sit. I trust you were comfortable last night?'

'Not five star but adequate, thank you.'

Owen looked at Cyril and shook his head. 'How many stars for keeping you safe?' The tone of Owen's voice left no one in any doubt as to his opinion of Freeman Freshman.

'I'm here, thankfully, Sergeant, that's all I can say. Hardly slept a bloody wink mind, the damn bed had more lumps than a brothel keeper's wife!'

Owen just stared. For two pins, he would happily knock the supercilious smile off his fat face.

'Mr Willis is now with us, Mr Freshman.'

Freshman frowned. 'Who?'

'Derek Willis, the gentleman you bumped into in the cellar at Ure Bank Top. He's with us. In fact, he's with someone I know very well, right now, as we speak.' Cyril leaned back, folded his arms and stared at Freshman. Owen slowly did the same. Neither spoke, they simply stared.

'Willis? Christ, Bennett, how many times do I have to say this, I didn't know him. He was bloody dead, his brains were hanging out for God's sake, he can't have gone anywhere. Scared me shitless when he fell out.'

'We took him into safekeeping, found him waiting in a van parked not far from where you met him.'

'You're not bloody listening. I didn't meet him. He was fucking dead.'

'We know he was in the cellar and we know that you were in the cellar by the clever discovery of both your DNA.'

'Thanks to Freeman, Hardy and W...?' Owen stopped himself. 'They're the people who discovered DNA. Makes our job a lot easier. So, we know that you and Willis were together in the cellar. If he were dead, as you keep on insisting, then who killed him?' Owen just stared waiting for Cyril to interject.

On cue and after a suitable pause, he did not disappoint. 'Did you kill him?'

Freshman's blood pressure was beginning to rise, as his complexion grew ruddier. His voice also rose an octave. 'He was dead. I came out and was intercepted by that nosy neighbour, that woman, Higginbottom. How many times do I have to tell you? I'm telling the truth. Why am I here, why did I come to you? If I'd killed this Willis bloke would I ring you and say, excuse me but I've found a dead body? Would I hell. Jesus, we all know you coppers couldn't find your arse even with your hand in your back pocket...' He stopped himself realising that his temper would get him nowhere.

'We found Mr Willis. Think on that,' Owen said in anger as minute flecks of spittle shot across the table in Freshman's direction. It was the only thing at this moment that he could attack him with.

Cyril put his hand on Owen's arm.

'Well, you obviously feel we're not capable of helping, we are, in your opinion, but a shower of incompetents, so here's what I suggest we do. One of my officers will take you to the safe house, you'll collect your things and then he'll drop you off at Harrogate railway station. You are free to go.'

Cyril stood and Owen followed. 'We'll be in touch. Your passport will stay with us for the time being. Good day.'

'What? I've been threatened, man!'

It fell on deaf ears. Within the hour, Freshman was heading to the railway station. Cyril returned to his office and Owen brought in a cup of tea. Cyril was vaping vigorously.

'What if someone kills him?'

Cyril raised a Gary Barlow eyebrow and looked at Owen. 'If, Owen if? If somebody kills him! You disappoint me, Sergeant, I was hoping you were going to say when. Don't forget, we have it on tape that we can't find our own arses therefore how on earth can we be expected to find his? If we can't, how on earth do we possibly protect it?'

Owen laughed.

Shakti came to the door. 'Sir, Christopher Nelson and Paul Gray have just walked into North Street Police Station and have asked to see DI Claire.'

'North Street, York? It's not open to the public is it?'

'An Inspector Preston is with them there now. DI Claire is on her way in from Fulford Road.'

'Get them moved to Fulford and please keep them separate. I'll meet her there.' He looked at his watch, shook it and checked again. 'It's 10:35. I'll be there within the hour. Can you also put a line watch on Gray's house?'

Cyril turned to Owen. 'We let one go and two return to the fold. Together!'

'Now that makes absolutely no sense,' Owen replied as he held out his hand.

'They came in two by two, Sir. Is there danger of a flood pending?' Shakti added in all seriousness.

'Now that makes more sense!'

Cyril looked at Owen's outstretched hand. 'What?'

'Last time I looked York was in Yorkshire, Sir.'

Cyril removed his wallet and handed over a tenner.

Owen simply smiled. 'Don't see many dodo skin wallets these days!'

***

Cyril and Owen drove into the Fulford Road Police Station, a large building constructed in the late seventies. Above the main entrance in large, white letters were the words, NORTH YORKSHIRE POLICE.

They were swiftly through the Reception area and soon nursing a coffee.

'Sorry the cup and saucer are odd, you wouldn't believe how long it took to get hold of those.' Helen frowned.

Cyril looked at the flowery-patterned china cup sitting on a white porcelain saucer. His mother would have said it was like a pea on a drum. He smiled inwardly. 'I'm grateful.'

She slid two copies of the statements taken from Nelson and Gray. 'They were separated from the start, even brought here separately. They make fascinating reading. To be honest I never thought that there'd be so much money in art fraud!'

Owen was still only half way through reading when Cyril turned the last sheet of A4 and started to make notes.

'Do we know where Bernadette Gray is right at this moment?'

'She's still in France, travelled with Eurotunnel on a flexible ticket as usual. Returns when the work is finished. I believe, according to Mr Gray, that it's a big contract. She's producing the graphics for a comic interpretation of *Les Misérables*.'

Cyril removed his phone and checked the signal strength. He dialled Shakti. 'Bernadette Gray? When did you last make contact?'

'I spoke to the publisher with whom she's working six days ago. I mentioned to you that she was working on something to do with *Les Mis*. They said her work was nearly completed.'

'Did you speak to her directly at any stage?'

'No, each time I rang her mobile it went straight to answerphone.'

'Thanks, Shakti.'

'Sir, before you go, I'm struggling with clearance for bank details for Natalie Grey, we have few details to go on. Lynn McGowen hasn't used her bank cards for over three weeks which is odd in itself, no transactions at all, in fact.'

'She's using an alias.'

'Concentrate on any Natalie Greys located within the Harrogate–Ripon area and be careful with the spelling. Try to tag in dates of birth with those we know, Paul, Bernadette, her work colleagues, Green and dare I say, Freshman. Be imaginative but think logically.' He was just about to hang up when a thought crossed his mind. 'Try Higginbottom, maybe a Natalie Higginbottom and as a last resort try Delmas, Bernadette's maiden name.'

'Sorry, Sir, didn't catch that.'

Cyril spelled out the names and hung up.

Owen turned to look as he finished the last page. 'Bloody hell, this is thicker than soup!'

'Before you ask, Owen, a Lowry-type sketch that an expert can draw in the blink of an eye on the back of a fag packet, supported by the correct provenance, would sell for £6,000 all day long. Think on that. Now let's go and meet our friends.'

***

Freeman Freshman tapped in the code to silence the warning tone on the alarm control box and then locked the door. He flicked on the lights and frowned at the object standing in the parking bay. However, within seconds he immediately felt his heart leap in his chest as he stared at the mahogany box, the fat, mannequin of a policeman grinning back at him. His senses seemed to tingle as he immediately scanned every visible corner of the warehouse. He listened but all he heard was his own pulse pounding in his ears.

'Hello!' he called feebly, hoping desperately that there would be no response. He checked the door a second time before quickly approaching the box. A note was resting on the top:

'A penny for them …?'

A copper penny lay next to the note. Terrified, he moved quickly to the office. He opened the safe and removed three bundles of cash before stuffing them in his inner jacket pockets. It was then that he heard the noise. It was faint, very faint, but it was definitely there. He listened again, his body flushed with cold, as the hairs on the back of his neck seemed to stiffen, as if someone had blown along his collar. He turned slowly and moved towards the door. It was then that the laughter started, laughter that once had been amusing but that had now turned sinister and oppressive. He closed his eyes hoping that it would all go away, but it only seemed to intensify.

***

Christopher Nelson had run through the whole story. He recounted his fears, his greed and more importantly, his developing understanding of the situation that had helped form his strong conviction that Nathalie Gray had been murdered by an associate of her mother's. Cyril had listened but remained silent. He was convinced that much of what had been said was sincere and honest, even though it amounted to an admission of guilt on his part.

'You know that Bernadette suffered severe bouts of depression from the day she had Nathalie. It's kept within the family, a secret, so you'll not find it on her medical records.'

Cyril made a note.

'Tell me about your dog, Lot. You wouldn't harm him so who did?'

Nelson sat for a moment surprised by the question; it was such a simple question from an extremely astute observation.

'I had a number of people work for me when we had the auction house, mainly specialists, porters and clerical staff. One, Peter Gregory, a porter I appointed when things were getting a little unconventional and more confrontational; the threats were getting bloody frightening actually. He seemed to find me and offered his services. Providing I was paying him well, he proved loyal. The threatening behaviour abated. I wasn't naïve enough to believe that he worked for one man, he was a mercenary bastard, still is I believe. It wasn't until much later did I realise that he worked for the person who was organising the paintings; ironically, he worked for the person who was threatening me! That's probably the reason why the intimidation lessened. I also discovered that the art fraud was but one string to that man's bow.'

'Did you have the name of the other ... boss?'

Nelson just shook his head. 'When I closed the business down, Gregory did the odd job for me, gardening, house maintenance at my home and that of my daughter. I also managed to find him work at the Conference Centre in Harrogate when they had the larger exhibitions. I believe he was a bouncer at clubs in the area, when they needed him. I think it's called security nowadays! That had nothing to do with my influence, I can assure you. On the day of my disappearance, he was supposed to take Lot and release him a few days later, but it appears that something happened. He told me that Lot had been badly cut on a barbed wire fence and he'd escaped and found his way home.'

'What I fail to understand is why all of this cloak and dagger intrigue? Why go missing? Why disappear?'

'Fright, Detective Chief Inspector, sheer panic and fear that something would happen to me before I could convey my knowledge to Paul Gray. I thought it was my only option after Nathalie's murder. You know that she confided in me, told me of her fears and of the threats that she'd received. I met with her in a Leeds hotel and she mentioned all of this. I was also staying at the Grand Hotel, Harrogate that dreadful morning that she disappeared. I saw your people at the scene and I knew then that something awful had happened. I was having dinner with old colleagues the night before but I did speak to her and it was then that she told me that she'd sent the only file containing the details of her research to Paul, her stepfather. She hoped that he would believe that she was innocent and that it would indicate who was behind the artwork deception. It was a warning to him. There was also a personal letter that I'm sure you've read. She despaired that he hadn't grasped the clues that she had previously sent. As I've said, I wasn't the only person who knew of this evidence; that became obvious when I received the video on the pen drive. Nathalie had shown me the one that she'd received and she knew the source. She made copies off and gave me the drawings that you found at Gray's works. I left them there in the hope that you'd put two and two together.'

'The chicken or the egg?' Cyril mumbled. 'Well done, Owen!'

'Sorry?'

'Nothing. So, who drew those?'

'After Nathalie had repaired the work at the Mercer gallery, she was told by the Curator that the police weren't interested. The young copper who attended to take a statement after the damage was discovered, simply smiled when he saw the painting.'

'I can assure you that no one is laughing now, Mr Nelson. So, if these people killed Nathalie why not kill you, after all, they know your every move through Gregory, surely?'

'Remember the words spoken as he looked out across the water. 'I really do not see the signal …' as the Admiral pretended to lift something and put it to his eye.'

'Nelson, raising his telescope to his blind eye,' Cyril commented.

'Correct. If I paid him well, Gregory would have two blind eyes and no hearing! I'm in a strong financial position, Detective Chief Inspector. Besides why would they kill a dead man?'

Cyril leaned back, his facial expression said everything. Nelson smiled.

'I have prostate cancer, a rather advanced form with only a limited life expectancy so I've no fear of a swift end by some thug, it would be less cruel than nature's planned way. I have kept this news from my family and I'd be grateful if you'd honour that, after all, it's not every man who is lucky enough to try to correct the wrongs he's done before he meets St. Peter at the pearly gates!'

***

Freshman stared down at the man leaning against the mahogany case. His eyes swiftly alighted on the sledgehammer resting next to him.

'Mr Salvatore wanted to say that he'd like his four paintings back and that he'd be prepared to excuse your error. He's also returning this with his thanks.'

Freshman's throat dried completely and he found his tongue sticking to his hard palate. He could only watch as the sledgehammer was raised above the man's head before it crashed down onto the top of the box. The glass fragmented and scattered across the floor as the hammer continued its downward trajectory, crushing the Victorian mannequin. It exploded in a cloud of fabric, porcelain and dust. Clockwork, mechanical parts seemed to fly in all directions. Freshman moved down the steps and stood looking at the destruction. The shattered remnants of the policeman's head lay between him and the broken box. The remaining eye staring vacantly towards him was complimented by the rictus, china smile. As if it had not tormented him enough, it rolled fractionally before finally settling on one side. The remaining eye closed and then slowly opened.

Gregory bent and collected the copper pennies that had spread from the ruptured collection box and put all but one into his pocket. He pointed towards Freshman and then began curling his finger as if summoning a naughty child to move closer. As he did so he raised his right leg allowing his foot to stamp and crush the remains of the porcelain head.

'Mr Salvatore says …' Gregory flicked the remaining penny into the air. '… heads he wins, tails you lose.'

The penny landed on the concrete floor, the sound ringing out as it spun briefly before settling on tails.

'You're fucking lucky, you have a choice! Maybe that's because Mr Salvatore needs your help. He wants you to look after two people at your house, just for a while; one you know. If you're agreeable and providing he receives the paintings back or if not, adequate compensation, I'll not have to use my friend there on you.' He pointed to the sledgehammer.

Freshman found his voice. 'I don't have them. I didn't touch them.'

'So, you simply pay.' Gregory held out his hand. 'I know you have the money.'

***

It took a few moments for the news of Nelson's diagnosis to sink in. If he were being honest with himself, Cyril suddenly found himself admiring the man sitting in front of him.

'I'm failing to see the significance of the drawings, maybe it's my inability to grasp all of the elements. I don't know Nathalie's work like you or her father do.'

'She probably drew them out of frustration, as an exercise and sent them home … I don't know. What I do know is that they came back to haunt both her and others but usually not for long; receiving the video was commensurate with receiving a black spot.'

Cyril thought of the pirate reference and the concealment of the pen drive that he had received behind the Turner painting.

'If you didn't fear for your life, why leave your family? Surely you must have considered that they might be targeted?'

'It was a risk that I had to take. I just thought that with the police presence, they'd leave them alone. Thankfully, until now, they have. I feel sure that I'd have been given the nod from Gregory.'

'So, where's Peter Gregory now, Mr Nelson?'

'Peter used to live in Harrogate but then he moved to live at his sister's in Ripon when she left. Ure Bank Top, I believe. I don't know the number.'

'Do you know her name?'

'Sorry, no idea.'

Cyril collected his papers and smiled at Nelson who seemed to relax. He returned the smile.

'One further thing, the van you used to kidnap Gray, where is it now?'

'Gregory has it, I asked him to get rid of it.'

'He did that alright. What about Willis?'

'Willis, my old porter? Haven't seen him since he left. Bad piece of work. Could never be trusted.'

'No longer. Found in your box van. Gregory certainly got rid of it, burned it out. You can now guess who we found sitting behind the wheel!'

Nelson pulled a face and held his hands up, his palms facing, Cyril, not believing what he was hearing. 'I've no idea about that.'

'We've only your word on that. Remember you're under caution.'

Cyril left the Interview Room and requested information about Peter Gregory. He gave Ure Bank Top as an address but knew it to be false.

'Anyone by the name of Peter Gregory living in the North Yorkshire area? I'd like details ASAP. I also want a stop on a Bernadette Gray if she enters the UK. She's driving a silver Citroën

C5 estate.' He checked his file and gave the registration number. He then dialled Helen.

'Any record of Bernadette Gray suffering from severe depression?'

'Yes, it's all on file.'

'Why wasn't I informed?'

'You were, but it was seen as an irrelevance at the time. Please check … Sir!'

That miss could well end up a home goal, he thought.

***

Sweat ran down Freshman's face as he considered his options. 'I know what was asked for the paintings. He put his hand into his inside pocket and removed one of the bundles of cash. Crossing to a table, he counted out the sum and passed it to Gregory who spread out the notes and fanned Freshman's face.

'And the house?'

Freshman went to his office, collected a spare set of keys from the safe and handed them to Gregory along with the alarm code. 'Make sure enough food is stocked as nobody will be going out for a while once they arrive.' Gregory in turn handed him a mobile. 'For incoming calls only, don't cock that up. By the way, I'd get rid of that.' He pointed to the remnants of the arcade amusement. 'Just in case the coppers come looking for one of their own. Get rid of old laughing boy there. I'll see myself out.'

'When will my guests arrive?'

'One will arrive later today and one tomorrow so you'll need to do some shopping.' He bent and picked up the penny and tossed it to Freshman. 'You can keep that, everyone should have a lucky penny, particularly someone who seems to attract a good deal of bad luck!'

Within thirty minutes, the remnants of the laughing policeman had been bagged. Originally, he was going to dump them in the skips that were on site but then thought better of it, dumping them instead amongst the overgrown hedgerows along Cinder

Hill Lane, a narrow, pot-holed track a mile from his warehouse. Looking at the other bags that were scattered randomly, he was not the only fly-tipper.

***

Lynn McGowen walked down the driveway to Freshman's house dragging a suitcase behind her. His car was in the driveway and the engine ticked as it slowly cooled. He had obviously not been home long. She rang the bell. There was no answer so she rang again keeping her finger planted on the button. Freshman opened the door cautiously; a dressing gown was wrapped around him and his hair was wet. His expression was more one of surprise. He looked her up and down in confusion and then at the suitcase.

'Bloody hell, it's you Lynn. Going somewhere? Do we have an appointment that I've forgotten about?'

'No, Freeman, you were told to expect me.' She pushed open the door and walked past him, the case rolling across his naked feet.'

'Fucking hell! Mind my bloody toes!'

'You need to get dressed and then you need to listen. If you can do that without the swearing, I'd be grateful. Now I need a drink! There's a slight change in the plan.'

***

Bernadette Gray had received several calls and messages from DC Shakti Misra which had been left on her answerphone. Realising that there was a problem, she had called the emergency number and had spoken with Lynn McGowen before her Eurotunnel crossing. She had been advised to miss the M20 so consequently had parked the car in the railway station at Folkstone West. It was a risk as there were numerous cameras around the car park. She paid for a twenty-four hour stay. Within the hour she was travelling towards St Pancras Station. She would then cross to Euston, wait and then catch the Manchester train that would arrive in Manchester Piccadilly at 17:05. She intended to leave the train at Wilmslow.

***

Lynn McGowen sat at the kitchen table, a large gin and tonic positioned in front of her. Freshman entered the room.

'I need at least one of what you're having!'

Lynn pointed to the side where a drink awaited.

'Firstly, why you? I've just been told that two people needed a safe house for a few days.'

'Freelance, Freeman. I've been working for Salvatore for a few years, started with Nathalie. It's been bloody good money. She was helping her father by sending the money she made from the paintings she produced. All was plain sailing until she saw a painting at auction that was not only fake, but was also her mother's work. She informed me that she had spotted it straight away. There was always a matchstick somewhere in the painting. Some artists add mice, she added a match. She always signed her professional work *Allumette*. She was right, of course! It was then that Nathalie stopped, said that it was getting too risky and so I contacted her mother. She replaced Nat; I forged the provenance when necessary. You've heard of sibling rivalry? Well here the mother was determined to outclass her daughter, but I have to say, she was clearly misguided, Nathalie was much the better artist.'

'So, you've been adding fakes for years?'

'A slow trickle of quality pieces. You bought some, I believe, well, quite a few, firstly from Pearl Street and then Ure Bank Top.'

Freshman just stared at her. 'You know there was a body in there, don't you? Bloody brains everywhere.'

'That's what happens when you steal from Salvatore. It's that simple.'

***

Cyril was watching the recording taken of Owen's interview with Gray when Helen entered. 'Did you check the file on Bernadette's depression?'

'Yes, sorry. Thank you. It was my error.'

'They've located Bernadette Gray's car. She passed through using Eurotunnel last night before the info had been reached by border control! The car was located parked at Folkstone West railway station, picked up on camera. Checking CCTV of the station and then all connecting stations for today.'

'Where can she get to?'

'Direct to London, St Pancras or she might have been collected there. Until we can spot her we have no idea.'

'Let me know what you find. What about McGowen?'

'Due back tomorrow. I've made an appointment to go and see her at eleven.'

Cyril thanked her and continued with the interview.

***

It was decided that Gray and Nelson would remain in custody, mainly for their own safety. Neither asked for a lawyer nor for bail. It was also agreed that their families would not be notified for the time being as it could jeopardise this stage of the inquiry.

Cyril spoke little on the return to Harrogate but rolled the electronic cigarette along his lips.

Owen was not convinced. 'I still don't get it, Sir, all this murder and mayhem over some poxy paintings pretending to be something they're not. I know they can command huge sums. But the risks!'

'What we have here is the very tip of the iceberg, if you like. We have the upper end but every day people are conning others with fake watches, trainers, handbags and even fake drugs. We live in a consumer society and people want to be seen wearing the best and the most expensive, even though it's not. The art market is on the periphery of all that. Money in the bank is worth bugger all at the moment and gallery owners know that and advise people to buy paintings or art, advocating it as a sound investment. In many ways, they're right but with that you bring in the crooks, the ones who will hoodwink the unwary. Look at all the antique-type programmes on TV where people try to turn a fast buck by buying at a car boot and then either selling on through auction or dealers. *'Flog It'*! Tells you all you want to know. Everyone becomes an armchair expert on Clarice Cliff or ...' He inhaled and then continued .... 'How many fake Rolex watches have you seen? Loads.'

Owen glanced down at the watch on Cyril's wrist.

'Don't say a word. This one's real! My birthday present to me.'

'Forty, Sir?'

Cyril just smiled, not acknowledging Owen's grin.

As they entered the Incident Room Brian Smirthwaite held up his hand.

'We have an ID on Bernadette Gray at St Pancras and she was then seen leaving the station before heading up Euston Road.'

'If she's heading for York and home she'd need King's Cross, but she's obviously not going home. She's been warned, that's why the car's been abandoned. What else do you have?'

'If we assume she's heading north then there's a Manchester train from Euston arrives ...' he checked his computer. '... approximately every thirty minutes.'

'Trawl CCTV again for Euston and the cameras on the Manchester-bound trains, as well as any station close to Manchester that they stop at. My bet is, she's heading north, it's just a case of knowing when and where.'

Cyril's phone rang. 'Bennett.'

'Shakti, Sir. We've located a Natalie Grey, correct spelling, been living in a care home in Pudsey, for the last three years. I'm trying to track down relatives to see if she owns property.'

'Thanks, Shakti. Keep me informed.'

Cyril went over to a freestanding easel and jotted down the words, 'My gut tells me that they're planning to meet and disappear.'

***

Bernadette Gray left the train at Wilmslow Station and headed across the road before passing through the leisure complex grounds. She was bound for Greenway, to the address that she had been given, a ten-minute walk away. The small case on wheels clattered along behind. She was tired and angry. It had always been so straightforward until she had received Nathalie's note and the laughing policeman images. Why could she not just have left her alone and let her finish what she had started rather than interfere?

It was the quality of Nathalie's images, the graphic genius that she was that had been the final straw, along with the threat to go to the police. Had she just turned a blind eye and not told Lynn of her intentions, then she might still be alive. A tear came to her eye, more out of frustration as she visualised Nathalie on the day that she had returned the painting that had failed to sell. She always had to go one better, then recently, she had to reveal that she was aware of what they were doing, belittling her mother and her efforts. Whether it was Nathalie's own guilt, Bernadette would never know. The fact was that she, Nathalie, had started it all that time ago and had taken great satisfaction in winning. She wiped her eyes on her sleeve. She suddenly had the strongest urge to talk to Paul.

She stopped and took out her phone. She dialled her home number hoping that Paul would respond but it went straight to answerphone. She did not leave a message.

The Police Communications Officer was vigilant enough to make a note of the number and immediately forwarded it to the Incident Room. Within ten minutes they would track the position from where the mobile call had been made.

Cyril waited patiently.

'Wilmslow, Sir. People believe that tracking calls is an exact science but I'm afraid that's not the case. She's near the railway station or was at the time the call was made.'

Cyril responded. 'Close down Greenway, Freshman's address. She's there! His fears were a sham. A pound to a penny he's up to his bloody neck.'

Owen tossed ten pence onto the table. 'I'm in!'

***

Bernadette noticed the black Land Rover parked higher up the road. Gregory had been waiting there since leaving Freshman's.

He had counted the money and hidden it. He had watched him return home and then had witnessed McGowen's arrival.

Bernadette had originally thought that it was a police vehicle but then once the tears had gone, she could see more clearly, that the vehicle was too old. As she walked alongside the car, the window lowered. 'Bernadette?' She stopped and looked.

'Lynn sent me. My name's Peter, we've met before. It's not safe here.' Bernadette looked up and down the road and then back at Gregory; she recognised him but could not remember exactly from where. He leaned over and opened the passenger door.

'Put your case in the back seat,' he smiled. 'We need to hurry.'

She was tired and frightened and simply followed his instructions. She had just closed the door when two police cars, all blue lights but no sirens, flashed by and turned onto Greenway. Gregory simply smiled. *Saved from the coppers' grasp.* He grinned and drove away, heading first for the M60 and then the M62. Bernadette allowed herself to relax for the first time since leaving her car eight hours previously. For her, it would be the calm before the storm.

***

'They've arrested McGowen and Freshman. SOCO have been called in. They'll be processed and then transferred to Harrogate as soon as. There was no sign of Gray. They're doing a sweep of the area and checking town centre CCTV.'

Cyril smiled to himself, pleased that he had released Freshman. 'Like bees to honey.' All he needed now was to identify and locate Gregory.

***

The Land Rover turned onto Pearl Street and drove to the bottom before returning along the backs of the houses. Gregory parked at the rear. Opening Bernadette's door, he helped her out. She had slept most of the journey and appeared dazed. He unlocked the gate and they went through into the yard. Bernadette looked at the mess.

'Where have you brought me?'

'We need to stay here for a couple of days and then you need to disappear. The police have your husband and Nelson and they now have Freshman and McGowen. The walls are tumbling.'

'Paul's done nothing.'

'Taken money, laundered your gains.'

She thought for a moment. 'Who's Nelson?'

He took two cans of lager from the fridge and opened them, handing one to Bernadette before speaking. By the third can he had finished explaining his understanding of Nelson's involvement.

'You worked for both of them and Nelson has told Paul that I was instrumental in Nat's death? So, Nelson didn't know you were involved?'

Gregory just nodded and then smiled in answer to the second question. 'It looks as though all the evidence about the paintings will now be with the police.'

'You could've got rid of Nelson.'

'If he'd got the stuff, then believe me, I would have but until he had it …'

He finished the cans and looked for more. He went to the shed remembering that he had stashed a bottle of vodka there. He yanked the door taking the top section away from the hinge. His memory had served him well. He grabbed the alcohol and the four small, wrapped paintings.

'These, I'm informed, are your work, they were nicked from the new Harrogate gallery. Cheeky sod had them stashed to sell privately. Salvatore sees them as a bonus for us to sort out. They'll not go on the Art Loss Register.' He tossed them irreverently onto the sofa, quaffing a quarter of the bottle before passing it to Bernadette. 'For you?'

Bernadette demurred but continued to unwrap the paintings.

'Dr Darwin Green was convinced that these were original. Put his name to them. Even the best-trained eye can be duped. He was such a simple man.'

'Who Green?' Peter's speech had started to slur.

Bernadette shook her head. 'No, Lowry. He said himself that he was a simple man who used simple materials: ivory, black, vermilion, Prussian blue, yellow ochre, flake white and no medium. He said that was all he ever used in his paintings but that wasn't strictly true, he used titanium white also but don't tell more than six people.'

She looked up. Gregory had finished the bottle and was spread, open-mouthed on the chair, a slight rumble of a snore emerging from between his yellowing teeth. She collected the paintings and stood. She needed to make a choice. She could stay with a man who might be a violent and cruel murderer or she could simply leave. She looked at Gregory's face and crept to the back door, through the yard and surveyed the piece of land used as allotments.

Within ten minutes she was walking onto Starbeck railway station. She would have loved to find a taxi, but knew that she might have to wait forever. As it was, the train arrived only eight minutes later and she was Harrogate bound, a five minute, two-pound ride. On leaving Harrogate station she was faced with a choice of taxi; there were four waiting in a row. She gave Darwin Green's address and hoped that he would be at home.

***

Cyril had clearly had enough for one day and phoned Julie. They arranged to meet and go out for dinner. He needed to clear his head. They now had Nelson, Paul Gray, Freshman and McGowen. No one seemed to know where to locate Gregory and now Bernadette Gray was missing. One minute she was in Wilmslow, the next she had vanished. Owen suddenly appeared in the doorway to Cyril's office and it was reminiscent of an eclipse.

'Bloody hell, Owen, come in, you're blocking the light!' He carried a cup and saucer as well as his usual leaking mug.

'Brought you a brew, Sir. Thank Crunchie it's Friday. Who was that other woman we saw on CCTV with Nelson?'

'Just an old customer of his.'

Owen put his mug down on the desk. Cyril just put his head in his hands. 'You didn't come in to ask that, it was added to the white board. Don't tell me, you're the bearer of good news or are you just the tea monitor this late in the afternoon?'

He looked at the grin on Owen's face as he lifted his mug. Cyril read out loud the words printed on it. '*Harrogate, 50, Arts, 50, Literature, 50*,' and most importantly, '*Crime!*'

Owen turned the mug to see it and spilled more.

'You'll never guess, Sir!'

'No, Owen. My job is about detecting, using all available evidence, connecting that and deducing what a possible outcome might be. Guessing, no!'

Owen took a piece of paper from his top pocket and, avoiding the ring of tea that now sat on the desk, he slid it to Cyril. 'What do you deduce from that?'

Cyril opened the screwed-up note and was surprised to recognise Julie's handwriting. He read it out loud. '*Give Hannah a call, she'd like that. J x*'

He looked up to see Owen smirking. 'And, have you?'

'Out tonight, a beer and something to eat.'

Cyril picked up his cup and held it towards, Owen. 'Wonderful news, Owen, simply wonderful. Cheers. You will change your … never mind.'

He regretted his actions as soon as he raised his cup as more tea cascaded onto the desk. Owen went to leave.

'Owen, as a matter of interest, where are you taking your young lady to dine tonight?'

'No idea, yet, Sir. Great though, isn't it?'

Cyril simply smiled, mopped up the tea and went for his jacket.

Chapter Eighteen

The taxi pulled up outside Green's gates. Bernadette paid and retrieved her case. The crunch from the drive made her heart race, as she tugged it through the pea gravel, leaving two parallel lines behind her. She had never met Green but Nathalie had mentioned him and Paul had spoken highly of him when he had visited Nun Monkton. She rang the bell. A breeze moved the rose growing to the side of the door. Its perfume burst into her nostrils and the aroma seemed calming. The door opened and Green looked at Bernadette and then at her small case.

'Dr Green?'

'Yes, how may I help?'

'We've never met but my name is Bernadette Gray. I'm Nathalie's mother. May I come in? I need your help.'

Darwin pushed the door wide and took her case. 'Please, come in, come in.' He looked down the drive for a car.

She turned and watched him. 'I came by taxi.'

He showed her to the lounge and made her comfortable. 'I must say that you look exhausted? May I offer you some refreshment?'

'In a moment, coffee would be perfect. It's been a difficult day. I'm, totally exhausted and I need somewhere to stay for a day or two. I want to be with somebody who knew Nathalie well, somebody who will listen, someone whom I can trust.' She leaned forward putting the case flat in front of her before opening it. From it she took out the wrapped paintings. 'Please look at these. This is where the story begins.'

***

Cyril was just signing out when Shakti called. 'Grey, she had three rental properties, two in Harrogate and Ure Bank Top, Ripon. I've just sent the authorisation for immediate action to all three addresses.'

'Well done. Keep me informed no matter what the time.' He checked his watch, it was 19:28.

***

Dr Green unwrapped the first painting and expressed surprise. 'Goodness me … I've seen these before!'

'You have, you checked them a few years ago. You added your seal of approval, signed that they were genuine.'

He smiled and removed the others. He stood them on the mantle piece and admired them with fresh eyes. 'For a rent collector he produced some beautiful, small, observational paintings.'

'No, for graphic artists Nathalie and I produced some fine work, don't you think?'

***

Gregory woke as the sun dipped behind the buildings opposite putting the room in shadow. He checked his watch, it was seven pm. He remained still, listening for Bernadette. Was she in the bathroom? Silence reigned. He stood before calling her name. He searched for the suitcase but it was not there nor were the paintings.

'Shit, shit, shit and fucking shit, you bitch! I fucking save you and then you run away. That really fucks me right off!'

He kicked the empty vodka bottle against the fireplace; the neck snapped but the rest of the bottle stayed in one piece. He cast his mind back and the only name that came into his head was Green. From working with Freshman he knew just where to find him. *Goodness they were like old buddies,* he said out loud. Green had booked him regularly to help move the antiques for the Fine Art shows. Suddenly his mood improved as he made his way to the Land Rover.

***

'Sorry, what did you say?'

'Nathalie and I did those. She did one, that one and I painted the other three. That one sold to the Harrogate gallery owner for £27,000.'

Green stared again. 'As genuine works, that would be a snip, an absolute bargain.'

'But they're not, they're fakes. Please, let me explain everything to you.'

Green made coffee and they settled down. Bernadette told her story.

It was Green who heard the car on the gravel. He looked through the side window and saw the Land Rover and Gregory looking at the tracks made by the suitcase. He took out his mobile phone and quickly found Cyril's number. He dialled. Cyril had just settled into a small, cosy booth in the Sorrento Italia Restaurant when he noticed the caller's ID.

'Sorry, a minute.'

Julie just smiled. She turned and noticed Owen and Hannah enter. *Great minds,* she said to herself.

'I'm on my way, stay calm. Sorry, Julie, this is serious.'

She pointed to Owen and Hannah, 'Surely not Owen, Cyril, not tonight?'

Cyril called the station for back up and firearms and gave a rendezvous location as he moved through the restaurant tapping Owen on the shoulder. 'You're needed. Sorry, Hannah. Please join Julie it's on me. Order what you like.'

***

Green dragged Bernadette and swung open the bookcase and the short door. Down there, you should be safe!' He closed both doors and straightened the books. The bell rang. Green mopped his brow and then opened the front door.

'Peter, from the Conference Centre? What can I do for you?'

Peter Gregory put his palm onto Green's chest and pushed him out of the way. 'Where's that bitch of a frog?'

'Sorry? Who?'

Gregory stopped, turned and with the back of his hand he slammed it across Green's face. 'If you say one more fucking word out of turn I can assure you that it'll be your fucking last. I know that she's here unless you've had Santa and his sleigh down your drive today. Now I'm happy to tear this lovely home of yours apart, destroy everything in it and that, my friend, includes you. This will be nothing compared to killing that silly bitch you worked with, Nathalie Gray and the woman who killed her. Remember Willis? Did him too, he was cooked to a crisp, so doing you will be a piece of piss. Where the fuck is she? In the end, you'll be in so much pain that you'll squeal.'

***

Cyril met the first team comprising four officers. Within minutes the two firearms officers pulled up. Cyril briefed them.

***

Green moved to the bookshelf and pressed it. A huge smile appeared on Gregory's face. 'Bloody hell, very James Bond, Dr. No?'

He opened the small door.

'After you just in case it's a trap. Not as green as I'm cabbage looking, no pun intended!'

They descended and Gregory smiled at Bernadette who cowered in a corner. 'We meet again, bitch!'

The doorbell rang.

'See who it is and get rid of them, me and the frog bitch here have some chatting to do.'

Green turned on a computer screen and looked at the image. 'It's DCI Bennett. He was coming this evening to collect some evidence from the Harrogate robbery, you heard about it? If I close the upper bookcase, he'll have no idea anyone is in the house. This room is secret or should I say, was.'

'Mess me about and she's dead.'

Green mounted the steps quickly and closed the doors before opening the front door. Gregory watched on screen.

'DCI Bennett, come in.' Owen followed. 'You've come for the evidence. One minute.'

Cyril looked at Green who raised a finger to his lips and then ran it along his throat. He opened a cupboard door and removed an empty envelope and handed it to Bennett. 'The envelope is empty a bit like the house and you can instruct your man here that he can tell it to the marines down in Men with Hill.' He moved his hand to the mark on his face where Gregory had struck him.

Cyril looked at the bookcase and back at Green. 'Thank you. I'll ensure that Owen does that.'

Green showed them out and Bennett made a point of waving. Gregory watched and smiled.

Bennett climbed into the car and quickly reversed out of the drive. Further down the road he stopped close to the other officers.

'What on earth was that about? Marines, Men with Hill …?'

'We wait. There's a camera positioned at the front door so work behind it. There are no other cameras.' He spoke to the two firearms officers. 'I want you in position to take out whoever mounts a threat when leaving the house. The Land Rover doesn't belong to Green. He's wearing a blue cardigan and black trousers. He's not a target. As I said, we wait.'

Shakti called informing Cyril that they had tracked the house used by Gregory and that SOCOs were on site.

***

Gregory came from the cellar as Green opened the door. He slapped his face gently. 'Good boy!'

They moved back to the lounge and Gregory spotted the paintings. 'Well, well, well, look what we have here.' He collected the paintings. 'Money, all that you have. Now! Credit cards and pin numbers too. Don't fuck with me.'

Green went to the safe and opened it. Gregory looked and smiled. 'You're being cooperative!'

'There's over forty thousand there, that's it.'

***

The firearms officers took up position and Owen waited, blocking the road a hundred yards away as a van did the same in the opposite direction.

***

Gregory emptied Bernadette's small case, stuffed in the money and then added the paintings. 'It's been a very profitable morning. Oh, one other thing, booze, two bottles of your best spirit.'

Green collected two bottles of brandy and Gregory tossed them in on top of the paintings before leading them towards the bookcase and the bunker. He went to the bottom of the steps and to the screen, ripping the cables out of the back. 'Remember that I might stay a while upstairs or I might just go. You'll not know either way, but I suggest that you don't appear from behind the cupboard whilst I'm there or this place will be your tomb.'

He left them, climbed the steps, closed the top door before moving the bookcase against the wall. Within minutes he was outside. He tossed the case in the back and then moved the Land Rover to the drive entrance. Immediately Owen positioned his vehicle blocking the way. The Land Rover reversed, swung left and ploughed through the flowerbed removing the wooden fence, before plunging into the field. The marksman took aim and the first shot destroyed the left rear tyre, the second shattered the rear window and then crazed the front screen. Gregory swung the vehicle back onto the road only to meet the van placed diagonally across it. The Land Rover accelerated, smashing into the side of the van; the airbag immediately deployed. Gregory floored the accelerator trying to push the van away but it ran into another vehicle behind it. Quickly he swung open the door to be confronted by Owen who leaned in and grabbed him whilst delivering two firm blows to his right temple. Gregory slumped like the deflated airbag in front of him. Owen shook his hand and rubbed his knuckles, but smiled.

Cyril stood and watched Owen walk up the drive. He brushed white dust from his jacket shoulder. 'Got to say, Owen that I've never seen you look so smart at work.'

Owen looked down at his shoes and trousers. 'One has to make an effort, Sir. I'll be known as Flash 2 if I'm not careful. Tell me, marines, Men with Hill. What's all that about?'

Cyril led him into the hall and went towards the bookcase. He took the small handle and pulled it open.

'Bloody Hell, Narnia?'

'No, Owen, sadly not.'

***

Julie and Hannah were drinking coffee and brandy when Cyril and Owen returned. Cyril noticed the upturned Prosecco bottle in the ice-bucket. He smiled. 'Successful evening, ladies?'

'Expensive, Cyril, very, very expensive!'

Cyril had to sit down. He called over a waiter. 'Two beers, two of your largest pizzas and another bottle of that for these patient ladies.'

Julie looked at Hannah. 'You'd better have your camera ready when Cyril's presented with the bill but you'll have to be quick before he faints!'

Owen simply picked up his pint and downed it in one.

Chapter Nineteen

Three weeks later, Cyril stood in the Incident Room they had used for the murders and the gallery robbery case; the white boards, apart from one, had long since been wiped clean. A large bouquet of flowers stood in an orange bucket. He finished writing the names on the board and, sitting with a cup of tea, he waited for the team to arrive. Shakti was first, quickly followed by Smirthwaite and Nixon. Within ten minutes all were present.

'I'd like to thank you for your dedication and hard work. It's not been an easy case and I also wanted to give you some information regarding those involved. Before I do that I should like to thank DI Helen Claire for her dedicated support in what was both a complex and a difficult investigation, especially when she was holding the reins.'

Cyril lifted the flowers from the bucket as Helen moved across to receive them. The applause and whistles were genuine and she had a tear in her eye when she thanked everyone for their support. However, it was her thanks to Cyril that brought the loudest cheer.

'To have you back, Sir, here where you belong, has been the greatest reward. You were very much missed of that I have no doubt.' She leaned in and kissed his blushing cheek.

He raised a hand and managed to control his emotions. 'I just want to sum up and close this case by mentioning the characters who have given us so much grief. Christopher Nelson is presently undergoing treatment for cancer. His knowledge that he was suffering from prostate cancer was the catalyst that spurred his mission to broadcast the corruption within the art world. Shortly after his arrest, tests have proved his diagnosis was understated, it's worse than he imagined. Sadly, the disease has transferred to other areas and the prognosis is a poor one. Paul Gray has been freed on bail. It's likely that he'll receive only a suspended sentence for handling stolen money. Originally, Nathalie Gray used the property at Ure Bank Top for McGowen, until she decided to step back. It was then that McGowen co-opted her mother, Bernadette Gray. She then worked predominantly from the same property and that's where the majority of art works were created. The house along with another one in Pearl Street was rented from a Natalie Grey, who has no link to the case other than being a landlady; the money was needed to pay for her care. We're trying to track the tenant but, so far, it's been a false trail. Freshman is guilty of knowingly buying and dealing in fraudulent works. All are charged with murder or accessory to murder with lesser counts of fraud and deception as well as conspiracy to commit fraud.'

Owen raised his hand. 'Mac was brought in by the Manchester mafia over McGowen's head. The fact that Monica Mac had failed to get the relevant information brought about her demise. We also believe that Willis stole one of the paintings, the fake Valette, we found and that's why he followed Mac to an early grave. Peter Gregory seemed to be the main man working closely with a Mr Salvatore. We also believe Salvatore is an alias. Gregory's DNA has now been found at Ure Bank Top, Pearl Street and Nelson's house. From his boasting whilst with Green and Bernadette Gray, we know that he was instrumental in organising Nathalie's murder, responsible for Mac's murder and that of Willis.

Shakti asked about Simon Posthumus.

Cyril smiled. 'Sadly, he's been charged with knowingly trading in fake art works, conspiracy to commit fraud and will probably serve over three years at Her Majesty's pleasure. To cap it all, he's also been declared bankrupt!'

The Chief Constable popped his head round the door. 'My congratulations on your commitment and dedication. I'm proud to have you here. SCO7 are delighted with Nathalie Gray's information. They've tracked two of the fraudulent paintings to a well-known public gallery and another that was traded through a very reputable auction house. These will only herald the start, I'm guessing. If the press gets hold of it they'll have a field day. My sincere thanks to you all.'

Epilogue

Cyril sat with a Black Sheep beer in one hand and his laptop resting on his knees as he watched a black and white documentary made in 1957 by the BBC about a Manchester man who became an artist because he missed a train. The music was reminiscent of the time that the laughing policeman was in vogue and he smiled. The doorbell rang. He popped the laptop down and went to answer it.

Dr Darwin Green stood at the door.

'I believe that owing to the circumstances of the last month or so you'd like me to cast my professional eye over your collection of northern art? You also said that there would be a beer in it for me!' He smiled and held out his hand.

'Just watching a fascinating documentary made by the BBC in 1957.'

Green looked quickly at the screen. 'I know the one. Very good it is too. Did they really speak like that then?'

Cyril just laughed. 'Before my time, Darwin! Please, take a look at my small collection of northern art and let me know if I've bought any fakes.'

Green stared at all of the paintings before returning to the Theodore Major. He stood, hand on his chin. Cyril held his breath hoping that this out of all his collection would not be labelled a fake.

'This one, Cyril ...' he said, shaking his head. He paused and then smiled, '... is a cracker!'

Cyril collapsed onto the chair and they both laughed.

'No, they are, in my opinion, authentic, but then I was the one who thought that Gray's work was sound! Maybe you need a second opinion. I need that beer, Cyril, and, more importantly, I think you do too!'

Dr Darwin Green removed a small oil painting from his bag and handed it to Cyril in return for the beer. 'I brought this with me. Thought you might be in the market for a Valette for your collection. Unfortunately, it's not cheap!'

Cyril unwrapped it and smiled. 'It's a Manchester scene, too.' He looked at it carefully under the light. 'It's fabulous. How much dare I ask?'

The End

A Note from Bloodhound Books

Thanks for reading Dying Art We hope you enjoyed it as much as we did. Please consider leaving a review on Amazon or Goodreads to help others find and enjoy this book too.

We make every effort to ensure that books are carefully edited and proofread, however occasionally mistakes do slip through. If you spot something, please do send details to info@ bloodhoundbooks.com and we can amend it.

Bloodhound Books specialise in crime and thriller fiction. We regularly have special offers including free and discounted eBooks. To be the first to hear about these special offers, why not join our mailing list here? We won't send you more than two emails per month and we'll never pass your details on to anybody else.

Readers who enjoyed Dying Art will also enjoy the first four books in the DCI Bennett series also by Malcolm Hollingdrake.

Only The Dead

Hells Gate

Flesh Evidence

Game Point .

Acknowledgements

Thank you to my wife, Debbie, without you I'd be nothing. X

It's hard to believe that this is the conclusion of DCI Cyril Bennett's fifth case. He and the rest of the team have now become a firm part of my family. It was sad to write the death of one of his colleagues in Book Four, forgive me! It was a difficult decision to plot Liz's demise and one that I didn't take lightly, but sometimes life deals devastating blows that make each and every one of us take stock and rethink our position. Bringing Cyril back from the chasm of his depressed state has been more of an emotional test than I could have imagined. I have to thank a truly inspirational lady for her professional guidance on this important, sensitive issue. **Linda Foster**, thank you.

Writing is such a pleasure but one that, for me, requires a good deal of support. Although I type the words, there are many people who, through their various skills, help form and wreak the raw material into a tangible structure. I must offer a massive thanks to the wonderful team at Bloodhound Books, the editors, the cover designers and all those beavering away behind the scenes. I shall be ever grateful to Betsy and Fred for having faith in my writing. They are the ticking heart of Bloodhound.

To, Christopher Nolan, Ross Greenwood and Mark Tilbury for their support for me as a newly published writer, it does make a difference. Thank you.

I am constantly humbled by the support I receive from the many bloggers who promote writers. Please keep doing what you do so well. Authors hold you in such high regard.

A big thanks to a number of groups: Crime Fiction Addict, Book Connectors, TBC, UK Crime Club, Let's do Books, Orchard Book Club and the Crime Book Club, all on Facebook. Your support is so valued.

I am blessed in having a dedicated group of readers who are always there to offer honest, critical insights into my work. Thankfully, they are still here! To Stuart, Chris, Margaret, Bill, Barbara, Tony, Eileen and Peter, my sincere thanks.

Thanks to **Carrie,** who always casts a critical eye over the second draft, your patience is appreciated.

Thanks **Danny Norkus** for his continued support

Thanks to **Bill Clark** for sharing his personal reflections.

Thanks to **Ben Kelly** for allowing me to add his name and describe his fantastic artwork in this story.

Monica Mac entered an online competition to have her name included. She also wanted to be an evil character. I sincerely hope that you liked your part.

Helen Claire – an inspiration in so many ways. Thank you.

Everyone has a guardian angel and I am no exception. Thank you for watching over me. x

Last, but certainly not the least, I have to thank you, **dear reader,** for your continued support. If you have enjoyed this latest Bennett book please help spread the word.

Malcolm

Lightning Source UK Ltd.
Milton Keynes UK
UKOW04f0609041017
310352UK00001B/115/P